W9-ADG-685

GETTING OLD
IS A DISASTER

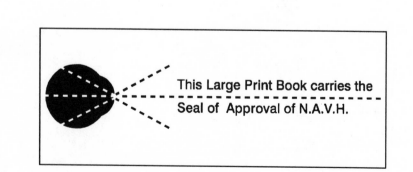

GETTING OLD
IS A DISASTER

RITA LAKIN

THORNDIKE PRESS
A part of Gale, Cengage Learning

GALE
CENGAGE Learning™

Detroit • New York • San Francisco • New Haven, Conn • Waterville, Maine • London

GALE
CENGAGE Learning

LIBRARY OF CONGRESS CATALOGING-IN-PUBLICATION DATA

Lakin, Rita.
  Getting old is a disaster / by Rita Lakin.
    p. cm. — (A Gladdy Gold mystery) (Thorndike Press large print mystery)
  ISBN-13: 978-1-4104-1429-8 (hardcover : alk. paper)
  ISBN-10: 1-4104-1429-9 (hardcover : alk. paper)
  1. Gold, Gladdy (Fictitious character)—Fiction. 2. Older women—Fiction. 3. Retirees—Florida—Fiction. 4. Women private investigators—Fiction. 5. Bank robberies—Fiction. 6. Florida—Fiction 7. Large type books. I. Title.
PS3612.A5424G46 2009
813'.6—dc22
                                              2008053444

Published in 2009 by arrangement with The Bantam Dell Publishing Group, a division of Random House, Inc.

Printed in the United States of America
1 2 3 4 5 6 7 13 12 11 10 09

This book is for Leslie Simon Lakin,
my amazing daughter-in-law,
with Love and Gratitude

BABY BOOMERS: THE THIRD ACT, OR, ENCORE CAREERS

Act One:

Even though I didn't know it at the time, I followed every trend.

I was born in 1947.

In the 50's I was the perfect student in school.

In the 60's I was the perfect teenager.

Then in the 70's the perfect hippie.

Act Two:

By the 80's I became the perfect yuppie. By then I was married. It was all about money and spending.

In the 90's women's rights! I divorced and started my own corporation.

Act Three:

I married the right man. Now the two of us spend our time being useful to others. We began our encore career. We opened a bed-and-breakfast to bring pleasure to people in a beautiful place. I thought I was such a rebel all my life, but now I know I'm just a variation on what 70 million baby boomers have done with their lives.

— Guiamer Hiegert, co-owner with her husband, Gary, of the Lost Whale Inn, Trinidad, California

INTRODUCTION TO OUR CHARACTERS

Gladdy and Her Gladiators

Gladys (Gladdy) Gold, 75 Our heroine and her funny, adorable, sometimes impossible partners:

Evelyn (Evvie) Markowitz, 73 Gladdy's sister. Logical, a regular Sherlock Holmes

Ida Franz, 71 Stubborn, mean, great for an in-your-face confrontation

Bella Fox, 83 The "shadow." She's so forgettable, she's perfect for surveillance, but smarter than you think

Sophie Meyerbeer, 80 Master of disguises, she lives for color-coordination

Yentas, Kibitzers, Sufferers: The Inhabitants of Phase Two

Hy Binder, 88 A man of a thousand jokes, all of them tasteless

Lola Binder, 78 His wife, who hasn't a thought in her head that he hasn't put there

Denny Ryan, 42 The handyman: sweet, kind, mentally slow

Enya Slovak, 84 Survivor of "the camps" but never survived

Tessie Spankowitz, 56 Chubby, newly married to Sol

Millie Weiss, 85 Suffering with Alzheimer's

Irving Weiss, 86 Suffering because she's suffering

Mary Mueller, 60 Neighbor whose husband left her; nurse

Joe Markowitz, 75 Evvie's ex-husband

Oddballs and Fruitcakes

The Canadians, 30–40-ish Young, tan, and clueless

Sol Spankowitz, 79 Now married to Tessie

Dora Dooley, 81 Loves soap operas; Jack's neighbor

The Cop and The Cop's Pop

Morgan (Morrie) Langford, 35 Tall, lanky, sweet, and smart

Jack Langford, 75 Handsome and romantic, Gladdy's boyfriend

Oz Washington, 36 Morrie's friend, also a police detective

The Library Maven
Conchetta Aguilar, 38   Her Cuban coffee could grow hair on your chest

Other Tenants
Barbi Stevens, 20-ish   and
Casey Wright, 30-ish   Cousins who moved from California
Yolanda Diaz, 22   Her English is bad, but her heart is good
Stanley Heyer, 85   Original builder of Lanai Gardens
Shirley Heyer, 80   His wife

Interim Tenants Phase Two
Abe Waller, 85   Stanley's friend
Louise Bannister, 60-ish   Femme fatale of Phase Six, interested in Jack

GLADDY'S GLOSSARY

Yiddish (meaning Jewish) came into being between the ninth and twelfth centuries in Germany as an adaptation of German dialect to the special uses of Jewish religious life.

In the early twentieth century, Yiddish was spoken by eleven million Jews in eastern Europe and the United States. Its use declined radically. However, lately there has been a renewed interest in embracing Yiddish once again as a connection to Jewish culture.

bubbala endearing term for anyone you like, young or old; a tasty egg dish

bar mitzvah at age thirteen a boy becomes a man after a ceremony accepting responsibility and religious law

kasha varnishkas cooked groats and broad noodles

kibitzer one who gives unwanted advice

kvetch whine and complain

mezuzah tiny box affixed to right door frame containing parchment with 22 lines of Deuteronomy

nachas joy, especially from children

nosh small meal

tsouris trouble

schmegegi buffoon, idiot

schlep drag, carry, or haul sometimes unnecessary things

schmear to spread like butter

Shabbes Sabbath

tallis prayer shawl

Torah the five books of Moses — Talmud law

yarmulke traditional skull cap worn at all times by observant Orthodox Jews

yenta busybody

Building Q-Quinsana

mailboxes & elevator

IDA 319 GLADDY 317 SOPHIE 314

TESSIE & 216 SOL

CASEY & BARBI 118

DENNY 119 IRV & MILLIE 114

ENYA 219 EVVIE 217 BELLA 216 HY & LOLA 214

MARY 314

mailboxes & elevator

Building P - Petunia
Lanai Gardens

Jack Langford lives in Phase Six.

The construction worker embraced the storm, letting the torrents of rain sting his face and soak his denim jacket. His hard hat offered little protection. His sopping tool belt weighed him down. But he was content to be the last man on-site. He knew how to finish a job.

The dim work light flickered with the splatter of the raindrops. Bolts of lightning illuminated the wooden billboard staked across the construction site: Lanai Gardens Modern, new one- and two-bedroom garden apartments. Three acres of lawns, Six Phases pools, recreation rooms. Fort Lauderdale at its finest. Opening September 1958.

A few more minutes and he'd go home. To a hot shower, his bottle of whiskey, and the news on the radio. He was always fascinated by the news in his reluctantly adopted land.

Meticulous and compulsive, he was annoyed that he could not find the shovel that he'd last seen near the tall piles of gravel. He debated whether to keep searching. Never mind, he told himself. He would dig it out of the mud tomorrow in the daylight. All he had left to do was tarp over the rest of the tools that were too large to be put in the shed. Then, home.

The booming thunder kept him from hearing the stranger until the man was standing before him, wrapped in a huge black greatcoat with a wide-brimmed gray felt hat obscuring much of his face. The construction worker startled, his boot clanging into a pile of pipes. Then he relaxed. Probably someone lost, needing directions.

The stranger didn't move as he watched the construction worker lay the last corner of the tarp down.

"Are you lost?" the construction worker finally asked.

For a moment the stranger didn't answer. "No, I am not lost."

The construction worker straightened, bracing himself, forming his huge hands into fists. He always had a knack for smelling danger. "What do you want?"

"I want you to die," the stranger said with unchecked bitterness. "Now."

A huge bolt of lightning lit up the site and at the same moment they both saw the hard staff and sharp blade of the missing shovel less than five feet away, sticking up in the mud. The two men lunged for it. The stranger got to it first and raised the shovel high, preparing to charge, but the construction worker was too quick for him. He grabbed at the shovel, twisting it, pulling it away, using his more massive body to throw the stranger off balance. The stranger held tight, desperate to regain control.

Lightning and thunder were as witnesses to this dance of death. Huge earth movers stood as silent observers as well. The stranger grappled mightily in his battle to keep standing. But he fell. Then the construction worker fell. Rolling, tumbling, neither losing his grip on the shovel. Mud blinded them, covered them, slowing their movements, but hatred and the realization that only one of them would survive kept them going. Raw animal cries belched from their throats.

Several minutes later, the victor lifted his eyes to the sky so that the rain would rinse them. When he could see, he bent down and stared at the dead man's face. He smiled grimly, then glanced around, determining his next move.

The work light barely silhouetted the killer as he ripped off his clothes and exchanged them with the victim's. It was a difficult, tedious job. The clothes were soaked. The fit

19

was bad. Carefully he searched his own pockets, making sure not to leave any evidence.

Then suddenly he saw it. And with a shudder, he understood. He stared at the man's body as if memorizing something.

He dragged the dead man along the sodden gravel until he came to a plywood-framed trench. His rage returning, he kicked the body, edging him closer and closer to the hole, until the dead man tumbled and fell in. He picked up the shovel. Over and over, he pitched mud and gravel in on top of the dead man, and finally, anger spent, his body heaving with exhaustion, he stopped. He spit into the dirt and walked away.

1
HOME

The airport van pulls up between the Phase Two buildings of our Lanai Gardens condominium complex. It's a mild September evening with just a bit of drizzle coming down. I'm home at last.

I sigh happily, getting out of the van. We are back from New York and I'm so glad to be on home ground again. At the same moment I wonder — where will we all go from here?

The girls and Jack pile out. I call them girls although there's not one of them under 73 — my sister, Evvie, and our three friends, Bella, Sophie, and Ida. They're also my partners in our three-month-old private eye business.

My on-again-off-again boyfriend Jack Langford, now definitely on for good, graciously pays the van driver, since the girls manage to fumble through their purses long enough, with sheepish smiles, for Jack to

21

take up the slack. He's immediately commandeered into lugging suitcases for each one of them. Suddenly my girls are helpless? Next year's birthday presents should be smelling salts in case they decide to take up fainting. But Jack good-naturedly carries Bella's bags, along with my sister Evvie's, up the elevator in the P building, to their second-floor apartments. Then he's down again and racing across the courtyard to schlep Sophie's and Ida's things up to the third floor of building Q. The girls are always one step in front of him, rushing to unlock their doors — their idea of being helpful.

I wait downstairs for the troop movements to cease. I can foresee that there will have to be some rules and regulations as to how much they use and abuse my guy now that we are officially an item. What a relief that the girls are finally happy about our relationship, after fighting it for so long. Or are they? We shall see.

Tiny Bella is all atwitter. "It's so nice to have a man around the house," she trills off-key, hanging over her balcony and waving down to me.

"I could get used to it," Sophie calls out from across the way, patting her skirt down, trying to smooth the creases out of her lime-green velour traveling outfit as Jack lugs her stuff into her apartment.

Ida insists on carrying one of her own bags, so she picks up her small carry-on. "I'm not helpless. Yet," she tells Jack as she grudgingly allows him to wheel the other case — which, from the way it is listing to one side, looks like she packed an elephant inside.

Some of our neighbors stick their heads out to see what's going on. Not a surprise. They always stick their noses into anything anyone does at any given moment. Newly-weds Tessie and Sol Spankowitz pop out of Tessie's apartment on the second floor of Q. Is it my imagination? The reluctant husband, Sol, looks like he shrank since he got married. Not like the Sol we knew as The Peeper, who scared all the women with his lecherous snooping. Super-sized Tessie looms over him, eating pistachio ice cream from a gallon carton.

Naturally Mr. Know-it-all, Hy Binder, appears in a flash, on the second-floor balcony of P. And right behind him is his parrot. I mean his wife, Lola.

"Look who's finally blown back into town," he calls out. "So how was the Big Apple? Anybody get mugged?"

"Yeah," mimics Lola, "anybody get

mugged?"

Bella, standing two doors away, beams at the two of them. "No, but we were in a parade and got a medal. We had a fabulous time."

Sophie has to chime in, calling across, "And look who we met up with in New York. Our very own Jackie."

Uh-oh, here they go. My entire life will now be spilled out of the girls' eager mouths into our neighbors' ever-inquiring minds. But what can I do? I love them even though sometimes I want to paste duct tape across their lips.

Years ago, our husbands all dead — or in Evvie's case, divorced — we formed a new family unit sworn to care for one another through thick and thin. Mostly it's more thick than thin. We are an odd combination — mixed nuts is what Evvie calls us. My smart, fast-talking sister is also my best friend. Then there's Bella, our sweet, diminutive shadow, who follows us everywhere; roly-poly Sophie, who sees herself as a fashionista, mad about clothes; and last but definitely not least, Ida, our curmudgeon and self-proclaimed man-hater.

Bella is breathless in the face of everyone's attention. "Have *we* got a big announcement to make."

Even Ida is grinning.

By now Jack is at my side, puffing a bit, and as the new male alpha dog of our little pack, he decides to nip this bud off quickly. "Ladies," he calls out. "We've all had a very busy day. Time to get some rest."

"Yes," Evvie says with a tad of sarcasm, "let's get some rest." I can't believe my eyes. Immediately they scamper inside their own apartments, waving cheery good nights as they do. Doors one, two, three, and four — closed and not opened again. I hold my breath in case one of them changes her mind. Jack and I stand there and wait. And finally the looky-loos retreat, too. It seems as if the show is over. But I know better. They'll all be peering from behind their venetian blinds to see what we do next.

My very tall darling bends down to whisper to me, "I can feel their eyes burning holes in me."

"Not to worry," I tell him. "They'll get bored as soon as their favorite TV show comes on."

"What do we do now?" he asks. "Do you want me to come up with you?" A reasonable question since now we are officially a couple.

"It might be a better idea if we go to our own places alone. Let's meet tomorrow and figure out a plan of survival."

"Good idea. But I don't care if the yenta brigade is watching. I *am* going to kiss you good night."

I'm so lucky to have this wonderful man. For a brief moment I let myself think of the life-changing events that occurred when we were in New York. It will take a while for me to absorb the truth about my husband's murder so many years ago. But it was Jack who gave this truth as his finest gift to me. It has finally brought us together — forever more, I hope.

And Jack kisses me. Beautifully. Lovingly. I cling to him, not wanting the kiss to end.

From somewhere I hear a low smattering of applause.

Jack, suitcase in hand, walks to his building in Phase Six, his jacket collar turned up against the drizzling rain. He hears a sugary voice calling out to him from the third floor.

"Hi, honeybun. Up here."

He glances up to see Louise Bannister waving a handkerchief. His upstairs neighbor is a flamboyant widow in her sixties, who, because she's a bottle redhead, is under the illusion she's a Rita Hayworth lookalike playing Gilda. As she leans over, her Chinese red robe reveals — as Jack assumes she planned — much cleavage.

"Welcome home," she says breathily. "We missed you while you were away."

"Thanks, Louise," he answers quietly so as not to disturb the other neighbors. She's hard to take, his overwrought femme fatale neighbor, but Jack has to admit that Louise is a darned good bridge player.

His eye is caught by two men coming toward the building. Both are dressed in the Orthodox Jewish tradition: black hat, suit, and vest; full beard and mustache.

Louise calls cheerily. "Abe, Stanley, look who's home."

To Jack, the two men, both in their eighties, seem an odd pair, but they're always together. Abe Waller squints, peering through his Coke-bottle eyeglasses, and nods in recognition. Stanley Heyer smiles openly and waves in greeting. Whereas Abe is big and burly, Stanley is small and feisty. Abe speaks rarely, and smiles little. Stanley is garrulous and upbeat.

"Well, gotta go, boys," Louise says, straightening. "See you soon, hon." She winks at Jack before turning to go back into her apartment.

"I can hardly wait," Jack says under his breath.

"Good trip?" Abe asks.

"Very," Jack answers.

"Just in time for some heavy rains," Stanley comments as he plucks a few dead leaves from a hibiscus bush nearby.

Jack smiles politely. Everyone knows that Stanley was one of the original developers of Lanai Gardens back in the late '50's. Apparently he liked it so much, he moved into one of the apartments himself when they officially opened.

The two men separate and go their own way. Stanley crosses the courtyard to building Y and Abe walks into his ground-floor apartment in Jack's building, Z.

Jack's finished gathering his mail and is about to head up the stairs when he hears another voice behind him. Dora Dooley pops out of her first-floor apartment. The petite eighty-one-year-old soap opera addict is always cold, and wears a bulky sweater and wool scarf no matter the weather. "It's about time you got back. My garbage has been piling up."

"I'll take care of it in the morning, Dora. I promise," he says in his usual patient voice.

Welcome home, he thinks ironically. Women to the right of me, women to the left of me. It's not going to be easy having some kind of life with Gladdy around here with all these clutching women.

The phone has already rung four times. Each of the girls called me to do what they always do: say good night, make plans for the next day, share last-minute thoughts of any kind. Bella is last. Finally, peace and quiet. It's wonderful.

The phone rings again. It's Jack this time. "I've been trying to reach you, but the phone's been busy."

I sigh. "It's a tradition."

"I can't stand not being with you. I wish it was morning already. Maybe I should wait until dark and sneak over. No one will see me."

"That's what you think. The native drums will beat your arrival. Got a better idea. Meet me at the bus stop at the main gate. Six-thirty A.M." This time he sighs. "Six-thirty A.M. all right. Until tomorrow, my dearest. I love you."

That night, I have a dream. In it, I see Jack sitting on the beach waving a Mai Tai at me. He's in swimming trunks wearing a big floppy sun hat and aviator sunglasses with a big grin on his face. He waves to me to join him. The girls and I are dancing around a maypole. All of them are sewed on to me with huge colored ribbons. As we dance I try to get their ribbons off. I want to pull free, but they won't let go of me. The music goes faster and faster and finally we all fall down.

I wake up in a sweat. I don't need Dr. Freud to tell me what that nightmare was about.

2
MATA HARI EXPLAINS IT ALL

I am sitting at the bus stop in front of the main gate of Lanai Gardens, on Oakland Park Boulevard, at six-thirty A.M., waiting for Jack. It rained last night. Lucky thing I brought along a towel to dry the bench. But it's a lovely morning. It's been a long time since I got myself up this early. Nice to hear how quiet things are before the mobs of people start their day.

Someone has planted a new grouping of camellias in a wired fence in front of the big Lanai Gardens sign and I am enjoying admiring them. So far two buses have attempted to stop for me but I waved them on.

It's about a six-minute brisk stroll from my apartment to here, maybe ten from his. I look at my watch. I know Jack will be on time. Sure enough, here he comes at a sprint down the long road from Phase Six.

He hesitates at the strange sight of me. I

give him a great big smile. He drops down next to me on the bench, puffing slightly. "Morning," I say.

"For a moment I thought it was Halloween. What's with the Mata Hari outfit?"

"You like the black hat with the veil? And the huge dark glasses? I picked them up at a garage sale years ago for a costume party."

"So, I take it you're in disguise?"

"You bet I am. I snuck out the back way behind the buildings. Nobody looks out those windows because all they'll ever see are the garbage trucks. You might consider the same route going back. If you want any privacy, that is."

"Is this the life you predict for us from now on? Sneaking around Dumpsters? Getting up at dawn? Meeting at bus benches?" He grins. "It's a little kinky, but if that's what turns you on."

He lifts the hat off my head and places it beside me. "The better to see you with, my dear," he leers. Then kisses me, and I kiss him right back. I feel like a teenager again, sneaking out to meet my boyfriend.

Another bus starts to slow. This time Jack waves it past. I didn't know we had such good public transportation around here.

Jack turns my shoulders so I am facing

him directly. "I have an easy solution. Let's get married. After the girls get over the shock, everything will become wonderfully boring. They'll get used to us being together."

"Nice plan, but it won't work."

"Why not?"

"Maybe that's what I'm afraid of — the getting-used-to part. See how fast the girls got you to pay the cab bill and carry up their suitcases? Soon you'll graduate to 'Jackie, won't you please run down to Publix and get me a jar of Hellman's mayonnaise?' Or 'Jackie, I can't plug in my iron,' or 'Jackie, could you change a lightbulb for me? I just can't reach the socket.' Never mind they've been doing all these things for themselves for years before Mr. Easy Touch came to town."

Jack laughs and pulls me close and kisses me again. "You forget what I did last night. I just needed to snap my fingers and they jumped at my command."

I shake my head. "Foolish man. You just imagine you've got control."

"No, I know I have."

"You won't believe me? I'll prove it. We promised we'd have a celebration dinner when we got home. Okay. Tonight at the deli. It's what I like to call show and tell.

After that, you'll understand what you're in for."

For a few moments we snuggle together, exchanging kisses and waving buses on. Early-morning traffic on the six-lane street is getting heavier. Maybe we'll die from the exhaust coming out of all those vehicles. Right now, I don't care. This is bliss.

"Yoo-hoo, Gladdy, Jackie!"

We turn around and, yes, here they come. My darling, predictable girls. They climb out of a car, thanking a neighbor for the lift to the main gate. They manage to pull a huge picnic basket after them. They are all smiles.

"You left so early, you didn't have time for breakfast," says Bella, placing the basket next to us on the bench. "So we put together a feast from all four of our almost-empty fridges."

Sophie says, "Just a little snack, a little cheese, some apples," as she pulls them out. "A *rugallah* or two. Some hard-boiled eggs . . ."

Ida adds, "Naturally a few bagels and cream cheese. Already *schmear*ed." She removes these, along with plastic silverware and napkins.

Evvie grins wickedly at me, enjoying the look of horror on Jack's face. "We even

34

brought a thermos of coffee and cute little plastic cups. Just like a family picnic in the park."

"Don't bother getting up, Jackie," comments Ida. "We're fine just standing here."

I add my own evil grin as I ask him, "Shall I pour, dear, or will you?"

He grimaces. "How did you find us?"

"Piece of cake," says Ida. "Tessie was vacuuming the venetian blinds in her Florida room and she saw Gladdy sneak out. You know what an early riser Tessie is."

Evvie had this to add: "Denny was driving back from the flower market with new plants for his garden when he saw Gladdy sitting at the bus stop."

Bella giggles. "Lola was beating her rugs on the landing railing when she saw Jack run by."

My sister smiles ever so sweetly at me. "So we put one and one and one together and we realized two people we know and love were up early and we thought how nice it would be to bring them breakfast."

"How kind," I say, tossing an equal dose of saccharine back at her.

Another bus pulls up and we hear the whoosh of the pneumatic door opening. I see the expression on my sweetheart's face as he eyes the lowered steps to freedom.

35

I say, "Don't even think about it . . . Jackie."

3
THE POOL

It is still early in the morning. We've had our impromptu breakfast at the bus stop bench. Jack went back to his condo. The girls and I have done our exercises, such as they are — a little walking, a little stretching, a lot of kvetching. Now we're ready for the pool. We're waiting for the "regulars" to arrive for our usual nine A.M. meet. Definition of swim: Ten minutes spent getting in the water, inch by inch, to get used to what they describe as excruciatingly cold. The pool is kept at 80 degrees, so don't ask. Then walking and talking as we slosh our way across from side to side in the shallow section.

Now we're sitting around one of the patio tables, its umbrella shielding us from too much sun, and using the time to go through all the private eye business mail that piled up while we were solving crimes in New York. We are job efficient. Sophie opens each envelope. Bella takes out each letter and flattens it for easy reading. She hands all bills to Evvie, who is our bookkeeper. We all read, discuss, and decide which pile to place the rest of the missives in. Our stacks include: boring, crackpots, whiners, just plain stupid, junk mail, and maybes.

Sophie holds up a letter. "Here's one from a guy who wants to know if our agency can find him a girlfriend. He says he's eighty years old and still a stud muffin."

"Hah!" says Evvie. "Boy, is he unclear on the concept. This is not a dating service."

Sophie crushes the letter and puts it in the "stupid" pile. "I'm sorry Jackie had to leave us right after our nice meal. How could his head hurt so bad that he had to lie down?"

Evvie laughs. "Gee, I wonder."

Poor Jack. The girls crowding over him on the bench was a little much, and the dropped bagel crumbs on his shirt were kind of irritating, but the last straw was when Bella, in her eagerness to serve, spilled orange juice all over his lap. I'd tried to warn him.

"What about this one?" Bella says, holding up a letter. "Her husband goes to the park every day, then gets lost and can't find his way home. She says he doesn't have Alzheimer's, it's just his short-term memory that's shot."

"I feel like we're Dear Abby with these letters," Evvie comments. "What does the woman want us to do? Pick him up every day and bring him home?"

Bella looks up, surprised. "How did you guess?"

"Tell her to get him a dog," Sophie suggests. "One with a good sense of direction."

"Or put a bell around his neck so his wife can find him." Bella giggles.

Ida says, "Listen to this. A woman in Margate says men keep stalking her and the police won't believe her."

"Men?" Evvie asks. "More than one?"

"Does she give any other information," I ask, "like her age?"

Evvie says, "The woman writes she's fifty-five and still a heartthrob." She glances at the enclosed photo, then passes it around for us to see.

"Maybe we should send her photo to that first guy whose letter we read," says Ida. "I smell a possible romance here. Heartthrob meet stud muffin."

Everyone giggles.

Evvie studies a newspaper article someone sent in a folded sheet of paper. "Hmm," she says, "get this. It's from last week's *Broward*

Journal. While we were away." She laughs. "You're gonna love it. 'Grandpa Bandit eludes police again. A gray-haired elderly male has robbed six Fort Lauderdale banks to date. Bank officials and police, who arrived quickly on each scene, are baffled as to how the bandit has made his escape time after time.' Wow. And what about this?" She holds up the clipping for us to see. "Someone scribbled across the article with a heavy black marker. It says, 'Catch me if you can, girls!' "

This gets everyone's attention. "Girls?" Ida says. "He means us? How does he know who we are? Is that his way of hiring us to find him?"

Bella looks bemused. "But how will he pay us if we don't know who he is?"

"Well, he could afford it from his loot when we catch him," suggests pragmatic Sophie.

"But why would he want us to catch him?" Ida says. "I don't get it."

Evvie pulls something else out of the envelope. "Well, look at this!" She holds up a tiny green feather.

"I wonder what that's for," Sophie muses.

A green feather? A challenge to us to catch him? Why? I'm intrigued. "Put that one on our 'maybe' pile," I say.

"Someone's coming," Bella says. "I guess the pool gang is starting to arrive."

Evvie looks up and scowls. "Oh, no. Here we go again. I thought he'd have moved out by now."

Shuffling toward us is Evvie's ex-husband, Joe Markowitz. His head is bowed. It's sad to see what a broken man he's become, so unlike the virile, exciting soldier Evvie married after the war. Evvie has still not forgiven him for his sorry treatment of her during their marriage and she won't budge from her position. She hadn't seen him in more than fifteen years when, to Evvie's surprise and annoyance, Joe recently turned up and rented an apartment in Phase Three.

Joe reaches our table. "Hi, Evvie. I heard you were back. I just came over to say hello."

There's a stain on his shirt, which is buttoned wrong. And his shorts are badly wrinkled. His clothes look shabby, like he's given up caring. So unlike the meticulous dresser he used to be.

Evvie stiffens. Her tone is curt. "Okay. Hello. And good-bye. We're busy here."

I shoot her a look to tell her to lighten up a bit. She shrugs at me, meaning she doesn't want to. All our lives my sister and I have talked in body shorthand.

"Take a load off," Sophie says, offering

41

Joe a chair that she pulls from an adjoining table. Evvie is not pleased.

"May I?" he asks pathetically.

Evvie gives him her shoulder. A very cold shoulder. More like ice.

He hesitates, then sits down. No one speaks. The girls pretend to busy themselves with opening envelopes as Joe stares hopelessly at Evvie.

Finally, Evvie's had enough. "Well? Speak your piece."

"I thought I could take you out to breakfast. I'd like to talk some things over with you."

"I've already had breakfast," she says loftily, not giving him an inch. "Anything you have to say, you can say in front of my beloved sister and my dear friends."

Ouch . . . when the drama queen wants to play mean, nobody does it better.

Joe stares at her with a hangdog expression. She turns away. Joe stands up. "Maybe at a more convenient time."

The rest of us are silent when he leaves. Nobody will look at Evvie.

"What?" she says testily.

"Get up," I say. My tone is to remind her I'm the older sister. "Your parents brought you up with some manners. Go and say something kind to that poor man."

Evvie stands and puts her hands on her hips. "Or what? You gonna spank me? We're grown-ups now."

"Then act like one."

We glare at each other. Then she stomps off like a kid having a tantrum.

The girls applaud me. "Back to our mail," I say, but I'm glancing over my shoulder at Evvie catching up with Joe. He's obviously surprised and pleased, but trying not to show it.

I can barely hear their voices. "I'm sorry I was rude," she says, obviously not meaning it.

Joe shrugs. "Beggars can't be choosers. I accept your apology. But I bet Glad put you up to it."

Evvie has the decency to blush.

Joe says, "She always was nicer to me."

Isn't that the truth? Evvie, in true sisterly loyalty, humphs. "Look, Joe, I just want to say, even though you've moved here, there's no reason for you to hang out with me. I have a life and it doesn't need you in it."

"I'm sorry you feel that way. I'll try to stay out of your hair," he says sadly.

"That's that, then. See you around."

I turn around quickly, so Evvie wouldn't see me spying.

Evvie walks away and heads for her usual

43

seat around the pool, her shoulder still stiff. I assume her attitude is as kind as he deserves.

"Oh, goody, here comes the gang," Bella announces. She sweeps the piles of mail into a basket and heads for our appointed lounge chairs, which are around the three-foot-deep pool mark. These seating arrangements have been set in stone for years.

Sure enough, as if a bell rang, the usual denizens begin to arrive from all directions. The Canadians stake out their camp at the deep end, near the diving board. Hy and Lola plop down on their chaises, near the shallow end. Tessie and her new husband, Sol, who used to swim in Phase Three, take their seats next to the couple.

Barbi Stevens and her cousin Casey Wright are across the pool, directly opposite them. They immediately start rubbing sunblock on each other's bodies. My girls watch with fascination, knowing the "cousins' " secret sexual persuasion.

Oh, but here's something very new since we've been away. Irving Weiss arrives with Mary Mueller. They are carrying snacks, towels, and books to read. He now has a chaise next to hers. Irving, whose life has changed radically since his Millie went into an Alzheimer's unit at a local nursing home — Irving, who's always avoided the sun like a plague — now has become a worshipper?

There are the usual morning greetings.

As I walk past them to join Evvie at our usual spot, I have to ask. "How is Millie?"

Mary's eyes tell me what I know already. But Irving is still in denial. "Mary drives me over there every day. I stay all afternoon by her side. She seems to be doing a little better each time I see her. Sometimes I think my Millie recognizes me."

I look around. I can see there are mixed reactions to this new "couple." I know everyone feels compassion for Irving, but there are negative responses to his spending so much time with Mary. Mary must be lonely, too, since her husband left her. Speculating on what they are doing or not doing together? I shake my head. What do they want from him? That he should sit in his apartment and cry all day?

Everyone settles in. Tessie drags a reluctant Sol into the pool. She splashes him playfully, he cringes, then she takes off, doing laps. Hefty as she might be, Tessie is lightness itself as she swims laps up and down the pool.

The Canadians, the "snowbirds" who come each year during the winter, read copies of their back-home newspapers and chat quietly amongst themselves.

Lola immerses herself in one of her endless collection of romance novels. Hy always leers at their lurid bodice-revealing covers. I bet they secretly turn him on.

Casey and Barbi have their laptops open and their hands fly across the keys.

Mary reads medical journals. She used to be a nurse and even though she's retired, she likes to keep up. Irving stares into space. By his mournful expression, he must be thinking of Millie.

The girls are already in the pool. Ida and Evvie are doing kicking exercises along the edge. Bella and Sophie are humming little ditties from old musicals or other songs they remember, wiggling their fingers in time as they walk back and forth in two feet of water — their idea of strenuous exercise. I recognize the tune as "Tiptoe Through the Tulips." Tiny Tim, of course.

Hy, like some bird of prey, peruses the group, looking for mischief. His wicked, paunchy face lights on me. The perfect target. Not that I don't expect it. I hide behind my new Janet Evanovich mystery. Her books always make me laugh out loud. I brace myself. With Hy on the attack, there will be no laughter from me this morning.

Only aggravation.

"So, Gladdy," he calls out, loud enough for everyone to hear. "What's the big news announcement? Bella dropped a spicy tidbit the other day. You and Jack Langford maybe ready to tie the knot?"

Trust me, I don't have to say anything. My girls will do all the talking.

Sure enough, they hop out of the pool, dripping and smiling, ready to reveal my secrets to one and all. Except for Evvie, who will try to remain loyal . . . until she, too, will succumb to the great idol, Gossip.

Sophie starts it. "Well, you know they broke up."

Bella: "And then they made up."

Sophie: "And broke up again."

Ida: "Get to the point already. They are definitely an item and plans may soon be in the making."

I pretend to read my book, but it's impossible to concentrate. I have to keep alert for damage control.

Barbi and Casey look amused. The Canadians always listen to our repartee; to them I imagine it's something like going on safari and watching the baboons at play. Terribly droll, what?

Bella blathers on. "Gladdy doesn't have a ring, yet, but maybe . . ."

47

I shudder. I cannot bear the idea of my very private life being thrown to the hyenas. I pull my floppy sun hat farther down on my face.

Sophie adds, "We're hoping to hear dates being mentioned . . . soon."

Ida says smugly, "A formal engagement might be announced one of these days."

Sophie jumps back in. "With a great big party possibly to follow. We think."

Hy is chafing at the bit. He jumps up, his annoyance running over. "So? So? This is your idea of news? Maybe this. Maybe then. Maybe soon. Maybe later. It's like pulling teeth getting facts out of any of you. Gladdy, 'fess up."

Everyone turns to stare at me. I bet I'm doing a perfect imitation of a deer caught in the headlights of a two-ton semi. I remain in that trance, hoping it will be over soon and they'll turn on somebody else.

Evvie grins, knowing how much my silence is annoying Hy. "Believe me, you'll be the first, or maybe the last, to find out."

Lola the puppet bounces up and down with joy. "You can tell us. When's the wedding date?"

That's it. Time to stop this. I turn to Hy, smiling insipidly. "So, Hy, no joke today? I sure missed your jokes while I was away."

What can I say? It's either that or me, and I want out of the spotlight.

Hy bows like the bantam cock he is, and holds his arms aloft, embracing everyone with his largesse. "Funny you should ask. I'm reminded of this joke. I look around me, and I see couples. Newly married couples." He indicates Sol and Tessie, who simper back. "New sorts of couples." He looks toward Irving and Mary. Irving looks embarrassed. Mary throws him a dirty look. "And now love has resprouted. Phase Six melds with Phase Two."

That's aimed at me. I smile, though it's more like a grimace.

Hy pulls Lola up. I guess this routine needs a stooge.

"There's this loving couple, see? Let's call them Hy and Lola." He grins.

Isn't he the clever one? Meet Romeo and Juliet of Transylvania.

"They're sitting on the couch in front of the TV and suddenly Hy puts his arms around her."

Hy does just that. He pinches Lola for a response, and by golly, she says, "Oh, darling, how nice."

"His arm moves down her shoulder to her waist." His actions continue to follow his words.

I pray he doesn't make his story X-rated.

He pinches Lola for the next response. I guess they've been rehearsing.

She goo-goo-eyes him and says, "I love it, darling, keep going."

Hy, the man and the character, is now moving down toward her bony hips. Believe me, I'm holding my breath. He wiggles his fingers along her legs.

"Oooh, aah," she gurgles. "Don't stop."

His hand is moving dangerously close to no-man's-land. I grin, amused by my thought.

Hy, the narrator, says dramatically, "And Hy stops."

Lola moans like she's got indigestion or something. But I think she is trying to act out ecstasy. "Ooh, my precious, why did you stop?"

Hy lifts his hand aloft, using his sunscreen as a prop. "Because I found the clicker."

There is a long moment of quiet. Then, as one by one we get it, the applause builds to a smatter.

I hope this dangerous duo of daftness isn't going to be a regular act.

Suddenly there is a huge cloudburst and rain starts to fall. Hoorah, saved by the weather. We all grab our things and run home before it becomes worse and we

50

get soaked.

But when I reach my apartment, it hits me — what was different about the pool scene today. Someone was missing. Enya, our concentration camp survivor, who is always there, reading a book and never talking to anyone, didn't show up. She never misses a day. I hope nothing happened to her while we were away.

It was all confusion. Driving rain and impenetrable fog. Bodies pushed every which way, prodded by bayonets, useless struggling, nowhere to run, lights zigzagging, pinning them down, their pathetic screaming turned into wailing. Clutching their loved ones, their soggy flesh herded, smashed together until they were one mass of seething humanity. Hopeless.

Enya wakes up. She knows she should get up, but she can't. Her body *feels* paralyzed.
The nightmares have come back.

4
Dance Around the Dumpsters

Jack covers his ears against the noise of the garbage trucks as they empty the trash behind my building. It's early afternoon and once again I've snuck away from the girls to be with him. We have yet to get enough time alone to make some plans.

"I thought you were kidding when you said we should meet here," he shouts.

Between the clatter of the garbage trucks and the heavy traffic on this back road and the ambulances that speed by in a direct route to the hospital across the way, we can hardly hear each other.

"Well, I figured no one would think to look for us in this place, but then again, I thought we were safe at the front gate," I yell back at him. "You've already learned there's hardly any way to have a private conversation around my girls."

"We're not in jail, you know. We could have met off the premises." He grimaces as

52

one of the trash men heavily drops the lid of the Dumpster nearby.

"Yes, but we have a visitor coming soon, so it wouldn't have been convenient. Guess who."

"Somebody I know?"

"Intimately."

"Really? Morrie?"

I nod. He looks at me, surprised. "My son, the cop, does house calls? I'm impressed."

"Well. Not quite. He's giving a lecture in the main clubhouse on avoiding senior scams and I asked him to drop by afterward to chat with us about an odd letter we received from the man who calls himself Grandpa Bandit.

"I've already filled him in on the phone about the challenge thrown down to us. Naturally, Morrie's interested in the article sent to us with the man's handwriting on it. He's coming by to pick it up. Care to listen in?"

"Sure. Why not."

I give him a hug. "So, quick, let's get to our own agenda. We need a plan."

"I have a plan. We go out to dinner. Afterward, we go to my place. Plain and simple."

"You mean I sneak away and come over? I can walk this back route most of the way." I pause. "Wait, that's a problem. I have to tell someone where I'll be. If they keep phoning and I don't answer, they'll panic."

"That's not what I mean. No more hiding. Tell them you will be with me tonight. All night."

I am pleasantly surprised and a little shocked. "Are you sure you want to go so public? You may regret it . . ."

He tips my chin up so I can gaze into his eyes. Those gorgeous blue eyes that I want to sink into. "Chicken," he says sweetly.

He knows what I'm thinking. He always knows what I'm thinking. We have yet to consummate our love. Not for lack of trying to find an opportunity, though.

"Be brave, my sweet," he continues. "Since you won't marry and make an honest man of me, then you have to deal with being a fallen woman."

"Are you sure?" I ask tentatively.

"Yes!" he cries out dramatically. "Shout it out. Be strong. Who cares if the whole world knows!"

"Gladdy. Jackie. Hello down there." We hear Bella's lilting voice from up above. We look and she is half-hanging out of her Florida back room window on the third floor. "Morrie got done early and he's already here. We're waiting for you two

54

lovebirds to finish sparking."

Sparking? I haven't heard that obsolete word since the 1930's. Is Jack really turning purple, or am I imagining it?

He sputters, "How do they do it? How do they always know where we are and what we're doing?"

I grin. "They just do. That's what makes them such good private eyes."

I call up to Bella, "We're on our way."

I start to walk toward the front of the building. "Come on, Jackie, your cover's blown. Now's your chance to tell the whole world, including your son, that we're sleeping together tonight."

Young, handsome Detective Morgan "Morrie" Langford is waiting for us, seated at a patio table on the lawn, with my girls gazing at him adoringly. Which makes him most uncomfortable. He is dressed casually for his lecture today. Chinos and a cotton plaid shirt and a tie, instead of the usual suit.

Whenever I gaze at him, I see the young man my Jack used to be. Many a proud grandma in Lanai Gardens has shoved photos of their unmarried granddaughters into his unwilling hands, hoping to make a match. He hasn't ever followed up. Very wise, I'd say. I've seen some of those grand-daughters.

Spotting us, Bella and Sophie immediately jump up and take each of Jack's arms and cuddle into him. They lead him to an empty chair. Poor darling — trapped again.

Morrie is clearly surprised to see his father being greeted so familiarly. But before Morrie can open his mouth, Jack waves his arms at him, warning him. *Don't ask. I'll fill you in later.*

Our police detective shrugs. I guess he isn't used to seeing his dad flustered.

"Hand Morrie what we've got," I tell Evvie in my business voice. She takes the article as well as the envelope and offers both to him.

"Thanks," he says. He briefly glances at the article, then places the papers in his shirt pocket. "We'll look into it." He changes gears. "So, girls, how are you all?"

"Wait just a minute. Not so fast," I say. "After all, Grandpa Bandit reached out to *us.*"

"Don't bother your pretty little heads. It's minor stuff."

I persist. "Maybe we can help you catch him."

"Don't waste your energy. This is small potatoes."

56

Evvie chimes in. "But according to that newspaper article he's robbed six banks. Isn't that a big deal?"

"This is police business," Morrie says severely, obviously trying to end the conversation.

Don't bother our pretty little heads? Translation: We should mind our own business. What a put-down. Yet again our earlier successes as private eyes mean nothing. And why? Because of the usual prejudicial attitudes — we're old, and assumed senile. And invisible. Who would take us seriously? Even Morrie still doesn't get it — and he's seen us in action. But that's precisely why we succeed — people don't see us as a threat. They assume we've lost our marbles. That's why they're careless of what they say around us. And then we nail them.

"But it's our case," Sophie says stubbornly, as she refills Morrie's glass of iced tea.

He's just as stubborn. "You have no case."

"Yes, we do, now." Bella says sweetly. She reaches over to pick an imaginary bit of lint off his shirt.

Morrie is getting hot under the collar. "You have no client. A client meets with you face-to-face."

Bella smiles at his naiveté. "Now, isn't that

silly? If he met with us, we'd know who he is."

Sophie jumps in. "Yeah, and we wouldn't have a case anymore."

"Where is it written that he hired you?" Morrie crosses his arms, determined not to let us steamroll him, which we are about to do.

Ida points. "In the article that you just pocketed. In his very own handwriting. He wants us to catch him, not you."

"Yeah," says Bella. "If he wanted you to catch him, he'd have written to you."

Morrie's face stiffens. Jack shakes his head, trying to signal his son. I can tell he's warning him to get out while he can. But Morrie blunders on. "So where's your retainer?"

Bella smiles. "Silly. We work on a handshake deal." She stops to think about what she's said. "That is, we'll shake his hand when we find him."

Morrie is behaving oddly — for him. He's usually not so nervous around us. He's hiding something. I wonder what's going on. I can tell by Jack's expression he has the same impression.

"Look," Morrie blurts as he stands up, "somebody is pulling your leg. Somebody you know sent you the clipping as a gag."

That stops us for a moment, then Evvie glances at me, both of us remembering. "Take a look in the envelope," she says. "You missed something."

Puzzled, Morrie opens the envelope and sees the tiny green feather. By the way his face goes from tan to red to gray, we've hit gold.

"That wasn't in the newspaper, was it?" Evvie says knowingly. "That's the information the police kept back."

"Bingo," I say. "Your bandit has thrown down his gauntlet, so to speak. In fact," I add, "do us a big favor, since we're so old and helpless, mail me a list of the banks that our client robbed, and their addresses."

Morrie is sputtering by now. "Wait just one minute . . ."

He's right, of course. The police don't want civilians pursuing cases on their own. They want cooperation and information, not meddling. Or interfering in a way that might compromise their investigation or their evidence. It's not just the bandit who's thrown down the gauntlet; so has Morrie, wanting us to keep out of it.

We are at an impasse.

Jack says, "Son, why don't you and I grab a cup of coffee and let the girls do what they are so good at — finding out anything and everything they set their minds to."

With a last glance at me, he winks and the two men take off. That is, as soon as Jack can get Sophie and Bella to let go of his arms.

I call after him, "Jack, you have an announcement to make. Remember?"

He grins. "Enough excitement for one morning. Later."

I laugh. The girls want to know what's so funny. I give them the same answer: "Later."

5
EARLY BIRDS

The girls are not happy. They're dressed for going out but so far they are getting nowhere. We stand in front of my building waiting for Jack to pick us up. It rained all day and there are puddles everywhere, so we are grouped in a tight circle under the eaves, where the ground is dry. Sophie's pantsuit is a study in peach. From top to toes, she is every shade imaginable. Even to her latest hair dye, sort of peachy brown. Bella is also monochromatic — all in pale gray, which matches her hair as well. The two of them color coordinate whenever we go out. Evvie, on the other hand, is in one of her many flamboyant caftans — a riot of color, no pastels for her. Her hair is still red, but the gray is coming back slowly. Ida — well, Ida dresses as if she's standing under a thundercloud. Very dark. Plain. No frills, no jewelry for our Ida. I'm in my usual beiges, tans, and whites, with a coral blouse and silk scarf.

We are already late. Bella couldn't find her glasses. Sophie couldn't decide between her beige flats or her peach sandals. It's already four-thirty, and I told Jack to be here by four. It's our first outing as a couple with the girls and I'm nervous enough about the outcome. The girls are already grumpy, not a good sign.

Much tapping of feet and glancing at watches. Finally Jack's vintage Cadillac casually pulls over to pick us up, just before five.

"Hi, ladies," he says, getting out and opening all the car doors. The girls climb in, not looking at him. Ida mumbles, "It's about time."

Jack looks at me and I shrug and say, "Go ahead, ask it. I know you're dying to."

"Why does anyone want to eat at four-thirty?"

"You'll see." I realize that Sophie and Bella have already scrunched their way into the front seat, so I don't get to sit next to my "date." I struggle to fit myself in back with Evvie and Ida. Thank goodness the Caddie is large and roomy.

We stand on the long, long, long, long line snaked around the strip mall parking lot adjacent to our favorite deli, the Continental, and apparently everyone's else's, too. Ida taps her foot. Bella, as usual, peers into every store window as we pass. Evvie is using my back as a desk, scribbling her latest movie review for the next issue of her Lanai Gardens newsletter. Jack stands next to me, his shoulders slumped, his eyes glassy. The line is hardly moving.

I gesture at the crowd. "Now you know. Short lines at four. Chaos after five."

Sophie adds, "And the prices are lower."

Bella pipes up, "And the kasha varnishkas sell out fast."

"I am more than willing to go somewhere else and pay whatever extra it costs." Jack is sweating. He takes his jacket off.

"No way," says Ida. "We refuse to be beholden to you. We are independent women and pay our own way."

"At least Evvie is smiling," he says, grasping at straws.

Evvie looks up from her notebook. "That's because I'm writing about George Clooney, that hottie."

After yet another ten sweltering, humid minutes, we finally get inside.

I see Jack glance around. He whispers to me, "Not many men here."

"You need reinforcements?" I ask.

"I might." He squeezes my hand. "I'd love to kiss your cheek but I don't want to embarrass you."

I laugh. "Honey, in this place, embarrassment knows no bounds."

We get our favorite waitress, Velma, formerly of Flatbush, Brooklyn. Thin as a blade of sawgrass. Greasy hairstyle circa 1950's, very puffy and large. Nickname: Motormouth. The girls like her because she always makes sure to give them big portions of dessert. She is thrilled to see us.

As she shoves the menus at us, she says, "So where you guys been? I thought you all died."

"Not yet," Bella comments mildly. The girls are used to Velma's hyperbole.

"We took a vacation." Sophie bites off a chunk of sour pickle from a dish of coleslaw and assorted pickles already on our table.

Velma, not much of a listener, runs along her own track. "Boy, you missed some excitement around here. Edna Glatz from Hawaiian Gardens choked on a bone and almost expired before our very eyes."

"No!" Sophie and Bella chorus in horror, as Jack attempts to concentrate on the three-foot-high plastic menu.

"If it wasn't for our manager, Mr. Kay, who knew the Heimlich maneuver, we would have a dead duck on our floor. Instead of on a plate." She chuckles at her joke.

I can see other customers waggling their fingers to get Velma's attention, but Velma loves to talk and is on a roll. "And one day Mary Lou Feeney's great-grandchild up-chucked on their table, all over the *plat de jour* and her new flowered sundress. Don't ask."

"Could we order?" Jack asks morosely.

Velma is pulled up short by this interruption of her news report. She pretends to do a double take, as if seeing him for the first time. She turns seductive. Her idea of sexy is batting her eyelashes.

"I didn't notice you have a man with you. And who is this Mr. Gorgeous?"

Jack blushes. I can tell that he's sorry now that he opened his mouth. Here we go.

Ida can't resist. "Meet Gladdy's intended. Jack, meet Velma."

Nor can Bella. "We're here to celebrate."

"Gedouddahere!" Velma screeches with excitement. She flashes a huge mouthful of horsy teeth at me. "Congratulations! This calls for an announcement!" She picks up a glass and a spoon and turns to the rest of the room. I grab her by her apron strings and tug hard. She turns back.

I glare. "No announcements. Please."

Velma reluctantly replaces the glass and spoon. She sniffs loudly. "I guess I'll take your orders now."

Dinner manages to glide along without too many annoyances. Sophie sends her chicken back — "Too tough." Ida complains her brisket is stringy. Evvie doesn't take her eyes off me while I'm looking at Jack and Jack is looking back at me. Usually I can read my sister's expression, but not tonight. Everyone's cheerful but there is an underlying tension. Kind of like waiting for the other shoe to drop. I am on edge wondering if Jack is going to make his promised announcement about my going home with him tonight. I'm hoping he doesn't.

The checks arrive. Velma gives them out one at a time, making goo-goo eyes at Jack when she hands him his. The girls get into their usual discussion about tips. They pull out their little tip chart and make their decision. Velma always gets their best. Twelve percent.

Jack says, "I really do want to treat all of you."

I add, "And I agree. In honor of our celebration tonight."

"Nonsense," says Ida. "I told you, we pay

our own way." She reaches into her purse and takes out her share.

Bella follows suit, digging down into her pockets. She pulls out crumpled-up dollar bills along with many, many coins, which she counts aloud.

Evvie hands him her check and folds her hands. She smiles sweetly at Jack. "I don't mind being treated on occasion."

Sophie grapples through her purse. Then again. And again. She throws up her hands in disgust. "I can't believe it. I left my wallet at home."

"Shh," Bella cries out. "I lost count. Now I have to start again." With that she flails her arms and accidentally knocks her pile of coins onto the floor.

Jack gallantly stoops down to pick them up.

While he is down there on his knees, reaching under the table, a drumroll sounds. More like someone banging on a pot. Even though it's still light outside, someone is flashing the light switches off and on. And a huge chorus of voices begins to sing, "Happy engagement to Jack and Gladdy, happy engagement to them . . ."

Jack, caught on his knees as if he is in proposal mode, practically cracks his skull leaping out from under the table.

All the diners in the restaurant burst into applause.

I shrug at Jack and point to the huge strawberry cheesecake lit with candles that Velma holds aloft as she comes toward us.

The bill is finally paid. By Jack. Why am I not surprised? The girls are about to stand up, when Jack announces. "Ladies, I have something to tell you."

I gasp. I can't believe he's actually going to do it. All eyes look to him expectantly. "Glad won't be going straight home tonight. I'll drop you all off, then Gladdy and I will go to my apartment."

Sophie and Bella don't get it right away. When Bella does, she blushes. Ida's head drops down as she rips what's left of the bread on her plate into little pieces. Sophie giggles. Evvie slyly smiles.

The awkward silence that follows is broken by Mr. Kay, the manager, who walks over to our table and hands me a plain white envelope. "Mrs. Gold, a gentleman gave this to me on his way out and asked me to deliver it to you."

I open it as the girls begin to come out of their comatose state. Inside is a plain white piece of paper folded in thirds. As I take it out a small green feather flutters onto the table. I pick it up as I read from the scrawled note, " 'Getting old ain't for sissies. Catch me if you can.' " There's more but the girls are already on their feet. I shove the note and feather in my purse and stand.

Bella fairly swoons. "Another note from the Grandpa Bandit!"

To Jack's astonishment, we all race for the door. Once outside we look around the parking lot.

"Look!" Evvie shouts.

We see a hand waving to us from the darkened window of a senior pickup van leaving the shopping center. We hurry to the curb, but are too late. Evvie quickly grabs her pen and takes down the model and license number of the van.

Back in the restaurant again, we question the manager. But all Mr. Kay can say is he was an old guy with gray hair. Figures.

6
JACK'S PLACE

From Jack's grinning and whistling, I gather the girls didn't throw him off as much as I feared. I guess the letter from the bandit with its green feather cushioned the shock of his announcement.

We dropped the girls off at Phase Two, thinking who knows what thoughts as they stared after us. Jack parked his car, and now we stroll, hand in hand, toward his apartment building. All I have brought to this evening's adventure is my toothbrush. I wish I'd had time to put on something slinky (not that I have much in that line). Or even a dab of perfume. But never mind, it's a beautiful evening. The storm clouds still hover, but the sky has striations of reds amongst the deep purplish-blues. And I'm with my darling man.

Jack swings my arm with his, like some happy five-year-old on his way to a party. "See how easy this will be?" Now he's the party clown putting on a smiley face for the birthday girl. His mood is contagious. I feel like a kid, too. I am fairly skipping along with him.

We hurry upstairs to his apartment on the second floor. Jack turns the key in the lock. I glance around discreetly, relieved to see that no one is watching. The grounds are fairly empty since it is dinnertime for most people — those who don't live by early-bird-special rules.

Jack's voice goes singsong. "I know what you're thinking."

I laugh. "I know you know."

Once we're inside, he makes a demonstration of double locking the doors. Dramatically, he pulls down the blinds in each of the rooms. "No one and nothing will spoil this evening. I give you my promise."

"And I'll hold you to it." I watch his shenanigans with delight. He's so good to be with. I feel so blessed. I also feel a little nervous about where this is going.

He turns off the phone ringer with a flourish. "There! We are alone in our little pleasure-dome cocoon. Nothing will disturb us."

With that he grabs me and kisses me, holding me tight to him. It's a wonderful kiss, and the hug that goes with it feels like

71

it may go on forever. I hope it does. We finally come up for air.

"Need a drink for courage?" he asks me.

"No," I whisper, trying to catch my breath.

We zigzag our way to the couch. "Shall I tear off our clothes before or after we make it to the bed?" Jack says this as he's unbuttoning his shirt.

"Wait," I say eagerly. "We need to exorcise old demons."

"Go on, exorcise away." Jack kicks off his shoes.

I am worried. Not so much about the act we intend to consummate — well, that, too, a little. My concern is, what will interrupt us this time? Something has on every other occasion. I have to voice it out loud. "May I remind you that in Pago Pago, just as were about to have at it, we received a fax that changed our plans immediately . . ."

"How could I forget?" Jack gestures expansively with his hands. "No fax machine here. No problem."

"And our silly fight that kept us apart for so long."

"Over and forgotten."

"In your New York hotel room, the phone rang, once again interrupting us with important news that had to be dealt with instantaneously."

"Phone's turned off. No news can find us."

I listen. The silence is wonderful.

"Nothing's going to intrude. I'm telling you."

"It will. I know it will."

"Nonsense." He pulls me down on the couch. Then onto his lap. "Thank God."

"Why 'Thank God'?"

"Because I don't need Viagra."

Kiss. Kiss. Ummn, more . . .

"Lucky us to have each other."

I snuggle closer into his arms. "No girls to interrupt."

"No thinking about the girls allowed. Shut it down."

"Done."

More kissing and murmuring of silly nothings. How happy can one be? His body fits so well with mine. I let myself sink into the pleasure of the moment. It's been so long . . .

The doorbell rings.

We freeze.

I moan, "No . . ."

He echoes my "No," then shakes his head. "I will not answer it."

We both jump up so quickly that we bang heads.

The doorbell rings again. Jack mutters irritably, "I am absolutely not opening that door."

The ringing is now followed by knocking and then a seductive female voice calling, "Come on, Jack, I know you're in there."

Now it's Jack's turn to moan.

Another voice is heard. A high-pitched one. "It's seven o'clock."

And yet another female voice, a wispy one. "I brought the cards."

Jack gets off the coach. I roll over into a sitting position, straightening my dress as best I can.

He whispers to me, "Don't move, they'll go away."

"Who are they?" I ask.

"My bridge partners."

A few moments later, Jack's cell phone rings from a side table, once again startling us. Jack snarls. "They aren't giving up." He glares at it as the phone keeps ringing, then finally it stops.

We wait breathlessly. Silence. He smiles at me, sensing victory, then grimaces as the pounding on the door begins again.

We look at each other. No use. Jack says, "One thing you can say about bridge players, they are tenacious!"

Moving to the door, he runs his fingers through his hair and turns on the lights.

"Damn, damn, damn . . ."

He struggles with the double lock, cursing. When he finally opens it, there is an immediate flurry of activity. One woman, nice-looking, in her fifties, wearing navy blue sweats, lugs in a small square folding table. Two other women carry packages. One of them, a redhead wearing a rather sexy sundress with a jungle/tiger print, moves easily to the kitchen. The one following her is taller and big-boned. Even though they see me sitting there, none of them has the decency to be embarrassed.

The sexy voice calls out, "We brought all the snacks this time because we knew you didn't have time to shop."

The taller one adds, "Mostly pretzels and chips."

As if in a trance Jack helps the woman in blue sweats unfold the card table.

I sit up straighter on the couch, trying to look casual and relaxed although I am neither. I'm actually frustrated and annoyed. I cross and recross my legs. This can't be happening again. It can't. Is this some cosmic joke?

Finally the trio turns to stare at me. The sexy woman stands much too close to Jack, who looks beyond sheepish.

"Hi," says the sexpot. "I'm Louise Bannister." With that dress, I expect her to growl.

The tall woman says, "I'm Carmel Graves, from one flight up."

And blue sweats waves cheerfully. "I'm Carol Ann Gutsch from two doors down."

"My bridge partners," says Jack, shamefacedly. "Tonight's our usual game night. I guess I forgot."

I get up from the couch and move on shaky legs. "I'm Gladdy Gold," I manage to say, my voice breaking. I can't even look at Jack. "I was just leaving," I stammer.

"No, don't," Jack says, holding tightly to my arm. He faces the trio of card players. "I'm terribly sorry, but I made other plans tonight."

"So I see," says Ms. Bannister, assessing her competition. "I wish you'd called. I could have made other arrangements and not wasted my evening."

Carol Ann behaves as if someone ran over her pet cat. "I was so looking forward to tonight. I circled it three times on my calendar."

Carmel also seems crestfallen. "Maybe I could still make it to the movies if I can find someone to drive me. I don't see too well at night."

They look to Jack, waiting. What a bunch.

The man-eater is trying to make him feel guilty because such a hot tootsie could have filled her dance card over and over again.

Carol Ann is making him feel even guiltier about her lonely night ahead, and Carmel is playing the "I'm so needy" card. Jack doesn't have a chance.

I touch his shoulder and shake my head. I say to the group, "Please, don't let me upset your plans." I give Jack a quick peck on the cheek and leave.

As I hurry toward the stairwell, Jack is suddenly behind me. "Gladdy, wait."

"Let me know who wins." I can barely stifle my sarcasm.

"I am going to insist we play another night. Come back in. Please." He tries to pull me into his arms, but the mood is gone. Talk about totally.

"I can't. Not right now. I have a splitting headache."

Jack tries for a smile. "Can't you see the humor in this?"

And I do. I laugh softly. Jack joins in. He says, "You think there's some conspiracy keeping us apart?"

"Probably. Go back inside before your harem girls melt into a pool of self-pitying tears. And beat the hell out of them. In cards, I mean."

He kisses me.

I warn him, "And watch out for the tigress in there. She's out to devour you."

I'm still laughing as I dash down the stairs.

Suddenly, the skies open. It's raining and of course I didn't bring an umbrella. Then I realize I left my toothbrush at Jack's. I slosh my way home, my feet getting wetter and wetter in my open heels. All the way I am giggling and muttering like a madwoman. "I cannot believe this, I absolutely, positively cannot believe this . . ."

7
ENYA IN TROUBLE

Enya thrashes about in her bed in the throes of a terrible nightmare.

Closer and closer. They are coming at last. There is no place to hide or to run. Huddled in their bedroom, the four of them cannot look at one another because the truth will be revealed in their eyes — they are doomed. Eyes, eyes. She sees *his* eyes and the terrible scar. Why is there no help? The pounding rain will drown them. They are hammering on her door. No escape.

As I dejectedly arrive back at my building, I am surprised to find many people holding umbrellas and standing around. I look up and see Ida on the balcony of our floor, staring across the courtyard parking area to the building opposite. She is holding a newspaper over her head against the rain. I turn to find out what's caught her interest.

Denny, our handyman, dressed in rain

gear, is standing in front of his apartment, staring up at the second floor. Evvie and Bella are on the walkway in front of Enya's apartment, 219, at the end of their floor. At the opposite end of the landing, Hy and Lola are standing in their doorway, whispering and gesturing.

Evvie is pounding on Enya's door. "Enya. Open up. Please?" Bella huddles right behind her.

I am up the stairs in moments, joining them. "What's going on? What's wrong?"

Evvie glances at me, surprised. "What are you doing here? You're supposed to be with Jack."

I'm not about to go into detail about bridge players barging in on us and trumping our love scene. "Never mind that right now. Why is everyone outside?"

"We heard Enya screaming and then it suddenly got very quiet. We're trying to find out what's wrong but she won't open the door."

I try the bell, with no response. We attempt to peer into her kitchen window, which is next to the door. There is some ambient light, but no movement. I take out my cell phone and dial her number. It rings five times. Finally a small soft voice answers. "Who's there?"

I sigh with relief. "Enya, it's Gladdy. Are you all right?"

"I need to sleep. I can't sleep."

"Please let us in. Just for a moment. Okay?"

She hangs up. I do, too. After a few seconds the door slowly opens. Enya, wearing an old gray chenille bathrobe, barely peers out. She looks haggard and frightened. I speak gently to her. "May we come in?"

She nods. Evvie turns to all the onlookers to signal things seem all right.

Ida calls from across the courtyard, "I'm on my way."

Bella backs away. "It's fine," Evvie tells her. "Go back to your place and rest." Bella, relieved of having to deal with something possibly frightening, does so.

The show is over. The onlookers return to their apartments. The rain stops.

I can't remember the last time any of us has been inside Enya's apartment. Years and years ago. And only briefly. She is a very private person and wants to be left alone. We've tried to include her in events, but she politely refuses. While her husband, Jacov, was alive, he brought her to all the seders we had and the Hanukkah parties. But after he died she didn't pretend anymore. She wanted nothing to do with celebrations, religious or otherwise. She's eighty-four now but it seems that, as far she's concerned, she died with her entire family in 1942.

Her home is laid out as all of our apartments are: tiny entry hall, equally small kitchen, dining area and living room next, and bedrooms off to the side. But unlike the rest of us, who've decorated our homes to our taste, Enya has kept hers sparsely furnished. She has never bothered to adorn it in any way. She still has the few pieces of basic furniture she bought years ago when she and Jacov moved in. There is no artwork on the walls. However, there are books, magazines, and newspapers everywhere — both in English and German.

Ida arrives and joins us.

Enya is shaking, though the apartment has the heat turned up high and the weather outside is warm and muggy. Now that I can look at her more closely, it seems as if she's aged overnight. We crowd the spotless kitchen. Evvie immediately starts boiling water for tea. I find a shawl on one of the kitchen chairs and wrap it around Enya's shoulders. Ida brings in a throw blanket from the living room couch. She places it across Enya's knees.

When the water is ready, Evvie prepares a pot of chamomile tea. She has to hold the cup for Enya, who can't control her tremors.

"This will warm you up," Evvie tells her.

"It was a terrible dream. It woke me."

I ask, "Do you want something to eat?"

"No, I only want to sleep and I can't anymore."

Anymore? That sounds ominous.

"Why not?" Evvie asks gently as she pours a little more tea.

Enya clutches the shawl tightly around her and bows her head. She doesn't want to speak, but we wait. Finally she lifts her head, her eyes glazed, as if we aren't there. "There was a storm the night they came for us."

She stops, lost in her troubled thoughts.

"A storm?" Evvie prompts. "Like the rain tonight?"

She shakes her head. "No, so much worse. They pulled us out of our home, without coats or hats and clutching only a few small personal things. We sat in the open trucks, wet and shivering."

Evvie, Ida, and I look at one another, distraught. She has never spoken to any of us of the horrors her family went through. Jacov did when she wasn't with him. But that was so many years ago. Why now? It's as if I'd asked the question out loud.

"I haven't had these dreams for such a long time." She shudders. "It's the storm. I can't bear the rain."

I remember Jacov telling us that Enya was a college professor in their native Prague. He was an architect. They were both married to other people, but they lost everything and everyone in the camps — Enya and Jacov were the only survivors in each of their families. They met in America after the war.

"I'm so tired." Enya pushes the teacup away and lays her head on the kitchen table.

We are at a loss to know what to do to help her. "Do you want me to call your doctor?" I ask.

"No, no doctor," she whispers.

Ida leans down and says softly, "Come back to bed, Enya dear."

She helps her up and Enya doesn't resist. The three of us walk her down the short hallway and into her bedroom. There is only a small light on the wooden chest of drawers next to the double bed, but it is enough for us to witness a shocking sight.

The entire wall opposite the bed is covered with photos and papers. From top to bottom, old, crumpled, torn family photos and documents. Jacov's smiling face and his equally smiling first wife in a marriage photo. Various happy shots of their four children before the monstrosity that took their lives. Enya's collection of her dead — her husband and two children, standing in front of an obviously expensive house, the two little girls in ballet outfits. Documents, possibly in German. Maybe marriage licenses. College degrees. School report cards, it's difficult to tell. The personal things they took with them that managed to survive.

The remnants from a country gone mad. Reparations finally offered for that which was irreplaceable.

Evvie and Ida help Enya into bed, then join me and share my shock. I can see it in their faces and they in mine. *This* is what Jacov and Enya looked at night after night from their marriage bed? The guilt of the survivors, so they would never forget? God have mercy on their souls.

Enya, almost delirious with exhaustion, cries out, "They're coming for us. Hide! Hide! Something bad is coming, something very bad!"

We rush back to her side. Ida covers Enya with the blanket, then turns to us. "I'm going to stay with her."

I look down on this tortured woman thrashing in her bed and I am in tears.

■ ■ ■ ■

When Evvie and I walk outside, it is raining again. Pouring. The wind now raging. I walk her to her apartment, two doors down. Hug her and kiss her good night. She offers to give me an umbrella, but I tell her not to bother, it will only blow away. Besides, my feet are already wet.

I run across the courtyard, head down against the wind, getting soaked, of course. Was it only this morning Jack and I got up at dawn and met at the bus stop to rendezvous? What a day filled with dramas! The girls showing up with breakfast and interrupting us. The gang at the pool interrogating me. Morrie telling us to mind our own business about the Grandpa Bandit. The crazy dinner at the deli, and let's not forget the bridge players showing up at Jack's apartment. With Enya's nightmares to end this stressful day, I want only to throw myself into bed and pull the covers over my head and sleep.

In my apartment I attempt to towel dry my hair. And try to think about this emotional seesaw I'm on. But I am beyond tired.

Suddenly I remember that the bandit's note had more to say — we forgot about it when we ran out of the deli to chase him.

Once again I call upon Scarlett O'Hara to guide me in times of tension. I dig the envelope out of my purse, and without reading the rest of his note, I toss it on the kitchen table and head for my bedroom.

I'll think about it tomorrow.

8
DAMAGE

Rain poured relentlessly all night, amid dramatic displays of thunder and lightning. The winds raged, making eerie sounds in the darkness — creaking and groaning as if the buildings could bear no more.

In the morning, Jack glances around as many of the residents of Phase Six group themselves in front of Z building in the early light. They seem a sorry collection, most still in pajamas and robes, shaking their heads, surrounded by the mess all over the grounds, and studying the building that is clearly in trouble. Z for Zinnia, Jack reminds himself. The rain has finally stopped, but the wind still howls and his neighbors all stand hunched over — even the palm trees are bending over. Windows have been blown out. The elevator has been seriously damaged. Carmel Graves reports the roof leaking in her third-floor apartment.

Stanley Heyer is also here. Right now, he

is pacing back and forth in front of his crumbling creation.

Dora Dooley and Louise Bannister stand on either side of Jack, clinging to him. Carmel Graves huddles into herself, staring up at her damaged apartment worriedly. A Canadian couple, Larry and Sylvia Ulan, look on with concern as well. Residents from building Y across the way lend sympathetic mutterings.

"Seems like the roof took a beating last night," Stanley comments. He'd already sent his roofer up there this morning to investigate.

"I was so scared," Carmel says. "I thought the whole building would cave in on me. I hardly slept a wink."

"Me, neither, all that thunder and lightning right on top of us," adds Louise, leaning closer to Jack as if needing his support — far too close for comfort.

Stanley makes notes in a pad he holds. "Fortunately, it looks like you people got the worst of it. The other buildings report very little damage."

"Lucky us," comments Louise.

"And notice the cracks along the sides," Sylvia Ulan adds, pointing. "This place is falling apart at the seams." Her husband nods in agreement.

"Well, I'll get on it right way," Stanley says, "but I got to warn you, with all these storms lately, there's hardly a worker available. My roofer told me he's already backed up into late October. I'll see who I can round up."

"Please hurry," Sylvia says, nervously clutching her husband. "Do what you can."

Stanley shakes his head. "Fifty years these buildings are standing. Never a big problem. Now this. Let's hope the storms don't get any worse."

The group slowly disbands, but Louise doesn't seem willing to let go of Jack. "Wanna come up for a cup of coffee?"

"I would love to, Louise, but I've got to get going. I —"

"I'll take you up on your offer," says Dora.

Jack tries not to grin. That's not what Louise had in mind. She never stops trying.

"Forget it," Louise says sharply. "I've got too much to do." With that she flounces off.

Dora shrugs. "What a ding-a-ling. Well, I got my soaps waiting for me. Who needs her swamp mud coffee?" And she's off.

Jack looks up again at his damaged building and shakes his head. Not a good sign. He wonders how Gladdy's building held up.

The way things are going around here, when will they ever find time alone? He's got to think of something.

The girls are fairly jumping up and down with excitement. Having finally read the rest of Grandpa Bandit's note this morning, I discover he intends to rob another bank. Today! This very afternoon, in fact. I quickly called the girls to an early-morning meeting at our usual patio table under our favorite palm tree. Our poor tree lost many a frond during last night's storm, Except for trash blown everywhere, though, our buildings didn't suffer too much damage. But because of the heavy wind, now starting, we change our minds and go back inside to my apartment instead.

First order of business is to check on Enya. Ida says she slept fitfully, but she is up and about this morning and seems in better spirits. So hopefully her nightmares will stop.

I know I have to call Morrie and give him a heads-up about the bandit. But based on his unfriendly attitude about this case, first we must make our own plans. Grandpa's going to hit the SunTrust on Oakland Park Boulevard, according to his note. Fortunately, we are familiar with that corner — we shop there often. Naturally Morrie will tell us to stay away, but we intend to find a hiding place nearby so we can watch Grandpa in the act. How can we resist?

Sophie reminds me that one of our favorite delis, the Bagel Bistro, is right across the street, so we agree to use that as our observation point. I advise the girls to dress in subtle colors so we won't be noticed. Sophie beams at that; she can hardly wait to coordinate her outfit.

"Grandpa's got to know we'll tell the police. How's he going to make his getaway with them there?" Ida wonders. "He must have a reason for wanting us to know his plans. This is going to be trouble for us, I know it." Always the cynic.

"Maybe this time they'll catch him," Bella says.

"And we get the credit for leading them to him." Sophie looks up from polishing her nails. Her newest color is Burnt Orange to match her latest hair dye.

Evvie smiles. "Wanna bet he eludes them again? He has to have an escape plan. I'm dying of curiosity to know how he does it."

The girls listen as I talk to Morrie on the phone. "No article this time. He wrote a real letter. Yes, I'll read it to you. He says, 'Today I'm hitting another clueless bank, this time SunTrust, between two P.M. and four P.M. Oakland Park branch. He also says, 'Getting old ain't for sissies,' and once again he writes, 'Catch me if you can, girls.' That's it."

I listen, and shake my head. I say, "Yes, Morrie, even though it's clear now this is our case, we'll stay away," with as much sarcasm as I can muster. Then I add, "And don't forget to send us the list of banks he's already robbed. Yeah, yeah, I know, it's in the mail. Sure."

When I hang up Bella does a little dance in anticipation. "This is gonna be so much fun!"

After the girls leave, I call Jack. He tells me about his damaged building and I catch him up on our bandit.

"Did you call Morrie?" he asks.

"Of course I did."

"And did he tell you to stay away?"

"Naturally."

"And you aren't going to listen to him, are you?"

I think a moment — do I lie or tell the truth?

Jack answers before I weigh this decision about honesty in relationships. "You're going. I know you are."

"Don't tell Morrie," I beg.

"I would never mix in with your business

tactics, but you can guess what I'm thinking."

"I know . . . I know," I say, feeling guilty.

We both change the subject at the same time and, saying the same thing: "I missed you last night."

The girls and I meet at my old Chevy wagon at one o'clock. We're hoping to get there a little before Morrie and his cops arrive. As agreed upon, we are all in pastel shades or light grays and tans. Except Sophie. Her idea of subtle is a bright yellow slacks outfit with a bright yellow ribbon in her hair. She's carrying a huge yellow flowery purse.

Ida shakes her head in disgust. "You look like a lollipop!"

Evvie says, "More like a deranged canary who escaped from her cage. Where's a cat when you need one?"

Sophie sniffs, annoyed by our attack on her judgment. "The walls in Bagel Bistro happen to be painted in sunshine yellow and I'll blend into the woodwork perfectly. So there!"

Huh. No arguing with Sophie's logic. We're on our way.

When we arrive at Oakland Park Boulevard, first we oh-so-casually check out the front of the bank and then take a brief stroll inside, searching for anyone who might look suspicious. Every gray-haired man is to be examined. There are senior citizens, but only four male gray heads. I snap my fingers and the girls get it. Each follows one of the men only to return moments later, saying that all four got into their cars and drove away.

"One of them almost hit a telephone pole backing up," reports Ida, "but let's not get into a discussion of how some seniors drive."

So, we hightail it out of the bank and over to our hiding place.

The deli is packed with the lunchtime crowd, but we're lucky — there's a table for four in a corner at the window with a perfect view of SunTrust Bank directly opposite. We drag over another chair so the five of us can all squeeze in. It's then I realize Bella isn't with us.

Evvie nudges me to look out the window, and there's Bella, still across the street, bent over, dropping money in a small cup. An elderly legless man, wearing a large torn straw hat, holding pencils, is propped up on a wooden block with skate wheels. It is a small drama. After Bella puts her money in his cup, he hands her a pencil. She shakes her head and steps back. The legless man says something to her and waggles the pencil at her. Finally she gives in. She takes her pencil and crosses the street.

Dear kind Bella, I think. There's no way she'd take the pencil and prevent him from another sale.

We are in a deli, so naturally everyone wants to eat. But I warn them not to take their eyes off the bank. Happy chomping commences as we watch the busy parade of passersby go back and forth and in and out of the bank.

Sophie points animatedly. "Look, there's Morrie."

Morrie walks past the bank with his good friend and fellow detective Oz Washington and several other men in plain clothes. The legless man tries to sell them a pencil, but they ignore his efforts.

The men spread out. Morrie and three others enter the bank. Oz and the two men with him cross the street and move to the left of the deli.

"Oh, oh. They're searching all the stores!" Evvie grabs me by the sleeve. We all watch as the three men disappear from sight. Bella guesses Oz is going to the lamp-shade place next door.

"They're having a ten-percent-off sale," she informs me. We wait nervously. Moments later they appear again, and suddenly I have a sinking feeling.

I bark, "It looks like he's coming in here. Everybody hide your face." We use napkins, menus, half-eaten sandwiches, squirming to look invisible — but sure enough, as Oz walks up and down the restaurant searching for gray heads, he reaches our table and naturally recognizes us. He is his usual gorgeous self — café-au-lait skin, wavy black hair, and a smile to break your heart.

Caught! This was a dumb idea, picking a place so close to the bank. Oz and I exchange glances. For a moment, I hold my breath. Oz winks and walks past us.

We wait motionless until he and his men are safely past our table.

Ida whispers, "Why didn't he say something? Such as 'Get out of here'?"

I exhale in relief. "I think he likes us. And I bet he doesn't tell Morrie that he saw us."

Two o'clock comes and goes. So does three. Luckily the restaurant has cleared out and nobody needs our table. My eyes are smarting from watching so intently. People enter the bank and exit the bank. But nothing. No robbery. Finally my watch reads four. I can see Morrie, Oz, and their guys take off. Oz glances in our direction and shrugs. Morrie looks annoyed.

Sophie is disappointed. "Grandpa lied to us and sent us on a wild-duck chase."

"Goose," Ida says.

"Who are you calling names?" Sophie huffs.

I calm everyone down. We gather our things, throw our trash into the proper receptacles, and leave. But when we turn the corner to where I parked my car, lo and behold, there's a familiar white envelope stuck in the windshield wiper.

"He *was* here," Ida says, grabbing for it. Sure enough, inside, there's his trademark green feather. We all peer over Ida's shoulder as she reads.

" 'Hi, girls, this was only a test. Just wanted to see if you were on your toes. Next time, weather permitting, will be the real thing. Speaking of getting old, did you know if you were age fifty on the planet Neptune, you'd only be three months old? By the way, loved the yellow outfit. And enjoy your other friend's new pencil.' "

We all gawk at Bella. The pencil! Grandpa's disguise was the old man pretending to be without legs, and Bella spoke with him!

"What did he say to you?" Evvie demands.

"Who?" Bella doesn't understand why we're all staring at her.

Sophie practically yells, "You were talking

to Grandpa!"

"How could I talk to my grandpa? He died in 1937."

"Oy," says Evvie. "Grandpa Bandit sold you your pencil."

Bella now takes it out of her purse and looks at it in amazement. "He did?"

My turn to ask a question. "The two of you had a conversation. He said something to you. What was it?"

She thinks for a moment. Short-term memory is a problem for her. Ask her all about that grandpa who died in '37, and I bet she'd have a volume to tell.

"I said . . . I said, 'I don't want to take your pencil. Save it for your next customer.' And he said, 'No, please take it, and maybe you want some more for your friends.'"

"Double oy," Evvie says.

Grandpa knew she's one of us. And knew where we were hiding. All the while, he was laughing at us.

Bella is unhappy. "I didn't want to give him more money so I didn't take any more —" She stops at the expressions on all our faces. "What?"

Ida is a study in aggravation. "Why didn't you tell us? We would have had him."

"At least describe him for us," I say.

Bella thinks. "I couldn't take my eyes off

the folded pants with no legs. And he had that big hat. I never looked at his face."

Ida is disgusted. "Never mind. Let's go home."

We all plop into the car. Bella is still mulling it over. "So how can he rob banks without legs?"

No one bothers to answer her.

She huffs in her own defense. "Anyway, I can always use another pencil."

9
LOOKING FOR CLUES

Today is library day — might as well go while the sun is briefly out, since threatening clouds hang overhead yet again. Even though my girls love to read, somehow they are always too busy to come with me and pick out their own books. So I find myself overloaded with their books to return and a list of what they want next.

I drop Sophie off at the nail place along the way. She chipped a few bits of polish while we were on the stakeout for Grandpa Bandit yesterday. I still find it amazing that whole stores devote themselves to applying nail polish — and where was it I read that now nail polish is supposed to be bad for you?

Evvie is at home working on a survey article about hurricane shutters, for her community newspaper. Should residents buy their own or should Lanai Gardens order them for all?

Bella is at her knitting group at a neighbor's apartment. Ida is teaching a class on pie-baking in the club room. So I'm on my own. Which, frankly, I enjoy.

I asked Jack if he wanted to join me, but he was busy with the men at Phase Six, dealing with building problems. They are taking roof measurements for the roofer, who they hope will be coming soon.

That's equally fine with me, since I'll get to visit with my librarian friend, Conchetta.

When I arrive, Conchetta is busy with an elementary school group on a field trip. I wave and head for the stacks to gather books. Another Carl Hiaasen for me — his Florida comedy mysteries are hilarious. He sure does have a monopoly of this state's underbelly of weird characters. Another Sandra Brown for Sophie. Another Catherine Coulter for Bella. Ida loves Michael Connolly. And Evvie, that frustrated entertainer, gets to read an autobiography of Marnie Nixon.

Amazing how these writers keep churning new books out every year. I wonder how they can do that!

I stop in my tracks at the bank of computers. One of these days I'm going to have to give in and learn how to work the darn things and keep up with the rest of the world.

I stack my take-out books on a reading table, glance at the instructions posted on the desk, and poke a couple of keys. The screen goes black. So much for my foray into cyberspace.

Conchetta comes to my rescue. "*Pobrecita*, the machine chewed you up and spit you out?"

I smile. "Something like that." We hug. Sweet, chubby Conchetta is a huggy kind of person. "Did I break anything?"

She plays with the keys, and like magic the screen comes to life again. "Let's say you put it to sleep."

I tell her, "I always have that effect on machines."

"What were you trying to find?"

What the heck. Might as well. The machine's here and I have someone who can work it. "How would you look up Grandpa Bandit?"

"First, I Google —" She looks at me. "You're kidding? Grandpa who? Wait a minute, I did read something about that name. He robs banks?"

"That's the very grandpa I mean." I fill her in on our new client as she listens incredulously.

She claps her hands. "I love it! He wants you to catch him. I wonder why."

I hazard a guess. "Maybe he feels guilty but can't turn himself in? Reminds me of a movie where the killer scrawled on a mirror, 'Stop me before I kill more.' You think Grandpa wants us to stop him from stealing?"

I tell her about yesterday's adventures.

While we talk, I watch Conchetta whiz along the keys. She says, "Let's check out some articles. Maybe pick up a clue. Here's one."

I look over her shoulder as she clicks on an article from a local paper, featuring an interview with a Ms. Sarah Byrne, of Plantation, who was the bank teller Grandpa held up in the Wachovia East Broward Boulevard branch robbery. The reporter on the scene comments that "Ms. Byrne was in such a state of hysteria from the horrific experience that she was sent home immediately to recover. She was unable to give the police any details about the notorious bandit, who has been plaguing local banks for the last six months. This was the sixth bank held up by the man the police call Grandpa Bandit. Many descriptions have been given by onlookers, but no two people have agreed on what he looks like other than that he is old and gray-haired."

I smile. "Well, next step for Gladdy Gold and Associates is to attempt an interview with the young, frightened bank teller."

"And of course you will report everything you learn to me?" Conchetta says.

"Naturally."

The elementary school kids are now charging the desk with their chosen books, their shiny new library cards out and ready. The two librarians behind the desk have their hands full.

"Sorry to leave you," Conchetta says, "but I better help out."

"You've already helped me." I wave good-bye and head for the door.

I hear an imperious voice call after me, "Just a moment, Mrs. Gold." It's Conchetta, putting on a tone of authority in front of the gawking children. "The moment you walk out you will set off the alarm."

Oops. I forgot to check out my books. I look with chagrin at the mob at the desk and dutifully go to the back of the line.

10
THE BANK TELLER

The five of us face the very young Sarah
Byrne as we all sip lemonade. We have our
most solicitous expressions on in respect for
Ms. Byrne's recent painful encounter.

"I hope you're feeling better." This from
Evvie.

"And not crying a lot anymore." Bella offers her sympathy.

"Are you under a doctor's care?" asks
Sophie.

Our witness perches daintily on a small
tapestry bench opposite us. We are sitting
on flowery chintz couches and spindly
antique chairs. Her house is charming and
beautifully kept up. Sarah, herself, is petite
and pretty and nicely dressed, in white
slacks and a black tee. Her curly blond hair
is tied back in a white ribbon. And she is
barefoot.

After we found her address — in the
phone book, amazing these days — we

called her. We explained who we were and what we wanted. She said she was more than happy to have us come and visit.

Now she stares at us in confusion. "What are you talking about? Why would I need a doctor?"

"Was it because of the shock of being robbed?" Ida wants to know.

A smile forms on Sarah's face.

She's smiling? Odd. "We read the newspaper account of your leaving the bank in hysterics," I tell her.

She walks over and refills our lemonade glasses. "That's a good way of putting it! Hysterics? Oh, yes, I left in hysterics. I didn't know whether to laugh or cry, so I did both."

Now we're the ones looking puzzled.

"You know why I invited you ladies over? Because I'm upset about losing my job. Because I miss my work. Because none of my old friends at the bank have the guts to call me. The bank fired me. I didn't push the panic button fast enough."

"Was that because you were frightened by being in danger?" I ask.

"Danger? But was I really in danger? I'm not sure. This was the weirdest thing that ever happened to me in my whole life." She pauses as she rolls her head in a stretch.

"Are you really private eyes? You're really looking for Grandpa?"

Evvie answers Sarah's question with dignity. "We certainly are private eyes. Who did you think we were when you gave us permission to come over?"

"I didn't know and I didn't care. I wanted the company. I thought you were a bunch of old ladies who were bored and nosy. And, by the way, thanks for the pineapple upside-down cake."

"Hmph," mutters Ida, baker of said cake.

Sarah drops to the floor in front of us. "Mind if I do a little yoga? I missed my class today."

Why not, I think. This is turning into a bizarre little episode. Next thing, she might want us to do push-ups with her.

"Start from the beginning," I say. "Please. The whole robbery incident."

We all lean forward as she twists her legs around in a way that I never thought possible outside of the circus.

"Okay," she says. "It was an ordinary day, maybe a little quiet. This old guy comes to my window."

Fashionista Sophie interrupts immediately. "Do you remember what he was wearing?"

"Honey, I remember every little thing

about him."

I tap Sophie, indicating that she shouldn't interrupt.

Sarah twists into another improbable position, resembling something like a figure eight. "He was about five foot four, thin, wearing gray pants and shirt and a Miami Dolphins baseball cap. He had on huge sunglasses with white rims, making it very difficult to see his face. He had kind of a Groucho Marx bushy mustache. Looked like a paste-on to me. And a big Spider-Man Band-Aid on his cheek. I only realized later that all that stuff was to keep me from really seeing anything of his looks other than the tufts of his gray hair sticking out."

Bella pulls her chair even closer so as not to miss a word of this amazing story.

Sarah continues, "He carried a small tote with the SunTrust Bank logo on it. He opened it up and pulled out a bag from Mickey's Deli, the one that's right across the street from where I work."

We are listening with open mouths. Her attention to detail is fascinating.

"He took out a rye bread sandwich and unwrapped it."

Now Sophie can't stand it. "He was going to eat his lunch?"

Sarah shakes her head. "He then tells me

he got turkey but told them to hold the mayo so it wasn't too messy."

Bella is gaga over what she hears. "What wasn't too messy?"

"His gun, wrapped up in the sandwich," Sarah says. "He insisted it was a real gun, but frankly, I wasn't sure."

"You gotta be joking," Ida says. "He's holding up a bank with a gun wrapped in a turkey sandwich?"

"I kid you not," Sarah says, giggling. "Here I am being robbed by an old guy dressed like a clown, carrying a gun in rye bread. I didn't know what to think. I was so weirded out, I didn't know whether this was a joke or serious."

We're all giggling now.

Ida pours herself more lemonade. "Then what?"

"Then he says, 'Give me five hundred and fifty dollars and forty-six cents or I shoot.' My hands were shaking; I could barely count out the money. He tossed it into the sandwich bag, thanked me, and tipped his baseball cap."

We are speechless. Finally Evvie says, "That's it?"

"Oh, I almost forgot. He dug out a small green feather and said, 'Robin Hood's my name, robbing banks is my game.'"

Sarah does another complicated yoga move then gracefully stands up and stretches.

Bella and Sophie applaud.

I've heard some strange stories in my lifetime but this takes the cake. "Did you tell all of it to the police?"

"I did indeed, but I don't think they believed me, what with all my nervous laughing."

I have to ask. "Why did you give him the money?"

She thinks for a moment. "That's a good question. Maybe it's because I thought he was adorable. Maybe because he reminded me of my grandpa. And because maybe he was loony enough to be carrying a real gun. I tell you, ladies, I was a nervous wreck."

She performs another long stretch. "And when I finally remembered to hit the panic button, he was already racing out of the bank."

11
ANOTHER TELLER TELLS ANOTHER STORY

Pallie Finchum is a very different experience from Sarah Byrne. No laughing here.
This one's a straitlaced bank teller who
reminds me of an old-fashioned school-
marm. Maybe it's the tight brown bun
perched on the top of her head or her
starched black suit. She's in her fifties, thin-
lipped, and very unfriendly. She, too, had
been mentioned in an article after one of
Grandpa's robberies. We called her. She
refused to speak to us, so today Evvie and I
track her down at lunchtime. The others
stay home because I tell them five of us
stalking her would be ridiculous.

We wait for Finchum to leave the bank.
Noon, right on the dot. She then enters
Fuddruckers directly across the street.
That's a surprise — the noisy youth-
oriented restaurant doesn't seem her style.
We manage to get a table right behind her.
She orders a chicken salad and iced tea. We

order a couple of hamburgers and Cokes. We let her read her book and eat in peace. While she sips her tea and before she pays the check, we get up and sit down next to her, Cokes still in hand.

Naturally she's startled. Very quickly we introduce ourselves and remind her that we'd tried to make an appointment. When she recovers from her shock, she says, "Get away from me or I'm calling for help."

"Please," I say, "just a few minutes of your time. We need to talk to you about the old man who held you up."

"It's none of your business."

Evvie smiles. "Actually, it is. He's our client." And she hands Finchum one of our business cards. I remember how Jack surprised me with these cards as a "new business" present. I've given out about eleven so far. These cards will outlive me.

The woman accepts it with the same attitude she might have shaking hands with an alligator. "Your client? That's preposterous."

"Maybe so, but it's true," Evvie tells her.

"Prove it. Tell me what he looks like."

I don't know quite what to say since we've never met our client. Nothing fazes Evvie, though; she jumps right in. "Don't play with us. You don't know what he looks like, either. He's very secretive about his appearance. He usually wears a disguise. I'm sure he was wearing one when he walked up to your window. The only thing he lets people see clearly is his gray hair."

Miss Bun-on-top-of-head pauses, but she's not giving up yet. "You'll have to do better than that. Tell me something you know that only the police and the bank and I know."

Evvie, former budding actress, is in her element. "Gramps, our master of disguise, comes up to your window and shows you his gun, wrapped in a sandwich. Usually turkey, and he holds the mayo so it won't be messy."

This information startles Finchum. She weakens a bit. "It wasn't turkey."

"All right, already," Evvie says, pretending annoyance. "So what was it? Pastrami? Baloney? What?"

Pallie Finchum finally relents. She leans over and whispers, "It was corned beef on a Kaiser roll."

"How much did he demand?"

"Forty-four dollars and seventy-eight cents."

I'm surprised by this but I don't show it. "And," I add, "he showed you the green feather and called himself Robin Hood."

The bank teller sighs. "That's exactly what happened. My life has been hell ever since. My manager says I can never tell this story to anyone. So do the police. Why would I want to tell anyone? It was too embarrassing. But I did tell my mother. I live with her."

"And?" Evvie asks.

"She was so upset, she wanted me to quit. How can I quit? I need the money."

She stands up from the table. "I have to go back to work. This robbery has ruined my job for me. Now my manager watches me all the time."

And with that she leaves us sitting there.

Evvie look at me. "First it was five hundred something and now forty-four and change. What in blazes is that about?"

"One of the first things I'll want to ask 'our client' if we ever catch up to him." I stand up. "Time for another meeting to figure out what we know."

We're in the clubhouse with the door locked and a sign tacked on that reads PRIVATE PARTY. KEEP OUT. We need to use the chalkboard. Outside, the wind is blowing, rattling the windows and doorknob, promising a new storm. Inside, we are cozy. Evvie pops some popcorn for us in the community microwave.

We list on the board what we know and what the police know.

"Keep calling it out," I say, chalk in hand.

Evvie: "He's always in a disguise, with distractions, so nobody really gets a good look at him." She hands out paper cups filled with popcorn and we nibble as we chat.

Ida: "He goes to the nearest restaurant and buys a sandwich to hide his gun."

As I write, I add, "He probably gets the sandwich at an earlier time or the cops would have caught him by now."

Sophie: "The two amounts of money he robbed were different. I'll bet they're different in each bank. That's pretty weird."

Bella: "Maybe he gets bored and changes it. Or maybe he forgot what he asked for last time." She ponders this. "I know I would."

I look at the chalkboard, where I've copied out the list of six banks that arrived in today's mail. Frankly I didn't think Morrie would really send it. "I bet when we visit these banks, we'll find some kind of restaurant nearby. And that will be the sandwich wrapper of the day. He's toying with the banks and the police."

Evvie says, "Morrie probably knows in his

heart that we can solve the case and is depending on us."

"Maybe," says Sophie. "I bet the cops are all frustrated because this old guy keeps foiling them."

Ida adds a clue. "I checked on the shuttle van that Grandpa got into the other night when we had dinner out. The driver said Grandpa didn't belong to the Golden Era Retirement Home, but he admitted the old guy tipped him for a ride with them."

"Did the driver describe him?"

"No, he never really looked at Grandpa."

Sophie says, "I like that he calls himself Robin Hood and leaves the green feather. He steals from the rich to give to the poor."

I'm not so sure of that. "Maybe yes — maybe no. We'll ask him when we find him."

The wind outside is picking up, rattling the windows of the building. "Everybody got their flashlights ready if the power goes out again tonight?" Evvie is always on storm duty. She gets the appropriate number of nods.

"Bella," I say, "you look puzzled."

"I still don't know how he can rob a bank without legs."

Ida throws a handful of popcorn at her. "Get it through your head already. He has legs. He hid them under the box he was sitting on."

She pouts. "It looked real to me."

"Which brings me to a few puzzling questions," I say. "Didn't Morrie tell us that the police warned all the local banks about him? So, why were the tellers surprised?"

Evvie refills my popcorn cup. "And how does Grandpa make his getaway?"

Ida says, "I'm guessing he hides things nearby, in his car. Or in a backpack. What we saw was a legless-man routine. I wonder how many other getaways he has in his bag of tricks?"

Evvie adds, "What I want to know is how he knows us — does he live here in Lanai Gardens? Is he someone we see often?"

"And we should pay attention to this map," I say, indicating the Fort Lauderdale map I've taped to the board. I used a marker to circle the locations of the six banks Grandpa has hit so far — all within a five-mile radius of one another. "Within this same area there are at least three more banks that haven't been robbed yet. I wonder where he'll hit next time? We also need to figure out if there is a pattern to how often he robs and if there is a similarity to the time of day . . ." My cell phone rings, interrupting my daunting list of next steps. It's Jack. I tell him what we're up to. I turn so the girls won't see me blush as Jack informs me he's coming to my apartment tonight for our next attempt at a "sleep-over."

"What was that about?" Evvie asks when I hang up. But I'm saved from having to answer her question when a loud burst of thunder and lightning hits right above us.

I quickly erase the board. Everybody hurries to the door. Evvie tosses suggestions as we go: "Keep safe. Pull the blinds. Stay away from windows."

We race back to our apartments, holding hands. But I'm not thinking of the amount of rain or the velocity of the wind or Grandpa Bandit — I feel warm and fuzzy at the thought of my own thunder and lightning show on for tonight.

12
LET'S TRY AGAIN

It's after midnight. The weather outside is wild — the worst storm we've had in many seasons. But indoors we are comfy. Jack and I are wrapped in a blanket and stretched out on my couch in the living room, in front of a romantic fire sizzling in the fireplace. Candlelight takes the place of the power we no longer have. Wine warms our insides. Our clothes are still on, but in much disarray.

"I really missed you," Jack says, nuzzling my neck.

I nuzzle him back. "It's only been three days, silly."

"It felt like a week to me."

"What have you been doing?"

"Helping out. Stanley Heyer's been leading a group of residents from building to building, looking for damage from all the recent rain. And what mischief have you and the girls been up to?"

"Trying to find our Grandpa Bandit. He's very elusive."

We kiss. Then kiss again. Our hands are exploring. Our breaths shorten. No need for words. I am happy to realize that even at our ages sex is still an active urge. And to think I was sure I would never have these tingling feelings again.

The candles are burning down. The room grows dimmer. Our bodies are well heated. I am softly moaning with pleasure. Jack indicates the bedroom. He's ready. I'm ready.

As we get up there's a knock at the door.

We stare at each other in utter disbelief. It can't be happening again.

"Someone's knocking?" Jack asks incredulously.

"Impossible. On a stormy night like this? Must be a branch hitting the door."

"Or maybe a whole tree falling down on the building," he suggests jokingly.

The doorbell rings. Then there is the sound of a key turning in the lock. In the near-darkness we see the door open, and a small apparition enters. At first I don't recognize it — it's all bundled up with rain jacket, large floppy rain hood, boots, and a broken, upturned umbrella.

It's Bella. She flings the soaking-wet

umbrella to the floor, drops the rain jacket from her shoulders, and kicks off her boots. She is wearing her favorite lobster and squid pajamas; her hair is in curlers. Her teddy bear is tucked in under the waistband of her jammies.

She slogs toward me, shaking her damp head.

"What are you doing here, Bella dear?" I ask gently.

She walks through the hallway and into the living room without stopping.

"The storm is scaring me. I don't want to be alone." Her voice is slurry and sleepy.

"But, Bella! Dear, you live next door to Evvie. Why did you walk clear across the courtyard to my building? It's dangerous out there."

She doesn't even look at me as she moves through the living room. "I tried Evvie. But she was sleeping so soundly she didn't hear the bell. I used the key, but she double-locked the door. So I came to you."

With that, she enters my bedroom.

Jack and I stare at each other. Jack whispers, "She has keys to all your apartments?"

"Yes, we all do, in case of emergencies."

"She didn't even see me."

"That's because she forgot her glasses." I smile weakly.

We tiptoe into my bedroom. Bella is already snuggled up in my queen-sized bed, comforter tucked under her chin, sound asleep. Her teddy bear rests on my pillow.

I can't help it. I start to giggle.

Jack scowls. "This is funny?"

The giggle becomes a laugh. "My turn to say 'Can't you see the humor in it?' "

Jack sighs, then gives in to a wry smile. We tiptoe back to the living room and sit down on the couch. "Shall we continue where we left off?" he asks dolefully.

I giggle again. "You know what this reminds me of? Being seventeen and having a date in the living room and trying to smooch while my parents were sleeping in the next room. No way. I mean, horrors, what if they woke up and saw us?"

"And now you have this woman well into her second childhood in your bed and you still can't make out."

"What if she wakes up and heads for the kitchen to get a glass of water or something?"

"You said she can hardly see without her glasses. She'll never notice us."

"It won't work." I sigh. "I'm sorry, Jack."

"I know," he says, sighing, too. "I guess I should head for home."

"No. Stay. It's awful out there." I leave

him standing there while I bring him a blanket and pillow. "Should I tuck you in?"

"Sure. Why not. Want to read me a bedtime story?"

I swat him playfully.

"And, darling Gladdy, I'll make sure to leave very early in the morning so Bella won't even know I was here. Okay?"

We kiss good night. As he rolls over in an attempt to get all of his over-six-foot-tall body comfortable, I head for the bedroom to my unexpected sleepover guest. Behind me I hear Jack mumble, "How far do we have to go to be alone? Tell me. I'll book us a flight anywhere. Just name it."

I pretend to count off names as I call back to him. "Timbuktu. Bimini. Lower Botswana." I can't resist using the new computer terms I overheard in the library. "Google Travelocity and pick somewhere."

13
THE NEXT MORNING

As I drink my morning coffee, I have the TV on low. I don't want to wake Bella. The newscasters making small talk agree that it was quite a storm last night, with winds up to twenty miles per hour. The screen shows image after image of downed trees and flooded streets and highways backed up for miles.

My original houseguest, Jack, did what he said he would: He woke up very early in the morning and snuck out. What a comedy of errors. I looked in on him around three A.M., during a bathroom trip. It's the first time I'd ever seen him asleep. His long legs hung over the couch. Poor thing, he looked so miserable, yet adorable. He probably thrashed around half the night trying to fit his body into that small space. Oh, well, one of these days I'll get to see him sleeping in my bed. I'm really looking forward to it. Waking up next to him — how wonderful that will be. To see him sitting opposite, having breakfast with me, is something I will treasure. Though the way the fates have had it so far, who knows when that will happen.

I'm sitting at my kitchen table, enjoying my fantasies, when Bella walks in. Talk about another kind of adorable. She stands there in her cute PJs, rubbing her eyes and holding her teddy bear. I can picture Bella as she was as a child, in that same posture. Sweet and gentle. And as usual, confused.

Bella asks, "What are you doing in my kitchen?"

I smile at her. "No, you mean what are *you* doing in *my* kitchen."

She looks around, realizing that indeed she is in my apartment. "I don't know. How did I get here?"

She sits down and I pour her a cup of coffee. "Don't you remember coming over here last night during the storm?" I indicate the cluster of rain gear that we both can see in the adjoining hallway.

"I did?"

"You tried Evvie's door but couldn't open it, so you sloshed across the courtyard to me."

She blows on the top of the cup to cool her drink. Bella likes her coffee lukewarm.

We sit there quietly sipping and enjoying the silence and comfort of longtime friendship. Suddenly Bella perks up, remembering:

"I had the funniest dream last night. I was in a strange bed and some man was standing over me, looking at me. Isn't that weird?"

I cough, sputtering my coffee slightly. "That's quite a dream. Did you recognize this stranger in the night?"

"No, it was too dark. But I think he was nice."

The sun is out, although it's weak and weary. Black thunderclouds darken the horizon.

Ida is at her mailbox when Bella and I exit the elevator. She looks Bella up and down, eyebrows raised. Bella is still holding her teddy bear. "Are those your pajamas you're wearing under all that stuff?"

"Don't ask," I say.

Bella blushes, and hurries across the courtyard to her building, where she passes Evvie talking to her ex, Joe. Before Evvie can comment, an embarrassed Bella scampers into their building's elevator with her eyes closed against curious expressions on anyone else's face.

Evvie and Joe are standing near Joe's old Ford V8. He's parked, with his door open, right in the middle of the street. I can hear their voices clearly.

"I don't want them," Evvie says loudly.

"Why not? They're just flowers." Joe is obviously frustrated, but trying to stay cool.

"So, what's the occasion?" My sister busies herself reading her mail.

"Does there have to be an occasion? All right, maybe it's a peace offering so you'll stop treating me like dirt under your shoe."

She snorts. "As far as I'm concerned, this war is still on."

"How about amnesty?" he begs. "After so many years."

"How about you shut your car door before another car bangs into it?"

As he does so, Evvie is aware of me looking their way and she beckons me to hurry over — I suppose to get her away from Joe yet again. As I cross the courtyard, I see Denny busy sweeping up last night's mess. Many of my neighbors are brushing leaves, and whatever else the wind brought, off their parked cars and balconies. Palm fronds and debris clog the street. Trash barrels are overturned. Denny waves to me and I wave back.

Joe is holding a lovely bouquet of flowers,

which he is attempting to pass to Evvie, who refuses them. I hate being put in the middle of the two of them.

We exchange good mornings. I wait to see how this will go.

"Lots of rain last night," Evvie comments.

"Plenty of wind, too," says Joe.

I can play the same game. "Nice flowers," I comment.

Joe eagerly says, "Evvie's favorites. Pink roses."

Ms. Contrary has to say, "That was twenty years ago. Now I favor yellow."

My sister, queen of the put-down.

Joe turns to me. Here it comes, me-in-the-middle. "Gladdy, tell her to have dinner with me. She keeps turning me down."

"I have no need to go out. I already have a dinner planned," Evvie says haughtily.

"Like what?" Joe demands.

"Like my leftover pot roast from last night."

Joe sees this as a possible break. "Then maybe I can share it with you?"

She shrugs. "Sorry, only enough left for one."

Just then Enya appears in front of the building. Seeing us standing there, she moves in our direction. Joe pushes the flowers into my arms. "I give up. Stubborn broad. Here, you take them." And he gets in his car and drives off. I give my sister my stern look of disapproval, but she doesn't care. She still won't give her ex an inch.

Enya manages a feeble smile for the two of us. "Thank you for your kindness the other evening."

"You're very welcome," Evvie says.

"Are you feeling better?" I ask. She still looks very fragile to me and she clutches a worn black sweater to her, as if she isn't able to warm up.

She shrugs. "It helps when the sun is out." She leans over to smell the roses I now carry. "Such loveliness in an ugly world." She shudders, then frowns. "I still can't help feeling something very bad is coming."

"You mean another storm?" Evvie asks. "We've never had a hurricane hit Fort Lauderdale, so you needn't worry."

She pulls her sweater tighter. "A different kind of storm. A storm like no other. Something evil is coming." Then she forces a smile. "Don't listen to me. I'm just a silly woman with a lot of fears."

I look at Evvie, then at the flowers, and then at Enya. Evvie nods. I hand the flowers to Enya. She is surprised. "Please take them," I say.

Evvie adds quickly, "I'm allergic."

130

Enya smiles and reaches for them gratefully.

Evvie pinches me and indicates I should turn to see something.

I do. It's Jack coming briskly toward me. Enya, her nose smelling her flowers, walks off to go on her usual morning stroll.

Evvie winks at me, then heads for her apartment. I go to meet Jack halfway.

"Hi —" I start to say, but he instantly interrupts me.

"I'm already packed."

I gaze at him, startled. "Are you going somewhere? You didn't mention —"

Again he interrupts me. "*We're* going. I made us a reservation in Key West. Tonight. Throw a few things in a bag."

"You really took me seriously? You actually picked out a place?"

He takes my arm, and marches me toward my building. "You won't need much. I don't expect we'll be leaving the room too often."

With that he playfully pats me on my backside. "I'll pick you up in an hour."

14
KEY WEST

The girls can't believe Jack and I, based on a few minutes' discussion, are actually going down to Key West. I can almost hear one of them say, *Just like that, you go on a trip? Without us?* But with Jack standing right there, they hold their tongues. Roughly 180 miles away, approximately a three-hour drive. I can't believe it, either, yet here I am. Everyone is standing in a tight cluster when I appear downstairs with an overnight bag. Jack's vintage Cadillac is parked right in front, with its trunk open and his duffel bag very much in sight. I watch my girls as they watch me hand Jack my case and stare at him placing it next to his.

No guessing what the two of us intend to be doing on this trip — the answer is as plain as the blush on my cheeks. I look at their faces, trying to read what they're feeling. No one says anything but Bella is grinning. Sophie pinches her in excitement. Ida is scowling. Evvie is absolutely poker-faced. When will I ever feel comfortable about this couple thing and my girls? Maybe only when we finally marry — ha!

Needless to say, others are watching the Jack and Gladdy show, too. Ever-present Hy and Lola stand on their second-floor landing, whispering to each other. Lola giggles. This should give them an entire afternoon of speculation and innuendo. I'm surprised they aren't waving a sign that says FALLEN WOMAN.

Jack sees me gazing at them. He grins, and whispers, "Scarlet woman, babe. I keep pro-posin' and you keep dozin'."

The girls wave as we head out. We pass Mary and Irving in Mary's car. I am sure they're heading for the hospital.

What little sun we had before disappears. The first raindrops begin to fall.

I'd been to Key West many years before, but this trip will definitely be different, very different. I'm going with a man who loves me and wants to be alone with me. I look over at him adoringly. He catches my glance and winks at me. I feel this tiny little shiver up and down my back. I can hardly wait until we get there.

I look at Jack and then at the sky. *Threat-*

ening is the word that comes to mind. Jack senses my concern. "Don't worry," he says, "I checked the weather report. All systems go."

We pass Miami. Jack thoughtfully packed a picnic lunch, so we munch turkey/cranberry sandwiches, brownies, and bottled water without stopping.

Leaving Homestead, we get onto US One, the Dixie Highway, which takes us all the way down to the Keys. I sigh. Only forty-three bridges and 110 miles to go. Rain threatening. Clouds black and grumbling.

First town coming up will be Key Largo. How can I not think of Bogart and Bacall steaming up the sheets in that famous movie of the same name? I look at my macho Bogart type driving happily along with a big grin on his face. But then again, I remember that movie also featured the worst hurricane in the United States up to that time. The Keys were very badly hit. The sky above us gets darker and more foreboding. Jack whistles some tune I don't recognize. Maybe it's the theme from *Titanic.*

"It's starting to rain," I say, "in case you haven't noticed." I singsong the child's tune: "Rain, rain, go away. Come again some other day."

"What's a little moisture," he says cheerfully. "Won't spoil our indoor sports."

"You have a one-track mind."

"And why shouldn't I, since we've been derailed so often."

By the time we reach Islamorada, the rain is seriously coming down. And the wind has picked up.

"Would this be a good time to tell you I really can't swim?"

"Swimming is not on the agenda."

"And I'm afraid of sharks."

"Who isn't? But we won't be swimming, ergo we won't have to worry about sharks."

I wish I had his confidence. "Maybe we should get a room closer in. Long Key is just right up ahead."

"Nah. Key West is great. Why, if you get bored we can visit Ernest Hemingway's house and see all the cats that live there or Harry Truman's Little White House or maybe even ride a dolphin . . ."

I reach over and pinch his arm.

"Wise guy. But the weather does look ominous."

"Not to worry. To an ex–navy man who rode out the storms in the North Atlantic, this is nothing."

"Nothing can turn into something," I say, still nervous. "You never told me you were in the navy."

He leans over and gives me a peck on the cheek. "There's a lot you don't know about me."

That's for sure. Now I'm getting the macho view of my man against nature. I hope nature doesn't win.

By the time we pass Marathon, the wind is howling and the rain is pelting down. It's hard to see out the windshield. Many cars are on the road, but they are going in the opposite direction.

Jack is still whistling. I close my eyes and pretend I'm asleep. But that's even worse. My imagination continues to paint dire scenarios.

I feel like I'm going "up the down staircase" as we fight our way through the heavy wind up the steps to the Brown Pelican Inn. People hurry past us, obviously on their way out, lugging their suitcases. Nervousness is written on their faces.

I would like to admire the charm of this pale yellow faux-Victorian B&B, but I can't tell much for the downpour.

"Lots of people leaving in a hurry," I say, trying to look at Jack, though I can't see his face clearly.

"Good," says Mr. Cheerful. "We'll upgrade to a better class of room."

At the desk, the checkout line is longer than the registration line, which consists of us! I stand next to him and leave it to the admiral to get us settled.

The manager introduces herself as Ms. Teresa LeYung, petite with long, lovely dark hair and almond eyes. She looks to be in her thirties. I timorously ask what the latest weather report is.

"Last report I heard, the storm was heading toward Puerto Rico, possibly south toward Cuba. But it will be bouncy here. Storm should subside by midnight. Not to worry." She's upbeat, but I detect concern in those pretty eyes. Jack is right; she offers us the bridal suite. No extra charge. Apparently the Midwestern newlyweds had changed their minds and canceled their reservation. Am I imagining it that the manager's hand is shaking as she hands Jack the key?

"You will keep us informed?" I ask.

"Absolutely," Ms. LeYung promises.

As we head for the elevator, I glance around the lobby quickly. It is a lovely place, done in good taste with French antiques. A few tourists are milling around having drinks, looking relaxed. So why am I still worried?

I admire our "bridal suite" — all white satin and peach lace with Laura Ashley delicate lavender floral drapes and bedspreads. It overlooks Mallory Deck, a huge outdoor party space where people gather by the hundreds each night to view the glorious sunsets over the ocean and be entertained by carnival performers. The ocean is an angry battleship gray. There are no cruise ships parked there this time. There will be no sunsets tonight. No people dancing the night away.

Jack hefts the voluminous basket of fruit, cheese, and wine. The ribbon reads, "Congratulations, Mr. and Mrs. Jim Lawler."

He reaches for a slice of pineapple. "I'm sure the Lawlers won't mind."

"I don't know," I say, "maybe they'll come for it tomorrow. We've gotten this by default."

The playful ex–navy man puns, "Yeah, 'de fault' being that those Midwestern wimps are no-shows, so the goodies go to us."

I sigh. "Keep making jokes. Then how come so many rats left the sinking craft? I sure hope you were never a captain in the navy — you know, the guy who always goes down with his ship."

"Nonsense. I've been in worse storms than this. Remind me to tell you about the time I was with a convoy in the North Atlantic in December near Greenland. Now, that was a whopper."

He bites down happily on the pineapple, licking the juice on his lips. It's a very sexy sight and I almost succumb to his mood. Almost.

He remains in amazingly good humor. It must be the storm turning him on, it couldn't be scaredy-cat me. I take my little overnighter to the bed and start to unpack. He's at my side in a flash. "Never mind. Unpack later."

He sits me on the bed, then slowly lowers me to a lying-down position. I can smell the slight lavender perfume on the delicately patterned Laura Ashley spread. Above my head I stare directly into the top-floor skylight. I wonder why a Victorian has a skylight. I wonder if the glass will hold. And whether there'll be a tsunami. Can the ocean climb three stories high? I ponder dozens of disastrous events as Jack leans over me and with his wonderful body blocks out the sight of the window.

For a few moments, I am able to get with the program.

Until I hear a cracking sound. Followed by an immediate crash of thunder. Jack either doesn't hear it or ignores it. He kisses me slowly, deliciously, his body tight against mine. I am torn between passion and terror.

Not a time for me to make jokes, but . . . "Did the earth move for you?" I ask.

He laughs. "Not quite yet for that, honey. Soon. I promise."

"Well, it is for me, sweetie. In fact, the whole room is shaking now. And not only that, but there must be a leak in the skylight."

"What skylight?" He turns his head just in time for a drop of water to land on his cheek.

"The one right above us, which just might totally collapse on us any moment."

Within seconds, Jack is off me and the bed. He pulls me up with both arms. "Why didn't you warn me?"

We rush to the windows and, clinging to each other, watch the storm rage. No more little squall — this is bad news. We can no longer see the Mallory Deck. What few sailboats were tied to the docks, bouncing about like toy toothpicks, have disappeared and there is nothing but bleak grayness everywhere.

The sounds of the storm are so loud, we barely hear the shouting and the frantic knocking on the door. Jack opens the door to the wide-eyed Ms. LeYung. She looks to be red-faced from having run up the three flights. She can't hide her state of panic.

"News from the National Weather Service. The winds have shifted and the hurricane is coming directly at us. Delta force winds, type four, at more than 150 miles an hour are predicted. They're giving us twelve hours' notice, but they think it will hit sooner. We've all got to evacuate!"

I automatically salute. "Aye, aye," says the ex–navy man's "mate," who is envious of Mr. and Mrs. Jim Lawler, in whatever warm, dry place they might be.

We grab our bags and race down the stairs after the manager. Other guests are running downstairs as well. Ms. LeYung is muttering, "Oh, God, I was here when Wilma struck. It was horrible."

In the lobby we meet up with the rest of the frightened guests. Ms. LeYung gives last-minute instructions to her staff, who are hurriedly pulling down the hurricane shutters all over the B&B.

"I'll be right back," she tells the working crew.

She starts for the door. Jack stops her.

"Wait. Don't you want us to help?"

She shakes her head. "Thanks, but don't worry. We'll all get out of here in time."

We join the guests anxiously waiting at the front door. "Follow my car," she tells us. "I'll lead you to the shortcut out of the city."

Bleak. All I'm aware of are bleak- and angry-looking clouds covering the sky. Jack struggles to see out the windshield. The car is rocking as he fights to keep it in control. Frankly, I'm glad I have no view. I don't want to watch the destruction that might be happening to all these beautiful little towns along the Keys.

Other cars also rushing from the Keys pass us, dangerously close.

"I'm an idiot," Jack says. "Putting you through this."

"You said it, I didn't." I lean over to kiss his cheek. "But you're my idiot and I still love you. Besides, how could you know the winds would shift?" I pretend to put a good face on it. "Isn't this exciting?"

Jack is glum. "Not the kind of excitement I had in mind."

"All is not lost. I've learned a lot of new things about you, Mr. Navy Man. Stubborn. Opinionated. Risk-taker . . ."

Jack cringes. "Don't say another word. And what I've learned about you is that you're loyal, though foolishly so, and brave."

I don't want to ruin his opinion of me so I don't contradict him.

I peer out, barely able to see from one side of the very narrow causeway to the other, thinking grim thoughts. To the left of us, all of the Gulf of Mexico. To the right, the entire Atlantic Ocean. Water lapping hard on both sides reaching out to connect in the middle. Coming closer and closer to our car. Eager to have at us and suck us in. Forever.

"Brave" me, hiding my eyes with sunglasses, shuts them and keeps them that way for most of the ride home.

15
GETTING READY

It takes us nearly five hours to make it back to Fort Lauderdale. The farther north we go, the less ominous the weather, but no doubt there's a real hurricane chasing our tail. Everywhere we look the escalating wind is heaving debris, forming bizarre kites in the sky.

Drivers on the road rigidly lean forward into their steering wheels, clutching them with all their strength. They're a study in fear. Everyone is speeding home or in any direction that might get them out of town as fast as possible. Their vehicles are rolling from side to side. Already, small-weight cars have overturned, some blown onto the shoulder. Jack's car radio repeats the same announcements over and over. The Atlantic Hurricane Center reports that as of four-thirty P.M., the storm has intensified, and that now the east coast of Florida is in severe danger. Ocean waves at Miami Beach were kicked up by the Category Four storm. Winds are gusting at 160 miles an hour. By now the expensive beach hotels had been evacuated. The waves had already destroyed five houses and damaged ten others. So far, the hotels are still standing. The news comes at us at a staccato beat, breaking up occasionally, but the message is loud and clear: Fort Lauderdale will be next, hit hard with a hurricane for the first time ever.

When we finally pull into Lanai Gardens, exhausted, we see more of the same. People driving out and away; others boarding up windows or scurrying to and fro with last-minute preparations. For the first time I'm sure everyone wishes we'd put up hurricane shutters. But in all these years we never needed them.

Jack parks the car in front of my building. It's a parking spot belonging to someone else, but this is no time to worry about the rules. As we get out I hear someone cry, "They're back, thank God!"

I look up to see Ida, hands clutching a jacket to her chest and neck, her hair bun unruly. Perched on our landing, she frantically waves at us. We hurry upstairs, not bothering to use the elevator, heads bowed, the wind pushing at our backs.

Ida throws her arms around me. "We

didn't think we'd ever see you again. They expect Key West to be hit in a few hours!" I think of the lovely Ms. LeYung and hope she gets out in time.

Ida pulls us into my apartment.

What a sight before us. Every light in the apartment is on. My highboy, the tallest piece of furniture I own, has been pushed against my living room windows. The rest of the windows were obviously hurriedly boarded up. Denny is finishing up last-minute hammering. His girlfriend, Yolie, acting as his assistant, is handing him nails. My floors are covered with mattresses and sleeping bags. The couch and chairs are circled in and around the sleeping bags. The dining room table is sky-high with snacks. The air, oddly, is filled with delicious smells.

Evvie runs to hug me. "Thank God you're all right. I was so afraid you wouldn't be able to get back in time." Her hug is tight, I hug her back. We hold on to each other for a few moments. For the first time I allow myself to think of what might have been, had we left any later.

"Welcome to Hurricane Central, Operation Gladdy's Apartment," says Ida. "We decided to use your place because it has the least amount of clutter."

Bella adds, "So we could be able to fill it

with the biggest number of people."

"And because if you returned very late, you'd be able to find us." This from Sophie.

"What's going on? Do you have a plan?" I ask. Jack stands close to me, holding my hand.

"You bet we do," Evvie says. "Every building has made sure no one is left alone. People are staying together in groups. We have a telephone outreach so we can check on one another, and we know where every person is. That means we all have the phone numbers of the apartments with groups staying in them. For as long as the phone lines stay up. About five to eight people have been placed per apartment."

"Yeah," says Bella, seated cross-legged on one of the mattresses. "The stores ran out of candles and flashlights so we're all sharing everything."

Sophie adds, "Everyone brought food from their apartments. And we figure before the power goes out we're cooking all the frozen food."

That explains why I smell pot roast. And chicken, too.

Bella adds, "And we made a ton of ice cubes to keep the stuff in the fridge from spoiling."

Evvie looks shyly up at Jack. "Sorry your

vacation trip was ruined."

"Me, too," Jack agrees stoically.

It's already getting much darker outside. I can tell from the tiny slits of sky showing through the rough plywood boards.

Denny and Yolie walk carefully over and around all the stuff on the floor. "Best I could do this fast," he tells us.

The girls hug the two of them and thank him in unison.

"Where are you and Yolie staying?" I ask.

"With Sol and Tessie and Mary and Irving in Irving's apartment." Yolie nods for emphasis. They head out the door, into the wind.

Evvie calls after them, "Be careful."

They wave and with heads down, holding hands, they run to the stairs.

Out of curiosity, I ask, "Where are Hy and Lola?"

Ida grins. "Home alone. They insisted on being by themselves."

Evvie looks at Jack. "You'd better get back to your place while you still can." As she says this, she hands him a sheet of paper.

I look at Evvie, upset. "What are you talking about? I want him to stay with us."

Jack glances at the list. He looks at me. "I guess I better go." He hands the sheet of paper back to Evvie.

"No," I say quickly. "That's ridiculous. We need you here. I want you here."

Jack shakes his head. "Evvie's right. My building has a number of women who live alone. Our Canadian neighbors all went home days ago, so Abe Waller and I are the only men left. He'll need my help. They must be frantic waiting for me to round them up into my apartment and I can't let them down."

I grab the list and look it over. I know they are right. Evvie looks at me. "I'm sorry," she says.

Jack gives me a quick hug and turns to the girls. "Take good care of one another."

With that he gets hugs from them and a chorus of "We wills."

With a last kiss for me, he hurries out. Before I shut the door, he calls to me, "We'll keep talking on the phone until the lines go down. I love you."

I shout, "I love you, too." But it's drowned out by the wind.

When I go back in, I notice for the first time that my bedroom door is closed, as is the screened-in Florida room.

Evvie sees my look. "We have all the furniture up against the screens to protect the inside as best we can, but I doubt it will help . . ."

"What about the bedroom? Can't we use that?"

"Of course, but right now our other houseguest is napping. Enya is also in our group," Ida reports.

I look around the room once more. Each mattress and sleeping bag has a pillow and someone's clothing on it. "That's pretty darned good organizing in so short a time," I say. I look at the faces of my girls. They are frightened but excited, too. And trying very hard to act brave.

"Thanks to Evvie," says Ida. "She mapped out this plan in her last newsletter."

I blush. I've been so involved with Jack; I'm probably the only one who hadn't read it. I look apologetically at my sister. She smiles knowingly.

Sophie adds, "The minute the TV said we were going to get hit, Evvie was on the phone organizing every building. Within an hour everyone was set."

Evvie comments, "A lot of people went to schools and community centers but we all voted to stay here."

Suddenly there is a loud smashing sound outside. We all jump.

Enya rushes out of my bedroom with sleep-encrusted eyes. "What . . . what happened?"

Ida puts her arm around Enya. "We don't know."

Sophie joins Ida and embraces the shaking Enya. "Anybody hungry?" she says. "The pot roast smells ready."

Enya sees me and comes to hug me. "You're back safe."

I nod. "We'll be fine. Try not to worry."

"We have three kinds of potatoes to choose from," Evvie says, starting for the kitchen. Everyone follows. "Five different veggies and three meats."

My tiny kitchen will have to hold all of us.

There is a poignant cry from the living room floor. It's Bella, struggling to get on her hands and knees. "Somebody help. I can't get up!"

We rush to her aid.

Partners, all of us. Through thick and thin. God help us through this night.

16
A NIGHT TO REMEMBER

We are all pleasantly stuffed, which helps make what's going on outside almost bearable. The girls are stretched out in the living room in nightgowns and robes, leaning against pillows, walls, and couch backs, contentedly watching a classic movie. Each of them has a flashlight at her side.

It's dark out and the storm rages around us. Every time there is a banging somewhere, we stiffen. But we are determined to keep things light, to soldier on.

Enya stiffly sits away from us on a chair at the dining room table, eyes closed, still dressed. She is somewhere else, lost in her troubled thoughts. She clutches her cup of tea, already cold.

I am in the kitchen cleaning up the mess we made at dinner. I had offers of help, but it's much easier for one person to move around in the small space. Besides, I need something to take my mind off the storm. I watch my girls and Enya through the small pass-through opening. Poor Enya, she seems almost in shock.

Believe it or not, the girls voted to watch this TV rerun of *A Night to Remember.* Evvie, our movie maven, explains that this is the famous black-and-white English version of the disaster. It came out in the 1950's. The girls are mesmerized by the almost documentary style of the sinking of the *Titanic.* I guess watching another disaster is better than thinking of the one we're in right now.

Bella giggles.

Evvie asks, "What's so funny? We're watching a serious movie. They're about to hit the iceberg."

"I can't help it. Two nights in a row I get to go on a sleepover." Bella burps, and then giggles again, holding on to her expanded tummy. "Maybe I shouldn't have had three different desserts, but how often do I get to eat peach pie, chocolate cake, and strawberry shortcake in the same night?"

Ida huffs. "You didn't have to stuff yourself."

"Well, it was gonna spoil."

"So what," Ida answers. "It's disgusting watching you pig out."

Sophie grins. "I'm with Bella. I loved having all those different main dishes. I vote Evvie's cabbage rolls were the best."

"Thank you ever so much," Evvie says modestly.

"And besides," Sophie adds, "what if we're stuck here for days and run out of food? We might need to feed off our own fat — I read that somewhere."

"But where's that adorable Leo DiCaprio and the cute English girl?" Bella wants to know. "Where's the love story?"

Evvie corrects her. "That's the much later version, in color. This one is from the point of view of a young man who worked on board."

"No kissing, no naked painting?"

Evvie shrugs. "Sorry."

A Night to Remember is interrupted for another update on our own catastrophe.

Sophie groans. "Just before my favorite part, where the captain starts shutting down the emergency doors."

"We interrupt this broadcast for a special report," says the announcer. And now for the third time this evening we are getting a repeat of the same fifteen-minute documentary. *The Eleven Worst Florida Hurricanes in History* flashes on the screen, once more preempting our movie.

This program has been playing in between

the actual on-the-spot news reports happening on our own streets. "Here we go again," mumbles Evvie, sitting next to a lamp; she'd been trying to read a book and watch the movie at the same time. "If it isn't another depressing news flash, it's this thing. They're ruining our movie."

Ida is knitting. Sophie and Bella are holding up skeins of yarn, forming them into workable balls for Ida.

I keep playing over and over in my head the trip Jack and I took to Key West to be alone. I think of the warm feelings I felt for him. I wish Jack had been able to stay with us. I want his nearness and his comfort.

The phone rings. I set out for the bedroom to answer. It's probably not any of our families. We've spoken to a few of them earlier. My daughter, Emily, worriedly called much earlier from New York and so did Evvie's Martha. We assured them that we are fine. But are we?

Sophie's son didn't call, but she's not surprised — her jeweler son in Brooklyn is very selfish and uncaring. I can't go into what Ida is thinking. She has family but there is a huge rift that she refuses to speak about, and she never hears from them. As for Bella, as she says, she's an orphan. And Enya, well, there is no family left for her anywhere since the end of the last World War.

I'm sure it's Jack on the phone. He's already called twice. As long as the phone lines stay open, I feel connected to him, and I need this connection, to know he's safe.

In the background I hear stentorian tones: "In 1919 Key West was hit by the most powerful hurricane in its history. The storm killed more than eight hundred people. In 1926 . . ."

I shut the door to block it out. "Hello, dear, everybody still in one piece?" I ask, keeping my voice cheerful.

"About the same. Except for a few battles about who gets to control the TV, the ladies are holding up. Of course, Dora keeps wanting to tell us what's happening on her soaps and all she's worried about is will she be able to see tomorrow's episodes."

"And what about dear Louise?" I say icily. "Is she still pretending to be terrified, so she can hold your hand?"

Jack laughs. "Meow," he says. "You're jealous. Admit it."

"Maybe a little, since she's the one with you right now."

There is a pause. "I wish it could have been otherwise."

"Shh, take care of your little harem." I

pause. "Just keep her out of your bedroom."

Jack laughs. "I promise to restrain myself."

I hear a deafening sound from his end of the line followed by a woman's scream, then, "Jack, get over here quick! I need you!" I recognize Louise's voice.

His voice tightens. "Something's happened. Better check on it. Hold on, be right back."

I listen with the phone glued to my ear. I hear women's voices crying out all at once. They sound terrified. But I can't make out what they're shouting.

Jack's phone goes dead.

I try redialing, but no luck. I can't get through. A copy of Evvie's list is on the dresser. I dial Abe Waller's number. Surely he'll know what's going on in their building. The phone continues to ring. But no one answers.

I try Stanley Heyer across the courtyard. His line is busy. In a panic I call the next number on the list, of someone in the Y Building. A man named Charles answers. I've never met him. I ask him to look out through the slats in his window and see what's happening in Z. He does so. He reports back that all seems okay. Lights are still on. I thank him and hang up.

I want to run out the door and get over

there now! But I don't dare. It's not possible anyway. I'd never make it. Maybe it's nothing too serious and the women were overreacting. Maybe, I pray . . .

I go back into the living room, sick with worry, but I don't intend to say anything. My group's scared enough, and there's no sense causing a panic until I know more. I pull myself together and try to hide my dread. The moaning and groaning sounds, mixed with whatever things are smashing outside our door, add to my fears.

The girls are mimicking what the announcer is saying. They've memorized these words from earlier broadcasts. "In 1928 Okeechobee; 1935 the Keys; 1960 Donna; 1964 Cleo. Betsy, Andrew . . ."

"I wish they'd name a hurricane after me," Sophie says wistfully. "This year we're gonna get Arthur, Bertha, Cristobal, Dolly, Edouard, Fay, Gustav . . . who makes up those names anyway? And why do they make them up in advance? They have names picked out all the way through 2012." She counts on her fingers. "Twenty-one names. Does that mean they're expecting twenty-one hurricanes to hit this year? Oy."

Ida says, as she untangles a knot in her yarn, "I read somewhere that three different ancient civilizations all predicted a comet would hit the world in 2012. That's the day we're all supposed to get killed, so why sweat it now?"

Sophie groans. "Why do you always have to be such a truthsayer?"

"You're trying to say *soothsayer,* but you mean *naysayer,*" Evvie corrects.

"Whatever."

Ida makes a face. "I'm only telling you what I read."

Evvie climbs over the sleeping bags to find the remote, when suddenly the TV switches to one of our local broadcasters. He's huddled inside a restaurant doorway, clutching his mike, his hands shaking, his voice quivering. Behind him a group of onlookers peers into the camera, too frightened to make faces the way people usually do when they manage to squeeze their way in front of the camera.

"We are in Melina's Greek Diner on University Drive right off Oakland Park Boulevard. We can hardly believe our eyes. The corner streetlight fell moments ago and the street sign just . . . blew away!"

The camera shifts and now we are witness to what's going on outside the door, from their point of view, as the announcer continues to report. We see what he is saying.

"We are on generator power, as all lights

are out in the entire neighborhood. Trees are tumbling haphazardly down the streets as water from broken mains turns this usually busy intersection into rivers!"

"Those poor people," Bella says. "How are they gonna get home?"

Even as the newsman continues to speak, the lights in my living room flicker and everyone responds nervously.

On the TV, we see fire trucks racing by, sirens screaming, gushing up huge puddles as they pass the cameras. "The store windows are exploding," the announcer's frantic voice shouts. "Everyone, move back!"

Sophie gets up on her knees and points at the TV. "Oh, no, across the street, look — there goes Bagel Bites!"

Bella utters a small scream. "A car just floated by. Did you see?"

We watch as a wrought-iron bus-stop bench at the corner falls over. The announcer is fading in and out. Their generator light is dimming and we can hear people screaming as the front glass panes blow out. The sounds and sights are terrifying. Suddenly the picture is gone.

A voice tells us, "We now return to our original broadcast . . ." And *A Night to Remember* is back on again. Just in time to see and hear people screaming and running for the lifeboats as the *Titanic* starts taking on icy water.

One by one the girls turn away from the screen. Our real disaster has trumped the movie. They are all silent. Enya moans, shaking her head from side to side. We all turn as strong winds whistle eerily through the uneven slats on the windows.

Evvie mutes the TV. "Enough," she says. "Let's do something else."

"Like what?" Sophie asks.

"I don't know. Talk about stuff. Somebody pick a topic," Evvie answers.

I jump in, wanting to get their minds off what just happened on streets that are barely a mile away. "How about telling a funny story about yourself."

They look at me, blank expressions all.

After a few moments, Evvie says, "Okay, I'll start."

With that, Bella and Sophie start passing out candy and other assorted junk food.

When we are all settled, Evvie begins. "During the war I got a job singing in this bar in Brooklyn. I was only sixteen but I lied about my age. And on a Friday night, after one of my sets, this old guy sidles up to me and tries to pick me up. He uses the corny line, 'Hey, girly, haven't we met before?' and I look at him and I look at him

161

and finally, I say, 'You know, we did meet years ago.' Now he's getting all heated up. He says, 'Yeah, where? Did we have a hot old time?' And I tell him, 'We met on Boynton Avenue in the Bronx. I was a kid and you were my babysitter. Herby, you old cradle robber, you!'

"Herby was so embarrassed, he backed up and ran for the door. I yelled after him, 'How come you're not in the army?' "

The group is entertained and distracted. Bella claps. Evvie turns to see my frown.

"You sang in a bar when you were sixteen and you never told Mom and Dad?"

"Oops," says my adventurous sister, grinning at me.

Sophie raises her hand like a kid at school. "I got one. I got a story."

All eyes turn to her.

"Remember when we all had to wear girdles?"

There are sighs of uncomfortable memories at that. Bella comments, "We had to wear them every day. Even if we only went to the mailbox."

"Even if we were skinny," Ida comments.

"I was the Corseteria's best customer," continues Sophie. "One day I saw this picture in the paper of a crowd of women burning their bras."

Ida nods. "In the sixties."

"Well, I was living in a cute house in Long Island at the time and I took all my bras and girdles out to the burn barrel in the yard and set fire to every foundation I owned. However, I didn't take into account that the rubber in the garments and the plastic stays would start the smelliest fire you could ever imagine. The fire trucks came and my neighbors hissed at me. When Stanley came home that night, he had a fit. 'Why, why, did you do it?' he screamed.

"I put my hands on my hips and said, 'Because I'm a feminist now.' He looked at me and screams, 'Well, you're a *fat* feminist, so put your girdle back on.' "

The girls and I are awash with laughter. I even see a tiny smile appear on Enya's face.

Bella waves at us. "Me, too. Me, too. Could I tell a sex story?"

We look at her in amazement. Bella?

"Must you?" says Ida.

"Go ahead," says Sophie, patting Bella on the back. "Ignore the man-hater."

Ida, on the other side of her, shoves her elbow sharply into Sophie's side.

"Ouch," Sophie cries.

Bella manages to stand up. "Well," she says in her wispy little voice, "my Abe never undressed in front of me. And I never undressed in front of him. He went into the closet and I went into the bathroom."

Incredulity on every face. The things you don't know about your friends. We push forward to hear better. Even Ida.

Bella continues, "I must say I was curious about what he did in that closet, so one night I got in with him." She beams. We wait, openmouthed.

"And?" Sophie says to encourage her before her short-term memory loss kicks in and she loses track of what she's saying.

"And from then on we had the best sex ever in that closet."

Sophie screams with laughter. Evvie and I join her. Even Ida loses it. And Enya is actually smiling.

Bella adds in all innocence, "I must admit, we did smell like mothballs when we got out."

"I love this," Evvie says. "Speaking of sex, you wanna know the first time I did it?"

I squint at her. "I'd certainly like to know, big mouth."

"Well, if you feel that way . . ."

"I could live without any more of your stories," says Ida.

Sophie pinches Evvie. "Come on, tell us."

"Okay, now that you've twisted my arm, so to speak. We were in a phone booth. In

Times Square. On VE Day."

Need I say the girls gasped at that? My sister, what a bold young thing she was. And I — I was always the well-behaved one. How boring, I think now in retrospect.

Evvie looks at me and giggles. "Don't worry. I was with my husband. Joe had just come home from the war."

Our laughter fades as suddenly there's another crashing sound close by and the lights go out.

17
UNINVITED GUESTS

We are in a total state of panic. I feel the girls scrambling to get off the mattresses and sleeping bags, bumping into one another, crying out in fright.

I grab my flashlight. "Find your flashlights and turn them on."

"I'll light the candles," Evvie says.

"Enya, where are you?" My light finds her standing up next to the table. She waves her arms at me to indicate she is all right.

I crawl on my knees until I'm able to stand: "I'll check the phones." I make my way, cautiously, along the walls to the kitchen. Just what I was afraid of. "Can't get a signal," I call out to them.

Evvie says, "Try the cell." I pick it up from the kitchen table. "That's dead, too," I tell them. All I can think of is not regaining contact with Jack. I can't stand not knowing what is happening over there.

Evvie tries to calm everyone. "Come on,

stay down and form a circle and light up the center with our flashlights. Let's pretend we're camping in the woods and we're sitting in front of a fire telling ghost stories."

Sophie says eagerly, "Should I get some hot chocolate and marshmallows?"

Ida groans. "Enough with the food, already. Besides, we don't have marshmallows. And we won't be able to heat up the hot chocolate. Can't you make believe?"

"Ugh," Bella says, hugging herself. "Too many insects. I hate the woods." She slaps at her arm as if something bit her.

Ida huffs. "We're making this up, silly. Stop slapping."

"I don't like ghost stories," Sophie says. "They scare me."

Evvie is exasperated. "All right. All right. We're not in the woods, we're in Sawgrass Mall. Shopping."

"Ah," says Sophie, "that's better. I could use a couple of things."

We move around, trying for more comfortable positions. The storm's roaring sounds are terrifying, the winds are howling. The building feels like it's actually shaking. I can hear dishes rattling in the kitchen.

Sophie shrieks as she hears a cracking sound above us. "Maybe we should have gone to a second-floor apartment. What if the roof caves in and blows us all away?"

Ida looks up fearfully. "If we were on the second floor and the roof caves — then the third floor will fall on the second floor and we'll all be buried alive!"

"Are we going to die?" Bella asks plaintively.

"Are you ready to go if we do?" asks Ida, curious.

Evvie gets angry. "What kind of dumb question is that?" She looks nervously at Enya, who seems not to be listening.

Sophie pipes up, "When they asked my deaf aunt Fannie if she wanted to go, she said, 'You bet!' She thought we were talking about going to the Hamptons."

Leave it to Sophie to break the tension. But then she asks, "Does anyone believe in an afterlife?"

"Not me," says Bella, "not 'til I know there's a there there."

Sophie continues, "My dead cousin Sooky once came back to me in a dream. She said, 'Don't bother, stay where you are, it's nothing much.' "

Enya speaks softly. "I wanted to die when they took my husband and children."

It's very quiet for a while after that.

Evvie locates the battery-operated radio and turns it on. She fiddles with the dial until she finds music.

"Maybe we should all try to sleep," I suggest. "Or at least rest."

The music is basic elevator stuff, but perfect for this occasion. Enya returns to the bedroom. The girls lie down. And one by one we settle into our makeshift bedding. Evvie hums along to songs she recognizes, sometimes singing the words with that beautiful voice of hers.

As I'm lulled to sleep, I can even believe the storm is lessening. I close my eyes and think, Jack, please be all right.

A horrific pounding awakens me. Because of the boarded-up windows I can't tell if it's still night. I think I'm having a nightmare, but I finally realize the pounding hasn't stopped and voices are shouting. We all begin to stir.

Evvie is up first. "Someone's trying to get in," she says fearfully as she climbs over us to get to the hallway. I'm right behind her.

"Get out of the way," I say, "when the door opens."

And I'm right. Once Evvie unlocks it, the wind slams the open door against the wall behind her. To our astonishment, Hy and Lola practically fly inside. The whooshing sound of the wind behind them is mind-boggling. It takes the four of us to get the door shut again.

Everyone is up now, even Enya, who hurries out of the bedroom. All of us stare at Hy and Lola as they drop down to their knees on the floor of my hallway, panting.

What a sight they are. In robes and pajamas, with ropes wrapped around their bodies. They are soaking wet.

Sophie runs to get towels. Evvie quickly dashes to put up hot tea. But then she remembers we have no electricity. She reaches for the one pathetic quarter bottle of scotch which has been in my cupboard seemingly forever, and pours two glasses.

"What happened?" Ida asks.

The couple can hardly catch their breaths.

Hy manages to croak out his words. "The plywood didn't hold. Our living room windows shattered and the winds raged in and threw our furniture all around. It was so strong, it knocked us down. We had to get out of there."

They tug off their sopping-wet slippers. Evvie hands them the scotch. Hy downs his quickly. Lola, trembling, sips hers.

"Lucky we had ropes in our front hall closet," Lola says, crying with relief that she is safe, "or we'd be dead now."

"We crawled on our hands and knees

through the cars, using them to shelter us. We made it across the way, tying the rope to fenders, telephone poles, streetlights, whatever we could hook on to and pull from," Hy adds.

Ida doesn't understand. "Why didn't you go to Irving, right under you?"

Hy says, "We tried, but with all our banging, they didn't hear us. We saw the candles in your kitchen window so we hoped you were still up."

Lola sips gratefully. Color starts to come back into her face. "It must have taken us an hour to get here."

Hy reaches over and pats her gently. "It only seemed like it, toots."

She shudders. "I thought the wind would pick us up and . . . and toss us away . . . like rag dolls."

I find a selection of bulky sweaters and sweats and the two of them go into the bathroom to change.

When they come out, toweling their hair, and in an assortment of my clothes, they sit down at the dining room table and we surround them anxiously.

Evvie asks what we all need to know: "What's going on out there?"

"I don't know," Hy answers. "It was hard enough trying to keep our eyes open to see

171

our way, and we had to bend our heads down against the wind. But I could tell a lot of our cars are damaged."

Lola moves closer to Hy, shuddering. "It was so pitch black. No light anywhere. Like the end of the world."

He puts his arm around her, comforting her. This is a Hy we've never seen. Caring, even strong. And brave. A kinder, gentler Hy? Perhaps we've been unfair to him all these years.

After a makeshift breakfast of cold cereal, milk, and juice (kept cool by the now-melting ice cubes), everyone is feeling a little better. The wind seems to be dying down. The worst might be over. Our battery-operated radio informs us that the storm is moving southeast along the Atlantic Coast, back toward Puerto Rico and Cuba. But it's still not calm enough for us to go outside.

No one is sleepy anymore. We lounge around the living room, listlessly waiting for it to be over.

Sophie moans. "I wish the TV was on so we could watch something."

Evvie comments, "Our *Titanic* movie is over by now."

Sophie complains, "But I wanted to see

how it ends."

Ida is sarcastic. "You know how it ends. They all live happily ever after."

Sophie is miffed. "They do not. Most of them drown." She hits Ida on the shoulder and Ida hits her back.

"Dummkopf," says Ida.

"Meanie," retorts Sophie. "I don't care. I'd watch anything right now."

Ida scoffs, "Why bother? There's never anything of interest besides the news, which is always depressing."

Evvie agrees. "No kidding. It's all dreck. Garbage produced by kids and watched by kids. And cable — the language, the violence, the filth. It's almost enough to turn you against sex. Disgusting stuff. Is nothing sacred anymore? No wonder kids today are a mess."

Even I have to put my two cents in. "I don't know why they don't have a senior cable station. We're nearly forty-eight percent of the population now. Where's our representation?"

Sophie jumps in. "Maybe that rich guy — what's his name? Turner, who Jane Fonda used to be married to? I like his channel with old movies. He could afford our idea."

Bella rhapsodizes, "We could watch really grown-up love stories, with seniors falling

173

in love and with clean language. That would be nice."

Evvie murmurs, "I wouldn't mind some dirty language myself."

Lola adds, "Grown-up family dramas where wise grandparents are listened to, for a change, so their silly children and grandchildren would learn some lessons."

"And fashion shows with mature-bodied women modeling," chimes in Sophie. "I'm sick of seeing all those bulimic girls who look like they just threw up."

"And those stupid sitcoms where everyone acts like morons." Evvie is in her element. "Our senior network would have intelligence and class. We'll be seen as sensible people living happily in this, the third act of our lives."

The girls applaud her little speech.

Hy, lying comfortably across one of my couches, comments, "Never happen."

We turn to him. Evvie, hands on hips, demands, "And why not?"

He gets up, stretches. "Those lovely shows you predict? Think of the commercials that will keep interrupting." Hy, frustrated show-off that he is, gets up and acts them out with gusto. "Here's the sponsors of your quality shows: Hey, you oldsters, get your Depends diapers so you won't embarrass yourself in public. One size fits all. Is that a bulge in your bottom? Or are you not glad to see me?"

Now he prances in between the pillows. "Teeth dropped out? How about our gluey dentures? Bald, but for us, not by choice and definitely not a fashion statement; hair transplant anyone? Need orthopedic shoes? Hearing aids that never work? Varicose veins. Knee replacements. Hip replacements. Pacemakers. Walkers. Wheelchairs. Rascal scooters when you can't walk at all."

We watch him in hideous fascination as he hops and skips through the bedding on the floor.

"Assisted living at End of the Trails Retirement Home. No waiting. Vacancies every day. Estate planning — don't bother; the kids will fight over everything. Reverse mortgages — get thrown out if you linger too long. Come and pick your own satin casket. Initials optional. Go choose your cemetery plot. Every one with a view. Overlooking the golf course."

Now he's jumping up and down, with his hand over his groin. "Gotta go, gotta go. Gotta go. Oops, too late." He squats.

"Enough already," shouts Ida, throwing a pillow at him. "You're disgusting."

"Yeah? And how about Viagra, that little

blue pill that gives you a thrill." He winks. "Gets you up when you're feeling down."

Lola gently says, "You might try them yourself, dear."

"Quiet, toots, who asked you?"

Evvie is seething. "Are you through yet?"

"How about prunes for your constipation and Imodium for your diarrhea? And let's not forget Vicodin and Digoxin and Detrol and fifty others. You think we got a lot of pill sponsors already, just wait . . ." Hy is finished. He takes a bow. "How about all that?"

"How about we throw you back into the hurricane," Ida says.

"Hey, who else is gonna sponsor you old relics? It ain't Mercedes and Versace and Helena Rubenstein. *Bupkes,* that's what you old broads will get. *Bupkes.* No one cares about what you want to watch!"

I sigh. That's our old Hy, back again by unpopular demand.

I leave the living room with everyone screaming epithets at him. Entering the kitchen, I'm surprised to see Hy has followed me. As I drink a glass of water, he grins. "Like the show?"

"You were pretty disgraceful."

"Yeah, ain't I always, but I sure took

everybody's mind off the hurricane."

Touché.

18
AFTERMATH

We are awakened by the sound of people shouting. And sunshine peeping through the uneven slats of my boarded windows. I can't believe I actually fell back asleep, especially since Hy's snoring nearly drove me crazy. But he did look cute cuddled up with Lola.

I jump up from my mattress, grab my sneakers, and quickly shove my feet into them. In the hallway, I open the front door carefully, then, realizing it's safe, I pull it wide. In moments, Sophie, Bella, and Lola, awakened by my activity, follow behind me as I hurry outside onto the balcony. Sophie and Bella cling to each other, jumping up and down. It's really over. Blessedly over. And we'd survived.

We see our neighbors down below, walking around, surveying the damage. What a mess it is. Most of the cars were hit. Some crashed into one another, some landed on roofs of others. Trees have fallen. Telephone poles are down. The street is a sloppy mess of wet trash. Broken glass is everywhere, and plywood slats that failed and fell. My neighbors wear boots and walk carefully amid the rubble, calling out to one another.

From inside, I hear Evvie say, "Phone's still not working. Power's still off."

Hy, in my kitchen, is complaining, "I'd kill for a cup of hot coffee."

Tessie and Sol, downstairs, in robes, wave up to us. She calls, "Everybody okay?"

Sophie calls back, "We're good. How's your group?"

"We're still here."

I can't stand the suspense. Why isn't Jack looking for me? He would have rushed over by now. I start down the stairs and yell back up, "I'm going to look for Jack."

Evvie calls, "Wait for me."

Still wearing the clothes we slept in, looking utterly disheveled, we hurry down what's left of our cement staircase, which, thank goodness, we can manage by holding on to the dangling wrought-iron rails. Behind us we leave the others dazed and bewildered, heading for their own apartments to assess what has happened during the night.

We cut through Phases Four and Five,

pretty much the same scene we just left. Stragglers wandering around looking for friends, going to neighbors' apartments to check the damage. The buildings are still intact, except for broken windows and destroyed Florida rooms; many of our screened-in porches didn't make it.

When we round the corner to Phase Six, I stop and cry out, "No!" I can't believe what's before me. Building Z — Jack's building — has collapsed! Evvie sees it, too, and grabs my arm. We start running as best we can through the debris.

A small group of people stand in front, staring and talking quietly. I look across the courtyard. Building Y is undamaged. But in Jack's building, the third floor has caved in onto the second floor, where Jack's apartment is . . . Was. I can't see his apartment. It is crushed underneath the floor above. I remember Ida's chilling remark. I'm frantic. I finally see people I recognize. One of Jack's bridge partners, Carol Ann Gutsch, is there. As is Abe Waller. Carol Ann is crying. A woman I can't identify has her arms around her. Carol Ann's clothes are torn and her face is cut and bloody. We run over to them.

My voice is shrill, I hardly recognize it. "What's happened to the people in there?

Where's Jack?"

Abe clutches at the yarmulke on his head as if to make sure it is still there. "We don't know. When I came outside I found Mrs. Gutsch here on the ground."

Carol Ann shakes her head, waving her arms impotently, crying harder.

I can barely let myself look back up. My God, are they still in there?

Abe continues. "We were lucky." He points to his far-corner first-floor apartment, which is about all that's left standing of the building. "Our people were able to escape when the building started to fall."

Evvie, who knows the list, says, "Jack also had Louise Bannister, Dora Dooley, and Carmel Graves staying with him."

I want to shake Carol Ann until she tells me what I need to know. I cut in. "What about Jack and the other women? You have to tell me what happened. Please."

Her words tumble out through her tears. "All I remember is we were sleeping on the floor in the living room. Then the crashing noise started above us and the ceiling began to cave in. Jack yelled for us to run. I was nearest the door and I got out first. I dashed to the steps as fast as I could. I was so afraid the steps would be gone, and I'd be trapped, but they were still there. I tried to look back, but I couldn't see with all the dirt and pieces of the building falling. I could hear Dora screaming, and Carmel crying that she couldn't find the door. I made it downstairs and ran into the middle of the street and I fell down. That's all I remember. I must have passed out. By the time I came to" — she indicates her neighbors — "they were bending over me —"

I interrupted. "But Jack and the others. Did you see them again?"

Carol Ann shakes her head.

A man holding a towel to his bleeding head says, "I live in building Y. I saw something. After Z building fell I ran back home to grab my flashlight. When I finally made it out again, I saw a car drive out. Amazing that any of the cars could be running."

I feel hope. "Maybe someone picked them up." I look around. "Does anyone have a car that hasn't been hit?" I'm miserable when all I see are heads shaking and all I hear is them mumbling no.

Suddenly a piercing scream comes from behind Jack's building. We all run. The easier way around the building is from the side of Abe's apartment, which had the least damage. Oh, God, I fear the worst. Will all their dead bodies be lying there?

When we turn the corner, we see a young

couple standing there staring down into what seems like a very deep pit where part of the building used to be. The man has his flashlight illuminating downward.

"What is it?" the man with the towel asks. "What did you find?"

The young man says, "We were heading to look for our friends in Phase Four and we took the back way because it was less of a mess, and we almost fell into this hole."

The young woman can barely stutter. "There's a dead body down there."

Abe's group crowd around, but I cannot move. Evvie holds on tightly to me. I shut my eyes.

"You're not gonna believe this," the man says. "It's someone dead, all right. But it couldn't have happened last night. That's a skeleton down there!"

19
THE HOSPITAL

It takes a few moments for me to process the information. A dead body. Buried deep. A skeleton. Thank God it can't be Jack — that's the only thing I care about. So where did he go? It had to be the hospital. Someone was hurt, or he would have come to me.

The hospital is right across the street. But Oakland Park Boulevard might be impossible to maneuver. We can take the shortcut through the back of Lanai Gardens. I grab Evvie and pull her with me. "Come on, we've got to get to the hospital! Now!"

We race through mud and dirt and rubble and more milling people stunned by what has happened to their lives in one night. The hospital seems not to be too damaged, but it's chaotic. Outside, dented cars that can still be driven are parked haphazardly; nobody bothers to use designated areas today. The streets are silent except for sirens. Probably every police car and fire engine is out and about today.

Inside, it looks like a war zone: Crowds of bloody, battered people are waiting to be helped. Crying relatives look bewildered and shocked. I try to get the attention of someone at the check-in desk, but it's mobbed. I'm not alone trying to locate lost people. The harried woman behind the desk, dressed in sweats, hair uncombed, who must have rushed over this morning, makes it clear she has little information yet. We will all have to wait.

Not my Evvie. She grabs my arm and we head for the stairs. We have all of us, one time or another, been here. We know the place backwards and forwards. We also know most of the staff. Most of our doctors use this hospital facility. We head for Emergency.

It, too, looks like a war zone. Bandaged heads and bodies everywhere. People lying on gurneys, waiting to be seen. Nurses and doctors hurrying from room to room.

"Let's split up," Evvie suggests. "Signal when you find them." She refers to the whistle we invented when we were teenagers and would lose each other in department stores.

I go from cubicle to cubicle, sometimes

185

seeing people I know, asking if anyone has seen Jack. No luck at all. It's almost surreal, our friends and neighbors all at once in such a situation.

I have a preposterous thought — I wonder where Grandpa Bandit is. Is he somewhere nearby? Never mind.

I'm at the last possible section, dismayed and frustrated, when I hear Evvie use our familiar whistle. I follow the sound around and about the nurses' station until I find her.

And Jack.

As I run toward him I see immediately that he looks all right. Unharmed. Dirty, disheveled, cuts and scrapes on his face, but definitely still in one piece. He sees me and runs to meet me. We kiss and hug. I feel like we're in a scene in a romantic movie.

"When I saw your building . . ." I begin.

"I couldn't leave my women charges to come to you. I was silently sending you messages and hoping your ESP was working."

We kiss again. "Is your gang all right?" he asks.

"Yes, we were very lucky."

He brings me to poor Dora Dooley, who is thoroughly miserable. "I broke my arm," she tells me. "I'm waiting for someone to put on a cast. And the TV isn't working. I could be watching my soaps!"

Poor one-track-mind Dora.

Then we check on Carmel Graves, who is swathed in bandages. "I feel like a mummy," she says with humor.

"Where's Louise?" I ask. "Is she all right?"

"She's fine," Carmel says, pointing. "She's over there visiting people she knows."

"Did you see Carol Ann?" Jack asks.

Evvie says, "She's okay, just shook up. She's with Abe."

"Thank God," he says. "I knew she got out, but I couldn't find her in the dark."

Carmel smiles at me. "He's quite a guy, your boyfriend. He carried Dora over his shoulder and held on to me tightly with his other arm. And with Louise hanging on to his jacket and staying very close, he got us out of there. I don't know how he did it. It was totally black and we only had my flashlight, which needed new batteries and was almost useless."

She and Jack smile at each other. "Some Boy Scout I was," Jack says. "First thing happened I lost my flashlight."

When we return to Jack's building hours later, having left Dora and Carmel with some friends, he is astonished at the damage. "That we got out alive is a miracle," he says. "And you tell me there's a skeleton?"

I take him around the back. By now there is a sizeable crowd circling the fissure in the ground and yellow tape has been hung to keep people away. A couple of police cars are parked nearby.

"Dad!" We turn to see Jack's son, Morrie, rushing toward us. Father and son hug. "Thank God you're all right," Morrie says.

"I asked every policeman I saw at the hospital if anyone had seen you," Jack tells him. "Then I ran into Oz Washington and he told me you were safe."

Morrie hugs me, too. Hard. Clearly he was worried about me, bless his heart.

"What's going on here?" Jack asks.

Another voice is heard. A familiar one. "That's what I want to know!"

I turn to see Stanley Heyer. The sprightly eighty-five-year-old comes hurrying toward us with, as usual, Abe Waller. Poor Stanley. A few days ago he thought it was just a roof that needed repair. Now he'll have his hands full with all of Lanai Gardens to deal with. He stares down into the deep crevice where the skeleton lies.

Morrie says to him, "We need to get the body out and do an autopsy, but obviously this is not a priority today, with the city in so much disorder. Can you tell us anything that might help?"

Stanley looks at the bones soberly. "One thing is clear: He or she is in the substructure of the building. I can tell from the cement and what's left of the framed trench around him. This poor soul must have been buried under the building before it was completed."

"Oy, such a terrible accident," Abe says, shaking his head dolefully.

"If I recall," Stanley says, "we were having many storms around that time, too. I guess he or she might have fallen in."

"Or," says a bystander, "maybe a person dug a hole in their apartment and threw someone in. On purpose."

Onlookers react with shudders at this gory imagination.

Stanley smiles ruefully. "That would be very hard to do. Since we have no basements, that person would have to dig through his living room floor. Everyone would be aware of the mess and the noise."

Some agreeing nods at that.

My probable future stepson, Morrie, says, "Speculation will have to wait until we know more. Meanwhile there's a whole city to take care of. I'll have a team on the scene as soon as I'm able."

I glance over at Abe Waller. His head is

bowed, his lips move in prayer. Next to him Stanley Heyer seems deep in thought.

20

THE MEETING WILL COME TO . . . DISORDER

Two days after the hurricane a meeting of Phase Two has been called. The clubhouse is filled to the brim, including residents of other Lanai Garden Phases, who are here to help. I've been told that seated in the rear is a group of people who no longer have livable homes.

In front, I sit with Jack and the girls. Except for the Canadians, who left before the storm hit, all of the Phase Two condo residents are present.

We gaze around, nodding to friends and neighbors, many in bandages. Most of us look disheveled because we still don't have hot water.

When Evvie is sure everyone is seated, she wends her way up to the podium. As our Phase president and secretary, she thanks everyone for coming and indicates our guest speaker, who comes forward.

"This man needs no introduction. We all

191

know him, since he has made it his business to know us. Before he retired, he was president of the Heyer Construction Company, which built our beautiful condominium apartments. He loved his creation so much he moved in, living here since 1958, when Lanai Gardens was built. Over the years this kind man has been a familiar sight, carrying a loaf of challah and a bottle of Manischewitz whenever a moving truck arrived and new people came to live here. He would personally greet each one that happy day with bread and wine as a symbol of friendship.

"For fifty years he has been our best neighbor and now, in our hour of need, our leader steps up to the plate to help us. A big hand for Stanley Heyer."

Stanley gets his deserved applause as we stand up to show our respect. Evvie returns to her seat next to me.

Waving his arms for us to stop and sit back down, he takes the battery-powered mike, which squeals, piercing everyone's ears. "You all know I've been meeting with each Phase about this terrible disaster. The very good news is that though many were injured, nobody died. The bad news is that our beautiful homes require a lot of work. I don't need to tell you how hard it will be to get help, with the whole city in disrepair."

Much murmuring at this. I think to myself how lucky we are to have a man like this in our midst. The mood among the residents is despair, but Stanley will give us hope.

"It will be a long haul. But out of bad comes good, and neighbors will reach out in whatever way they can to help one another rebuild. Everyone in Lanai Gardens who has a construction skill, please sign up to help. Every Phase president will start a list of those who have a service of some kind to offer. Today Evvie Markowitz will start the Phase Two list."

Barbi and Casey raise their hands and stand up. Barbi speaks: "As many of you know, we own a computer research service. We deal in accessing information, which can be very helpful in getting services for those in need. We will explain our company's many uses to those who wish to contact us."

Casey adds, "We're available to anyone free for the next three months."

They sit down, to much applause. Evvie writes their names on her Phase Two list.

A woman I've seen before, from Phase Four, jumps up. She is colorfully dressed in what looks like a gypsy outfit. "Let me introduce myself. I am Madame Margaret Ramona, once known on the stage as the woman with a thousand identities. If you want to have your tarot cards read and find out what is in store for the future, get in touch with me. Free. For a while," she adds quickly.

Evvie leans over and whispers, "She stole that idea from Lon Chaney."

Ida puts her two cents in. "Like who cares. What a character."

Many other hands go up. Evvie speaks from her seat. "Meet me later and I'll get you all on the list. For now, let's let Stanley wrap things up."

The hands go down and Stanley speaks again.

"Thank you, one and all, for your generosity. People have opened their homes to their friends and neighbors whose apartments are unlivable. And today, we meet here to continue the same in your Phase.

"By now nearly everyone has been relocated. There are only a few still in need of lodging." He indicates the group in back. "Good friends, please come forward."

All eyes fix on the people who move up front, bunched together. There are seven in all. Among them, in front, are Dora Dooley and Abe Waller, looking forlorn.

Stanley puts his arm around Abe and says to the audience, "I, myself, wanted Abe to live with us, but with my large family, there is no room."

I whisper to Evvie, "Where's Louise? How come she's not up there?"

"I've been meaning to tell you. You won't like it, but she's relocated to your building. And worse, on your floor."

"What!"

"Shh," says Evvie. "Later."

"Looky, looky who's there," Ida says, poking Evvie. "Your ex."

Evvie spots Joe Markowitz in the back of the group, hiding behind a larger man.

"What's he doing there?" she asks, chagrined.

Ida says, "I heard his rental apartment was taken back by the owner, to do repairs."

Evvie quips, "Maybe they ought to put him up on an auction block and sell him off. To the lowest bidder."

"Don't be nasty," I say.

Sophie says poignantly, "Who's gonna want Dora? Or Joe? By now all the nice neighbors have been taken."

A woman rises. She introduces herself as Fran Duma. "My parents went back home to Quebec. Their apartment, P218, is available for as long as needed. They were apprised that Mr. Waller needed a place and I'm authorized to offer it to him."

195

Evvie and I exchange surprised glances. I say, "That's the apartment between you and Enya."

Abe walks over to Fran and bows to her as she hands him the key. "Please thank them for me."

While people are commenting, Jack suddenly gets up from my side and starts to move. I tug at his jacket to stop him. "Where are you going?"

He looks at me, his face blank. "I need a place to stay."

Startled, I say, "What are you talking about? You've moved in with Morrie."

He shakes his head. "He's got enough on his mind. I'll only be in the way."

I whisper, "Jack, cut out this nonsense. Please."

He shrugs. I hold on to his jacket.

People stare from me and then to Jack, as if at a tennis match. And a buzz goes round the room.

I say, "This is crazy."

He says, gently removing my hand from his jacket, "I'm being practical."

He moves toward the front. I feel myself turning red.

Even my girls stare at me, bewildered. He keeps going. Joe, grinning, makes room for him at his side.

Evvie pokes me, amazed. "What's Jack doing?"

"I wish I knew."

There's a moment when all stare at Jack, who's joined the people in need of lodging.

A hand flies up and a high-pitched voice calls out, "I have an extra bedroom. I'll be glad to share with Mr. Langford."

The room turns to Louise, now standing, looking sexy in some kind of slinky outfit with giraffes on it. How does she do it? With a smashed-in apartment how did she get a new dress? She takes out a house key and waves it. "Q317 is available, Jackie!"

The room erupts in shocked excitement.

Sophie hisses, "That brazen hussy!"

Bella says, "That brazen hussy just told us she's gonna be your next-door neighbor!"

Sophie gasps in alarm.

Evvie pokes me. "Do something!"

I can't believe Jack is putting me in this position. I mumble, "I'm going to kill him when we get out of here. I ought to let Louise have him."

Tessie nudges Sol in delight and she begins clapping. Others join in. Mary and Irving turn and glare at her.

Hy can't resist and calls out, "Okay, any other offers for Jack Langford, very tall, handsome ex-policeman? A valuable man to have around the house."

A woman in the rear shouts, "He can put his shoes under my bed anytime."

Lots of laughter at that. The buzzing gets louder.

Evvie, furious, jumps up, stalks to the podium, and bangs the gavel. Stanley moves off to one side, confused about what's going on.

Evvie growls, "Let's have some order around here."

"Hey, Evvie," Tessie shouts. "How about Joe? Your ex needs a place to lay his tired head."

Joe perks up at that and smiles widely.

More enthusiastic clapping. If there's one thing my Lanai Gardens neighbors love, it's to turn rowdy. Especially after the tension of the last few days, laughter is a relief.

Hy fuels the fire. To the cadence of clapping, he stamps his feet and recites, "Evvie and Joe. Evvie and Joe."

Lola, ever the dutiful wife, adds, "And Gladdy and Jack!"

Louise yells, "Hell with that, I have dibs on him!"

That's it! I'm out of here. I march from my seat to the exit as Evvie bangs the gavel and shouts, "Meeting's over!"

The last words I hear come from Dora

Dooley. "Hey, what about me? Anybody got a TV with batteries?"

Jack catches up to me as I'm crossing the small bridge behind the pool. "Gladdy, wait!"

I call over my shoulder, "Haven't you humiliated me enough for one day?" Below me the ducks quack as if they are a chorus to my misery.

He tries to touch my arm but I pull away, on the move again. "What new quality did I learn about you this time? Mean-spirited? Someone who likes to embarrass women?"

"I was trying to get your attention."

"In front of fifty people?"

"I've tried and I've tried. I keep proposing and . . . nothing."

I stop running and turn to him. "And that . . . that performance was your way of wooing me?"

He shrugs. "The act of a desperate man. What can I say? I was waiting for you to ask me to move in with you. An act of God gave you a great big signal. The decision was made for you. It's *beshert* — meant to be. How about this poor guy who just lost his apartment — everything he owns, gone forever. How about this being a perfect time to say, *Gee, Jack, why don't you move in with me?* You could help me shop for new clothes. I'm terrible at it. I don't even have a coffeepot, and this was your opportunity to say, *Jack, darling, think of the breakfasts we'll have together.* And the lunches and the dinners. We could spend our days together looking lovingly in each other's eyes."

I think of all the same fantasies I've had and I feel awful. I feel like such a bad person. "But . . . I thought you wanted to stay with Morrie."

"Yeah, right. I'd much rather be sharing my son's one-bedroom house on his lumpy couch in the living room, and taking away his privacy at the same time."

"But . . . but Sophie and Bella are staying with me. They're still frightened and don't want to be alone."

"They're not alone. They have each other. Or they can bunk in with Evvie or Ida. Or any of the fifty willing people at the meeting. Any more excuses?"

He gazes at me imploringly. I think of the man I accompanied to Key West with such love light shining in his eyes.

"None." I melt into his arms. "What a fool I am."

He hugs me tightly. "And now all of Lanai Gardens knows it."

"It will take a little while until I get Soph

and Bella out."

"I'm known for my amazing patience."

We kiss long and deeply. "Say it," he says. "Come on, it will only hurt for a minute."

I look into those gorgeous eyes. "Jack Langford, will you live with me?"

He lifts me up and whirls me around. "It's about time, babe."

And once again, the sound of applause, as who knows how many of the fifty are outside the clubhouse, *kvell*ing at our love scene.

Jack bows to them, then attempts to pull me into a run. But I stop him. "In my hurry I left my sweater in the clubhouse."

He says, "Go get it and meet me at my old building. I want to see if anything's happening." He takes off, and I attempt to pretend indifference as I pass my amused audience.

I expect the clubhouse to be empty, but as I'm about to step inside, I see Evvie and Joe. From the look of them, they're in the middle of an intense conversation. I should leave, but can't stop myself from listening.

Evvie is shouting, "What are you trying to do to me? I'm having a nice retirement, and you barge in."

Joe speaks softly, pleadingly. "Do you want me to get down on my knees and beg? I will if you want me to."

Evvie softens slightly. "No, I just want you to go away and leave me alone."

"And I want to make up for what I did to you in our marriage."

She backs away slightly. "So apologize already and get it over with. No, don't even bother. I accept your apology in advance. So, go back to New York."

"I hate the weather, I can't take the cold anymore."

"I'm sure our daughter will make sure you're nice and warm."

"No, I can't go there . . . I mean, I won't. I don't want to do that anymore. It's a small house. They need their space. It's not fair to them."

"So go live with *your* relatives. I'm sure your sisters will be thrilled to have you."

His voice climbs higher a notch. "I don't want to, Evvie. I want to be with you! I need you, Evvie. I love you!"

This stops my poor sister in her tracks. She gasps in astonishment. "Joe, please . . . don't." Then angrier, "Don't you dare say that to me!"

I back away from the door. I can't bear watching anymore.

21
THE SKELETON

I hurry to meet Jack at his building. By now, what's left of the structure is yellow-taped. In the sharp sunlight, I look up to the crushed second floor. It looks even worse than it looked on that first gray morning. I shudder to imagine what might have happened.

He's not in front. I become aware of people hurrying to the rear, and I follow them. There's quite a crowd hanging around behind the yellow police tape, including Stanley Heyer and Abe Waller. I see Jack, and I join him, not wanting to miss a thing.

I watch the cops. Besides Morrie Langford and Oz Washington, there's a medical examiner and a team of police. They're all in hip boots, what with the ground still muddy from the storm. The sun is out, but it's weak, barely illuminating the scene. The cops have brought their own powerful work lamps.

At the bottom of the cave-in, which seems to me about five feet deep, a couple of the gloved policemen carefully bag the skeleton and place it on a pulley.

Once the remains are hoisted out, the cops gather up what else might give them clues as to what happened to this person so long ago. They send up bag after bag of their findings. Other cops carefully lay the items down on a large tarp on the ground. We try hard to see what's there. Looks like a few scraps of fabric. Some shredded, sodden pieces of paper. When they retrieve a gray mass of something that looks like metal, Stanley gasps.

Oz and Morrie turn to him. "Something?" Morrie asks.

Stanley is shaken. "It looks like a piece from one of the helmets my men wore on the site."

Oz lifts the yellow tape for Stanley to enter. "Come and take a closer look," Oz tells him.

Stanley nervously moves toward the wretched-looking items on the tarp. "Yes, it could be."

Now Oz and Morrie talk in lower voices, but my hearing is sharp and I hardly miss a word.

Oz comments, "The cloth looks like it

might have come from a plaid shirt. We'll
know better when we have it analyzed at
the lab."

"Remind you of anything?" Morrie asks
Stanley.

He sighs. "Yes. One of my workers went
AWOL the day before we poured the con-
crete."

Morrie says, "It could save us a lot of
trouble if you can remember his name."

"Johnny Blake. When we first saw the
skeleton, I had a hunch and went through
my old records. He was new on the job. My
foreman, Ed Luddy, hired him while I was
away on business."

"Could you describe him for us?" Oz asks.

Stanley shakes his head. "That's what I'm
trying to tell you. I never met him. By the
time I returned, Ed told me he hadn't
shown up one day. I didn't think anything
about it since we hired a lot of itinerant
types who took off the moment their part of
the job was done."

"Where's Ed Luddy? We'd like to talk to
him," Oz says.

Stanley says, "Dead nigh on seven years.
Lung cancer got him."

"Anyone else still around who might remember?"

Stanley manages a wry smile. "You're talking to an eighty-five-year-old man. Do you imagine any of those other men are still with us?"

The cops place the bags and tarp in a van. Morrie and Oz remove the equipment they brought. Morrie hands Stanley a card. "You think of anything else, call me. I'll be in touch with you after the lab work is done. Might take a while."

The show is over and the onlookers scatter. Morrie and Oz come over to us.

Oz says, "Are congrats in order? Hear you two lovebirds are setting up house together."

I look at my love, amazed. When did he have time to report this news update?

"True," says my Jack proudly, putting his arm around me. Showing off now that he's captured his prey. Me.

"And I was so happy with you living with me," Morrie jokes. "So was my girlfriend. She loved having you around on her nights over."

Morrie winks, and I of course turn and blush. I grab Jack's hand and pull him away with me. He and I walk back to my place, hand in hand. All around us is a new kind of chaos. Tow trucks haul away battered cars. Resident men clear the streets of rubble, filling all available Dumpsters. Resident women come in and out of apartments, tossing damaged items. Everyone calls out to friends and neighbors. Who was lucky to be spared? Who wasn't? Cheerful voices and resigned ones.

Lanai Gardens is determined to rise again, and I've also got a new future to look forward to — living with Jack.

22
Days of Adjustment

All in all, damage to Fort Lauderdale was less than expected. With the exception of Z building, thankfully no apartments were destroyed. But major repairs may take at least a year. Life will be different from now on.

With the changes going on around Phase Two, you almost need a scorecard. What's good and not good: We have electricity again. Though the phones are erratic, cell phones are working overtime.

We did reach our families and everyone knows we are fine. They were sad that Jack lost his apartment, but delighted he is going to live with me. The unspoken question is — when's the wedding?

I get through to Conchetta, and learn her large family suffered only minor damage. She informed me the library will open again after the volunteers finish picking up all the bookcases and reshelve the salvaged books and tape the broken windows. No mail delivery yet. Some cars are operational and those are busy carrying neighbors to and from the places they need to go. Mine is still functional, but it reminds me of a big hunk of metallic cottage cheese, irrevocably dented. Publix, our big supermarket, is a mess, but the sign outside promises the store will be open for business soon. Our banks are open. Sophie bemoans the loss of her beauty shop — gone for good.

What's obvious is a sense of excitement with all the comings and goings. No lolling about the pool these days (the bottom is cracked). We are a beehive of productivity.

As I wander about I catch many snippets of conversation:

Hy and Lola moan about no glaziers being available to replace their apartment windows. "I can't sleep with that draft," complains Hy.

"And I can't sleep with that draft from your mouth complaining about it," says his much-put-upon wife. Seems to me like the dutiful wife is cranky from sleep deprivation.

Bella explains how she managed to get stuck with Dora Dooley as a roommate: "I don't know how it happened. She just followed me home. What could I do? So I let her in."

Evvie: "You never heard of 'just say no'?"

Ida: "You won't get her out again."

Sophie: "It'll take forever 'til they rebuild Z building."

Bella: "Oy!"

Dora, popping out of Bella's front door, announces, "I need a recliner. Why don't you have a recliner? How am I supposed to sit on a straight chair to watch my shows? And I need a *blanky* to keep me warm. And why don't you have sweaters? I'm freezing in there."

Bella, eyes like saucers, hurries back inside to wait on her demanding roommate.

Later in the day, Ida and I watch from across the courtyard as Evvie, Bella, Hy, and Lola greet their new second-floor neighbor with welcoming gifts of casseroles. Abe Waller is suitably grateful. He opens the door to his borrowed apartment, which is next to Evvie. Just then, on the other side of him, his other neighbor, Enya, appears, to see what's going on. Head lowered, she shyly says hello. Abe bows to greet her. Enya quickly retreats inside.

Their attention is drawn to the elevator as an excited Joe, lugging a bulging suitcase, comes out.

"Hi there, everybody," he says cheerfully. "Here's your other new neighbor."

All pivot to watch Evvie's response. But Evvie gives nothing away. She opens her door and hurries inside. Joe nods to the others and follows after her.

"He looks like a sad-eyed puppy," Ida comments to me.

From my balcony, another day: I'm with all the girls, and hands on hips, we watch Louise move into Q317, the apartment next to Sophie, which is only one apartment away from me. And three away from Ida. None of us is smiling as she turns her key in the lock and gives us a bright phony smile. "Anyone play bridge?" she asks, knowing damn well what the answer is. The only one on the floor who does is — my Jack. If he dares to play bridge with her, I'm going along. I can play dummy. Yeah, right. Ha-ha.

This evening Jack is moving in — with nothing but a toothbrush and some hurried shopping for a few necessary items. Tonight my life changes forever.

I clean up my apartment. Well, sort of. Dirt is everywhere, on everything. The slats on the windows couldn't keep out what the fierce winds blew. The washing machine room is working 24/7.

I do the best I can. The markets are low on fresh food. My first dinner alone with Jack will be catch as catch can. The girls are solicitous. They are aware of tonight's importance. They offer what goodies they have in their refrigerators.

Sophie and Bella call me just about every hour on the hour, for constant moral support. Bella spends a lot of time in Sophie's apartment because Dora is driving her crazy.

I wonder how Evvie and Joe are doing. It's two days now. Haven't seen her or Joe. I hope they aren't killing each other.

I dress up for dinner. Do my hair. Lather on the makeup. Then ten minutes later, I wipe off most of the makeup. Back to simple beige slacks and a white cotton shirt. I don't know how to behave. An old song pops into my head. Was it Sammy Davis, Jr., who used to sing "I gotta be me"? But who is "me" these days?

It would be nice to sit in the Florida room and have a drink before dinner. But my sunroom is a mess. The screens all blew out; furniture is strewn every which way. I guess now I should call it an open porch. Trouble is, everything is broken in there. My bookshelves, my reading lamp, my stereo, my family photos. All smashed. Most of it will have to be thrown away. Besides, all I have in the fridge is some lemonade. So much for the cocktail hour.

I hear a knock on the door. Then it opens. All kinds of silly things run through my head. I gave him a key, but I guess he felt he needed to warn me. What do we say to each other? How am I supposed to act?

I hurry to the hallway. There he is, holding a small bouquet of flowers and a bottle of wine. He has on new clothes — tan windbreaker, tan khakis, and a navy blue sports shirt that goes wonderfully with his eyes. He grins at me. "Hi, honey, I'm home."

I laugh. I play back. "Hard day at the office, dear?"

He puts his gifts down on the small hallway table and grabs me and hugs me. "I couldn't find a florist with any flowers, so I picked these in the park. As for the wine, I grabbed the first bottle I could find. I hope you like cheap sangria."

We stand there looking at each other. "So, what do we do next?" I ask.

Jack emotes from the movie *Marty:* "I don't know, Marty, wadda you want to do?"

He walks me into the kitchen and peeks into the pot to see what's cooking. "News flash," he says, "I have a job." He picks up a spoon and dips into my pot of chicken soup. "I'm no longer retired."

"Tell me," I say. We each grab a bowl and fill it with soup. He carries the bowls to the dining room table. I bring the salad, napkins, and salt and pepper. For a touch of festivity I light the two candles that are on my table.

"I've been recruited. Along with a lot of other retired cops. To help keep law and order. And how was your day?"

As he digs into my hearty soup, I begin to tell Jack all the gossip going round.

It's like we've been together for years. And it feels wonderful.

I sigh happily. Here we are enveloped in one another's arms on the couch, finishing off the really bad sangria. Soft music plays. We have been talking nonstop since dinner. It's nearly midnight and my eyes are closing, but I never want this evening to end. What is wondrous to me is that Jack and I are already close friends, before we've even gotten to the sex. Though not for want of trying. I smile, thinking of the irony.

I look at him. He looks at me.

"Dare we?" he asks.

I know he's referring to heading for the

bedroom.

"We're covered," I tell him. The girls won't call — they know I'll kill them if they do. Our relatives know we're safe. "Unless we have a sudden new hurricane, or the building burns down, all systems are go."

Jack is funny. I love his humor. He begins to tiptoe to the bedroom, stopping each moment to see if it's all right to take the next step. He takes another, still smiling and looking back at me. I can't help laughing. He's so cute. Can one call a man in his seventies cute? But he is — playful, upbeat, a happy man at heart. He makes my spirits fly. I begin to follow in his footsteps.

The doorbell rings, piercingly. Again and again.

The phone rings at the same time.

"What the hell?" Jack says.

"Maybe it's Halloween and we forgot the candy" is my exasperated response.

"You grab the phone," he tells me, "and I'll get the door."

Since I can see the door from the kitchen phone, all at once I know the news. My girls are standing there, faces pinched. Joe is with them. Evvie says, terrified, "Millie escaped from the hospital."

And on the phone it is Mary, informing me of the same thing. "Irving is hysterical.

We're going out to look for her. We need every car that's working."

I tell her, "Yes, we'll be right down."

Jack and I grab our jackets and follow the girls to the stairs. As we run, Jack asks, "How could she get out of an Alzheimer's facility?"

Ida informs us, "When the electricity went off, the locked doors opened. They assume she just walked out."

"Did anyone call the police?"

"The nursing home did," Evvie says. "They've only just called us. We don't know how long Millie's been gone."

Downstairs Tessie and Sol and Mary are already in Irving's car. Ida, Evvie, Joe, Bella, Sophie, and I squeeze into my car and Jack's. Denny's truck holds him, Yolie, Hy, and Lola. The battered vehicles squeal as dents scrape against tires, but at least we are still able to drive.

With relief I think — thank God Jack and I still had our clothes on.

23
A NEW WORRY

The gated nursing home in Margate is located on a half acre of grounds with wooded areas. The local police grimly tell us they've covered every inch of the facility, every room inside, every outbuilding. And are still at it. They suggest we surround the area outside the gate.

Though the nursing home itself is very quiet, a small group of staff greet our scruffy, anxious gang of fifteen. The home personnel are beside themselves. A Mrs. Stapleford, who seems to be in charge, reports to the shaking Irving, "We thought everyone was secure. It wasn't until eleven o'clock bed check that one of our staff realized that Millie had stuffed pillows under her blanket and was gone."

Another nurse says, "Nothing like this has ever happened here before."

A third says, "It's unbelievable. Those doors are heavy. How could she have had the strength to open them? We only just got our electricity back an hour ago." She cannot look at Irving and turns away.

Evvie asks, "When was the last time you saw her?"

"When we distributed meds at seven P.M. We left her lying in her room. Since the hurricane, our patients seem more comfortable staying in their rooms."

Jack comments, "So she could have gone out anytime since seven, but before the electricity came back on."

The nurses nod. What we are all thinking is she's been out there on her own for maybe five hours. God help her.

Practical Mary asks, "What would she be wearing?"

The night nurse says, "Just her nightgown, I'm afraid. Her slippers are still under the bed. Her robe is still in the closet."

Irving sobs at that.

Mrs. Stapleton suddenly remembers. "Oh, we left each patient with a flashlight. She must have taken it with her."

For some reason, that fact gives me hope. I don't know why.

"Then what are we waiting for?" asks Tessie.

Once outside the gates, the hardier ones of

us spread out on foot, the rest pile in the back of Denny's truck. Denny drives very slowly, for his passengers' safety and for them to be able to search. I'm glad Evvie remembered to bring the flashlights we used so much just a few days earlier. Our "on foot" group agrees to stay close, two or more, never alone. The plan — to meet back at the gate every half hour on the hour.

Through the dark neighborhoods, we call out Millie's name. We look in every yard, every empty doorway, ever mindful of hostile neighbors and dogs. Dogs do bark and neighbors come out, but no one has seen anything. We travel from street to street, Denny's truck and our waving flashlights the only movement in the night.

Joe and Evvie are with us. I notice Joe reach out to take her hand. She hesitates, then lets him.

"Haven't seen you in a couple of days," I say, making small talk, even though my eyes are darting every which way. "How's it going?"

"Things are fine, just fine," says Joe.

Evvie grunts. "Why can't he learn after fifty years to put the toilet seat down?"

Joe huffs, "Where is it written it has to be that way? You women make all the rules. What difference does it make? Up. Down.

219

Up. Down."

"The difference is," she says tightly, "at night, half-asleep, in the dark, when it's up, I fall into the toilet, you idiot!"

"Over here," Hy shouts excitedly. We race to the sound of his voice. But when we get there, sadly it is a homeless person sleeping in a large brown carton in an alley.

We regularly trudge back to the gate. Hour after hour, we forge on, but with no luck. No Millie anywhere.

We are exhausted and cold. The police suggest we go home. They will continue on. They'll call when they find her, they tell us optimistically. But Irving shrivels up into himself. He has lost hope.

We gather in front of our two buildings. Even though it is near dawn, no one seems to want to go to bed. Yolie, bless her heart, has made pots of coffee for us. Irving sits at the picnic table and we surround him with our love — each of us taking turns insisting that Millie is an amazing woman. A survivor. Courageous and beautiful. But in our hearts we are talking about the Millie we knew years ago. Before that plague came upon us older people.

Abe, wakened by hearing us, has come down to join us. He leads us in a prayer for

Millie. I watch the sky, about to turn into day. It will be a beautiful one. Mother Nature has trampled us, done her dirty work, and now she teases us with sunshine. Until she has another mood swing — as Hy calls it, Mother Nature with PMS — and gives us another blast of misery.

We swivel at the sight of a vehicle turning into our Phase. A taxicab pulls up and the driver gets out.

"I got a passenger in back," he says, not even showing surprise that this group of people is sitting outside at this odd hour. "Picked her up when she flagged me. Hey, I got an old mom, too. Felt sorry for her. I was going to drop her off at the police station, but she insisted she knew where she lived."

He opens the car door and Millie graciously steps out, one hand holding up the hem of her white cotton nightgown, the other holding her flashlight, still on. Her face lights up in a smile at the sight of us.

The cabbie asks, "Somebody gonna pay the tab?"

24
THE EARTH MOVES

What a night! But all's well. Irving informed the police and the nursing home that Millie is with him. She doesn't recognize Irving or anyone else, but her bed is familiar to her and all she wants is to sleep. Last night's Gang of Fifteen, as we are calling one another, will take turns watching Millie as the others rest. Jack and I bow out.

Well, here we are. Six A.M. In my bedroom at last. We throw ourselves on top of the bedspread, still in our clothes, kicking off our shoes. Jack mumbles before he drops deeply into sleep, "How do I *not* make love to you? Let me count the ways. Pago Pago. New York. Key West. My bedroom. Your bedroom . . ."

The last thing I remember before I pass out, too — Jack is snoring and I'm laughing.

I think I'm dreaming. But I'm not. My eyes

peel open and I see the clock. It's eight something. We are moving in slow motion. He helps me off with my clothes. I help him with his. Clothes are tossed. We kiss. I suggest a shower to get rid of last night's grunge. He doesn't care. He suggests later. Together. Arms and legs entwine. I don't know where one of us leaves off and the other begins. We are still tired, so our movements are unhurried. We are whispering nonsense as our bodies respond, ignoring our words. I say, "It's been such a long time." He says, "It's like riding a bike." I say, "I never rode a bike in the Bronx. My mother wouldn't let me." He says, "I have a bad back, it could go out any second." I tell him about the arthritis in my knees. "I might cry out in pain." We name all our old-age ailments. He tells me, "I have battle scars." I say, "I'll show you mine, if you show me yours." I giggle. He says, "We'll work around them." What we are doing to each other has us sizzling. We moan in pleasure. He says, "I think I hear the phone." I say, "No damn way." He says, "Kidding." We are no longer talking. We are in the moment, in the second, enveloped in bliss, peaking to rapture.

"The earth finally moved," I say afterward. He says, "It's about bloody time."

25
STANLEY ASKS A FAVOR

It's our first morning of living together. Getting up was hard to do. Coffee was an incentive but lovemaking was the more intense craving. Will I ever again think of the shower as just a place to wash? Our bodies might be aging, but our spirits are young. And willing. And capable. Forget the gymnastics of our youth; this is a whole new experience of experimenting with what we still can do.

Breakfast is at ten-thirty. And I silently thank my girls for giving up their early-morning phone call ritual. I'm still in my robe. Jack is dressed in one of the two outfits he owns — the one he didn't wear yesterday. We are on our third cup of coffee when the doorbell finally rings. I wonder which one of the girls it will be. Or perhaps all of them.

To my surprise, Stanley Heyer stands on the threshold, holding a small brown paper bag. "May I come in?" he asks.

Of course I let him in. I'm embarrassed, to say the least. Our first visitor, and it turns out to be the most religious man in all of Lanai Gardens. Can he see the blush on my face? But the little man seems not to notice.

"I brought bagels." He hands the bag to me.

I thank him and we tell him to sit down and join us. As I'm about to pour him a cup of coffee, he shakes his head no. I try to offer him a bagel. He says he already ate. He is being polite. My kitchen isn't kosher.

He begins, "You are probably wondering why I'm here."

Jack says, "Whatever the reason, you're most welcome."

"Allow me — the good news. It will take a while to clear the rubble, and to secure the building so it will be safe to enter, but then you and your neighbors will be able to get into your apartments again to gather up whatever has not been destroyed. I've already informed the others in Z building."

Jack is properly grateful. "That's a relief. Hopefully we'll retrieve important papers and not have to make endless reports to endless government agencies."

I agree. "Especially since the lines will be horrific."

Jack shakes Stanley's hand. "Thanks,

you're a godsend."

Stanley accepts this shyly. "I wouldn't say that." He sits up straighter in his chair. "However, I've just come from the police station with disturbing news. They finished the autopsy. The poor man's head was bashed in. They found bone fractures in the skull. And on some parts of the skeleton. No accident. It was murder."

"How awful," I say.

Jack asks, "Will they investigate? The department is overloaded and I doubt they have the manpower or the time."

Stanley nods. "You hit the nail right on the head." He clasps his hands together on my table. "Who knows when or if they'll ever find out anything. That's why I'm here. Gladdy Gold, I want to hire you to investigate."

I'm surprised. "I don't know what to say."

"Listen, let me tell you what I know." He grimaces. "It's true what they say about old age. I don't recall what I did yesterday, but I can remember fifty years back like it *was* yesterday."

I nod in agreement, but don't respond, not wanting to break his train of thought.

"The crime happened about this same time of year. The weather was stormy. We were late laying in the foundation. So many delays in the construction. So much mud. Men leaving for warmer climates and other jobs because they couldn't wait any longer for the weather to change. A lot of aggravation, but I won't bore you with my *tsouris.*

"As I said, my foreman, Ed, had hired a new man during the week I was in Chicago. Family situation. A relative in trouble. Ah, I digress. I already mentioned the worker's name was Johnny Blake. Ed told me he was a large man, a good worker, but he didn't talk much. He told Ed he came from Tampa. Somewhere near the Gulf. The day I arrived home, the storm was at its worst. But the next day, we had a break in the weather and we decided we had to get the foundation done. Fast. Ed was surprised Mr. Blake didn't show up for work. He believed Mr. Blake wasn't the type who would walk just after getting a job he needed. Besides, his locker still had his things in it.

"But we had plenty of other problems on our plates and I assumed the man would come back for his stuff one day, so I stored it. And I forgot about him. Until now."

"Do you remember what was in his locker?" Jack asks.

"Yes. But I didn't find out until after the job was done — when we closed down our on-site work office, I remembered it. I opened the locker, but there was very little in there. A change of clothes. Another pair of work shoes. A denim jacket with a wallet with a few dollars, and a key in the pocket. And a Christmas card signed 'your sister Lucy.' I thought it was odd that he left those items, but I was too busy to give it any more thought."

Jack and I look at each other. "So," I say, "it can be assumed the key was his house key and Mr. Blake wouldn't have left without his wallet before going home that night."

"Anything might have happened," Jack comments. "Maybe it was an attempted robbery. Or someone thought he could steal equipment and this man, Blake, tried to stop him."

"Do you still have the things from his locker?" I ask.

Stanley smiles. "Does not a pack rat save everything? I am such a pack rat. Actually it's in a storage locker that Esther has been asking me to empty for years." He shrugs, guiltily, as if to say "You know how it is."

Jack says, "Get whatever you have to the station. They have a good forensic lab. His stuff might be of some help."

"I will," Stanley agrees. "Then maybe it will prove to my wife that I'm not just a *shmegegge*."

I laugh. "No way are you a fool, Mr. Stanley Heyer!"

The phone rings. I excuse myself and answer. It's for Jack. I hand him the phone. He listens briefly and tells me he's wanted down at the station. They have work for him.

Jack kisses me good-bye. In front of Stanley. But Stanley is lost in his thoughts.

"See you tonight, gorgeous," Jack says, on his way out.

Stanley gets up. "I should not take up any more of your time. But my conscience is bothering me that I didn't look into this. He must have had family — this sister Lucy — who never knew what happened to him. At least let me make it up to them. Find out who they are and let me inform them."

He looks at me with an expression of pain. "I won't sleep well until I know I have done my duty to the poor man."

He looks so forlorn standing there beseeching me with his eyes.

"I'll try, Stanley. I will."

Needless to say, the girls are standing right outside my door as Stanley leaves. They waited until Jack left and now the coast was clear. They greet Stanley as they rush inside.

"So? How are things?" Sophie cuts right to the chase as she sits down at my kitchen table and helps herself to a bagel. "We just happened to see Jack leaving."

Bella adds, grinning, "And he was whistling."

"Things are just fine," I answer, taking cream cheese and butter from the fridge and setting them on the table. One severe look from me means this subject is off-limits and that's that.

Ida leans against the kitchen door and gives me one of her raised-eyebrow looks, but I'm telling nothing.

"I wish I could say the same," Evvie kvetches as she pours her own cup of coffee. "Joe is making me nuts. 'Should I fix the venetian blinds? Should I take down the boards in the Florida room? Should I do this, do that?' I wish he'd leave me alone."

Bella huffs. "I'll change places with you in a minute. That Dora is driving me up a wall. Why don't you have strawberry jam? What kind of apartment doesn't have cable? Could you run to the store right now, I need my pills . . ."

Sophie jumps in. "I told Bella to ask for rent."

Bella says, "And what does my new boarder say? Her checkbook is in her apartment, her destroyed apartment."

Sophie again: "So we tell her she can

always go to the bank."

Bella: "And she says her bankbook is gone, too."

"I hate to break in on all your miseries," I announce. "But we have a new job."

The girls stop, mid-chewing. I have their immediate attention and I fill them in on Stanley's assignment.

Ida asks, "How can we find out about something that happened so long ago?"

"Especially with practically no information at all," Sophie comments.

Evvie says, "First stop, our girls in Gossip. If anybody can track someone down, Barbi and Casey can."

"Wonderful," says Bella. "At least it will get me out of the apartment."

"Ditto," says Evvie.

26
GOINGS ON

We watch Irving and Yolie bring Millie out of his apartment. Millie smiles brightly and waves to us even though she doesn't remember who we are. It's heartbreaking to think back on the dear lady she once was. Always positive and interested in everything around her. A good friend when you needed one. She and Irving were crazy about each other. Now here is this shell of a person; her vacant smile has no substance behind it.

As much as Irving wants to keep her home, Millie needs round-the-clock hospital care. As wrenching as it is, Irving must take her back.

We all take turns hugging a giggling Millie, trying to put a good face on how we really feel.

Just as she is about to be helped into Irving's battered car, she swivels, startled, as if she were waking from a dream. She looks around, suddenly seeming to know where she is. "Irving?" she says, reaching out to touch him. He jumps, shocked. It is Millie again, come back.

One of us gasps. I think it is Sophie, but I don't turn to see. We are mesmerized.

Millie clutches at Irving's shirt. "Don't let them put me in a box. Promise!"

He leans his head into hers. "I won't. I promise." Through his tears, he hugs her.

Then, as if a light went off, she is the Alzheimer patient once again. Lost and bewildered. Irving and Yolie help her into the car.

Irving sobs. "It's like losing her all over again. She was so happy to be home."

We stand there silently, as we watch the car pull away.

We remain near Irving's apartment tearfully, arms around one another.

But suddenly Tessie says, "Look, there's Bingo Bob. He's back at last." Bingo is the nickname of our mailman, who spends all his free time with his wife in the bingo parlors. Well, it's something to take our minds off Millie.

We hurry toward our mailboxes. Hooray. It's been days and we've missed our mail delivery. He tries to fill the boxes while the girls are eagerly grabbing their mail out of his hands before he can even insert the envelopes.

"Neither rain nor sleet can stop the U.S. Postal Service," Bob emotes in his high-pitched voice.

"Yeah," says Ida. "But a hurricane can."

"We're very glad to see you," Sophie says. "How are you doing at bingo?"

"The Indian casinos are shut down 'til further notice," he reports grimly. "Even the churches are too busy these days."

Sophie groans. "Now, that's bad news. I was looking forward to playing."

As I flip through my mail, a familiar square white envelope catches my eye.

I beckon the girls to join me. Away from listening ears. We head for our usual picnic table. Sure enough, it's from our old friend Grandpa Bandit. I rip open the envelope.

Ida comments, "I wondered if we'd ever hear from him again. What's the old geezer got to say this time?"

I read, " 'Happy you all survived the storm. Back to business — if we don't get hit with another hurricane. First I got to get my car running. Getting old is not for sissies. But the good news is: The older you get, the more money your old junk will be worth on eBay. Further instructions to come.' "

The familiar green feather is enclosed.

Sophie stamps her feet. "The postmark is Fort Lauderdale. He lives in Lanai Gardens. I just know it. Let's get a list of all the cars that need fixing." She stops, realizing how impractical that is, since all the cars were affected.

Ida says, "But who could it be? He doesn't sound like any of the men who live here."

Evvie shrugs. "Even with six Phases, we haven't met everyone. It's easy for someone to keep a low profile."

Bella says, "Round 'em all up and we'll drill 'em 'til we suss him out."

We look at her, amused at her vehemence. "Yeah," says Ida, "great idea."

As we head out for Gossip, I glance up, to see Enya moving along on her balcony, toward the laundry room, carrying her basket. I wonder if she's had a chance to talk to her new neighbor, Abe. Evvie looks to me and winks. I know we share a feeling. Maybe these two people can reach out to each other — they, who have known so much pain, and have history in common.

27
NEIGHBORS

From outside, Enya hears the sound of the whirling dryer. With her basket firmly placed under her left arm, she opens the door with her right. She moves toward a vacant washer and stops abruptly.

Abe Waller is standing near the dryer, his empty basket on a plain brown wooden chair under a small unframed mirror. This is a utilitarian room with just the basics: two washers, one dryer, and a sorting table. The room is steamy and too warm. There is no air-conditioning in here. But one small louvered window, half-open, lets in a small breeze.

She is taken aback to see him, immediately uncomfortable. She hopes her new neighbor doesn't feel he has to speak to her. For a moment she is motionless, but poised to flee. Enya's eyes glance downward, to avoid looking directly at this large, overwhelming man. He is new to the building and won't know she does not make small talk to anyone, let alone strangers. She starts to leave, saying, "I'm sorry. I didn't know the room was occupied."

Abe wipes the sweat from his forehead with a handkerchief. "No, please. I am moments away from completion. Do not let me disturb you. The machine is yours to use."

She returns, opens the door of the empty washer, her back to him so he will not see her personal garments.

He, too, turns away, toward the small mirror. He takes off his Coke-bottle glasses and wipes the steam from them. Enya looks up and sees him reflected in the mirror. Then, not wanting to embarrass him, she quickly looks downward again.

The dryer comes to a halt. The room grows silent. As Abe removes his dry laundry, he attempts small conversation. "It was very kind of the people to allow me to use their place."

She pours soap powder in, and chooses the wash she wants, then places the quarters into their slots and turns the machine on. As she upends her garments into the machine, she says, "Yes. Mr. and Mrs. Duma are nice people. Very quiet."

"I promise to be quiet also."

She looks up at that, discomfited. "I did not mean —" She breaks off.

"I am not offended." He finishes removing his dry clothes and places them on the table and starts folding with great precision. "Forgive me for my forwardness, but your accent . . . May I ask where you are from?"

"So many years in this country, I don't lose it. I am from Prague originally. And you?"

"From Munich." He pauses. "That was a long time ago."

They are silent for a few moments, absorbing this information. She places her empty basket onto the bench. She tries to hide how tense she is, even though he seems a gentleman.

Abe finishes folding. He lifts his basket and moves toward the door.

As he passes her, he looks down at the numbers on her left arm. She immediately gasps, trying to hide them with her hand. She is not used to people staring at them, but then her eyes are drawn to just below the wrist of his long-sleeved shirt. He, too, has the damnable numbers.

Their eyes meet for the first time. Hers, watery and weak. His covered with strong glasses. He says very softly. "We are members of a very exclusive club, *ja?*"

Her head barely nods.

He opens the door and bows. "Good day, Frau Slovak."

28
GOSSIP

"Any luck?" I ask Barbi and Casey as the girls and I return. The cousins needed a couple of hours to research our new assignment. The girls were happy about that since there is a deli nearby that they like and we had a leisurely lunch.

Now we seat ourselves on the usual white chairs around the white table in the totally white room. Since this isn't our first visit, we no longer react to the strange working conditions of this all-white high-tech office located in a strip mall.

Barbi starts. "Given the fact we're dealing with dates so far back, even so, we did find quite a number of Lucy Blakes in that time span in the Tampa area . . ."

Casey continues, "Having a relative named Johnny, who was deceased, narrowed the options down to very few. We'll print out what we have."

I enjoy watching the two women as they

swivel their desk chairs around and slide across the room to their twin computers. The girls continue to be awed at these two unusual women who we know are pretending to be cousins.

"So," asks Ida, making conversation, "are you getting any clients since the hurricane?"

"Just one other, so far," Barbi answers, reaching for the paper coming out of the printer. "One gal, kind of a character, wore a weird, lumpy outfit, wanted to know about cities in Georgia. Ones that didn't get bad weather."

They come back to where we're sitting. And hand us copies.

"Got a hit on a Lucy Blake Sweeney. In Tampa."

Casey says, "Could be a fit. She's seventy-seven years old. Actually written up recently in the local paper — something about a strike at a local fishery on the Gulf."

"Well, that's a place to start," says Ida.

Barbi says, "Just thought we'd check some obits for that era. Blake's a common name and these are the two nearest 1958. A John Adams Blake died in '59, but he was age sixty."

"Wrong year and age," says Evvie.

"And this one, John Willis Blake, age twenty-seven. Could be the right age, but he died in March. Six months earlier than what you're looking for. Small obit notice, no information about any remaining kin.

"That's about it," says Barbi.

Sophie is excited. "Why don't we call that Lucy woman anyway? Maybe they didn't have a body and just had a funeral because they thought he was dead."

"Wait," I say. "We can't just call and say, 'You don't know who we are, but by the way, your brother didn't die when you thought. We found your brother's skeleton, and he died here.' This is a long shot."

Ida says, "But it's all we have right now."

Evvie says. "What if our skeleton isn't her brother and we just stir up a lot of confusion?"

Bella jumps in. "And what if she has a heart attack because we scared her out of her wits?"

I hold up my hands to stop the flow of what-ifs. "I need to talk to Stanley and ask how he wants us to handle this."

We thank Casey and Barbi and head back home. The noise level in my car's a crescendo.

Bella says, "Why don't you take Dora for a while?"

Sophie says, "You shouldn't have taken

her in the first place. So why should I get stuck with her?"

"But I can't stand it anymore. I thought I was deaf, but she's deafer. The TV is blasting me out of my apartment. Ida, maybe you'll take her for a while?"

Ida sneers, "Over my dead body."

Evvie says, smirking, "Don't look at me. Unless you'll trade her for Joe."

Bella blushes. "I'm a single woman. I couldn't live with an unmarried man in my apartment. That would be a sin."

It takes a moment for her words to sink in. *I'm* the single sinner living with an unmarried man. Joe and Evvie don't count because they were once married.

"Bella!" Evvie says agitatedly.

She looks around, confused. "What? What did I say?"

It gets very quiet. We reach Lanai Gardens and I park in any old spot. We no longer have assigned spaces, what with the abandoned wrecks not yet cleared away.

"Well, it's good to be home," Sophie says to cover the uncomfortable silence as we climb out of my car.

I'm not about to touch Bella's line with a ten-foot pole.

Once back in my apartment, I call Stanley

and tell him what we'd found out. He listens to the information and says that he wants to think about our next step.

I try to nap, one of my favorite pastimes. There's something about drawing the shades and lying down on my bed and closing my eyes midday that is so appealing. I usually drop off the instant my head hits the pillow. Not today. First, my bed has new meaning for me. I think of Jack lying next to me every night from now on. His reaching for me and pulling me close and then our sleeping together like two well-worn spoons. I never thought I was lonely until he moved in. Now I know how much I'd been missing.

How brave women are who live alone, whether by choice or not. We all put a good face on it, but it's never easy. Not easy raising children alone. Not easy having to bear all the responsibility in life with no one to share it. And hardest of all is to face that empty bed at night. We make peace with our lot, whatever it is. It's that or go mad. But lucky are those who find true love and companionship. As I did with my first husband. And now, with this wonderful man. I am twice blessed.

Why all this philosophizing that won't allow me to sleep? It was Bella's remark. I know she didn't mean it to hurt me. And it didn't. But it made me remember that one should never take good fortune for granted. Life has a habit of whisking it away on a whim. How well I know that.

My mind reels round and round. After an hour, I give up trying to nap, get up, and go into the kitchen to make a pot of tea.

I concentrate on preparing dinner as I sip my tea. Well, this is another piece of the puzzle of living alone or not. Ordinarily I just throw something together for myself, and quite often munch from a carton, just standing in front of the open fridge.

Now I'm back to planning meals, shopping for food, and cooking. Even though it's fun to see my man enjoying home-cooked meals again — who knows how many cartons *he's* eaten out of — I put this on the con side of the column. The pros are enormous, but still . . .

A timorous knock on the door, or did I imagine it? No, I have a visitor. There's Bella standing outside, carrying a covered dish with something that smells wonderful.

When I let her in, she waits in my hallway, tears forming. "I'm sorry. I didn't mean what I said in the car."

She walks into the kitchen and reveals her gift. "I baked you a peach pie, your favorite.

I'm a very bad person."

With that I put my arms around her and tell her she is anything but. "I'm actually glad you said it. It made me think."

"No, don't try to make me feel better. I love you and I love Jackie and I even loved his dead wife, Faye. I wouldn't hurt any of you for anything." Now the tears are rolling down her face.

I grab a dish towel, the closest thing, and hand it to her. She dabs at her eyes.

"Come on, sit down, and join me in a cup of tea."

"No, I can't. I won't. Jackie will be here soon and you have to get his dinner ready. Please say you forgive me."

"I forgive you, honest."

She hands me my towel and heads for the door. "You can give me back my pie tin anytime. I'm in no hurry."

With that she's gone. Okay, sin forgiven. But there it is, the unstated contract, meals to be made. Is he going to expect me to do that every single day? Wait just one minute . . .

Jack walks in. I'm in a frenzy of cooking. He comes up behind me and kisses the back of my neck. "What smells so fabulous?"

"Pot roast, baked winter vegetables, potatoes au gratin, and a huge tossed salad with balsamic vinaigrette, and peach pie à la mode for dessert."

"Yum. I'm already drooling," he says as he now kisses the top of my head. "No more eating out of open cans standing in front of the refrigerator. Ever again."

I wheel around, spatula in hand. "I have two questions for you. Will you marry me? And do I have to do all the cooking?"

29
AN EVENING AT HOME

What a splendid evening. Jack is so thrilled about my finally using the *M* word, he is eager to prove he doesn't only love me for my cooking skills. He demonstrates how much he loves all my skills. Okay, I get the point.

Some couples create prenup agreements about money, real estate, and jewelry. Ours is about chores. Which ones we hate to do and which ones we actually enjoy. We have fun making lists. And we fool around before, during, and after. He's perfectly willing to do half the cooking (he says he makes a mean lasagna) or we can go to restaurants anytime I want. Ditto on housework. (He loves ironing. Huh? Who loves ironing?) As well as taking clothes to the cleaners (fine with him) and food shopping (together — we'll make it enjoyable). Checkbook reconciling. Banking (he likes it, he can have it), and so on and so forth.

What we are in total agreement on is that we are both willing to share the sex. Ha-ha-ha. Little joke there.

"Glad," he says to me as we microwave popcorn for an evening of watching old movies on TV. "No spreading the word yet. Not until I put an engagement ring on your finger."

"I don't need a ring to know I'm yours."

"Well, I need it to keep the other guys away."

"Yeah, right, there's a line of them from here to Publix, just waiting for you to dump me."

The popcorn dings in the microwave. "Showtime," I say, kissing him.

We've both seen *Miss Congeniality* at least three times. That's the Sandra Bullock movie where she goes undercover at a beauty pageant. We throw lines out before the actors get to speak them. And chortle and giggle at the remembered scenes.

A moment of unhappiness seeps through. I wonder what Evvie and Joe are doing. Was their dinner table just another combat zone? Are they watching the same movie — Evvie, who I know loves this movie, and has seen it with me the last three times? Are they in different rooms? Left to laugh all alone? Or not laughing at all? In a perfect world those married couples out there would give up their old foolish battles that no longer matter, and as that '60's hippie slogan goes, "Make love, not war."

Evvie hears the front door open and she can sense Joe walk in and hover behind the couch where she is sitting. "Can't you find something to do and not bother me?" she says without turning around.

She's settled comfortably in her living room in front of the TV, watching *Miss Congeniality,* and she doesn't intend to let Joe spoil it for her. It's one of her favorite movies. She takes a sip of her tea and then a bite of her chocolate chip cookie, not looking at him.

"I could go to bed, but you're on the couch."

"Sit in the kitchen and read a book or something."

"I wouldn't mind seeing the rest of the movie with you." Before she can cut him off, he says, "Please, Ev. Let's stop this fighting. Can't we have a truce?"

For a moment she doesn't answer. "Come on and sit down, then." She grudgingly moves over to make room for him.

He quietly sits down next to her. Then a moment later, "Evvie, I need to talk to you."

"Only at commercials." She pulls at her cotton skirt to make sure his leg isn't touching it.

"It's a commercial now. I have to tell you something. I've been meaning to tell you since I moved in."

"Say it fast. There've already been six commercials. The movie will be back on in a minute."

"I didn't tell you the truth about why I moved here."

Evvie's eyebrows raise. "So?"

He hesitates, then leans over and whispers in her ear.

"What!" she shrieks in response, turning to stare at him.

"I can't stand saying it out loud. Please don't make me repeat it."

She looks at him, stricken. "I don't know what to say."

"Please don't say anything. Let's just watch the movie. I beg you."

They sit there side by side, but Evvie no longer sees what's on the screen.

Our movie is interrupted by the phone. As I go to answer it, I ask Jack to tell me later what I'll miss. We both laugh at that.

It's Stanley again.

"I couldn't wait," he tells me. "I had to

call the woman, you know, the sister?"

"What did you say to her?" I sit down at the kitchen table. This might take a few minutes.

"I didn't say too much. I told her I needed to talk to her about her brother, Johnny. Something that happened a long time ago. She sounded very nice on the phone and naturally asked what it was regarding. When I told her it was too complicated and took too long to explain, she said she'd be glad to meet with me. I'm surprised she gave a stranger her address."

"Sounds encouraging. When are you going?"

"Well, I had it in mind that maybe you would come with me? A woman along would make her more comfortable. I hope it won't be a waste of our time, but I feel I need to know."

In the background I hear Jack laughing out loud. I wonder if it's the scene where Sandra Bullock jumps off the stage and takes a flying leap at the startled Texan carrying a gun. "If you think it would help. When?"

"I was thinking tomorrow. We could hop on a plane and fly across to Tampa very fast. I already looked up flights and we could leave by nine A.M. And I MapQuested

252

where she lives."

"Very organized, Stanley. All right."

"Thank you. As my dear mother used to say, *A katz vos myavket ken keyn mayz nit khapen.*"

"Sorry, Stanley, my Yiddish isn't that good. You'll have to translate."

"Literally it says, 'A meowing cat can't catch mice.' But what it means for us is that we can't just talk about doing something, we've got to go out and do it."

I say good-bye and hang up and happily get back in time. I didn't miss Texan-with-the-gun scene after all. I snuggle under Jack's shoulder, prepared to enjoy the rest of the movie with, dare I say it, my husband-to-be.

30

GLADDY AND STANLEY TAKE A TRIP

I enjoy my short early-morning plane ride with Stanley Heyer. Despite being acquainted with him for more than twenty years, I really don't know him that well. I'm familiar with the fact he's been married to Esther for a very long time. That he has two grown children, and now three grand-children. And that he takes his religion very seriously.

Maybe it's my guilt over Stanley's being aware of my living with Jack that makes me blurt out we are getting married. Talk about Jewish guilt. Well, there's also Catholic guilt and Protestant guilt. And on and on. But I find it amusing that at seventy-five I want this pious man to think I'm still a nice Jewish girl.

He is thrilled. Naturally he asks the expected question: "So when's the wedding?"

"We haven't gotten that far yet, but hopefully soon."

"A good man, Jack."

"I know." Now I'm sorry I brought it up. I'm always embarrassed answering personal questions. I change the subject. "Tell me about Esther. How is she?"

His face lights up. "Fine. Fine. I'm blessed to have a loving wife for fifty years. What more *nachas* could a man want?"

"How did you meet?" The countryside down below seems so wonderfully peaceful. How ironic. Not that many miles away from where we are overwhelmed with the damage done by the hurricane.

"Interesting you should ask. It was 1959. I had joined the neighborhood temple. On my very first Shabbat, after services, a beautiful girl with long curly red hair and big brown eyes was introduced to me, but I was too shy to say more than hello. But I saw her step outside alone and I worked up the courage to ask her if I could walk her home. My excuse was that a young lady should not have to walk home alone in the dark. She said she always came to services with her friend, but her friend was sick tonight. To my amazement, she agreed." He smiles broadly. "And one thing led to another."

"That's a lovely story."

255

I stare out the window for a few minutes more. I'm enjoying this difference in the lush Florida landscape when one gets away from the east coast beach cities. I turn to Stanley.

"And Abe Waller?" I say, just to make conversation. "You and he have been friends for a very long time."

"Yes. Best of friends for more than forty-nine years. That's another good story to tell. It's about six months later. I come home one night from temple and I see a man standing in Phase Six, looking from one building to the other. I ask, 'Can I help you?' He says, 'I'm thinking of moving here. Is it a good place to live?' I smile. 'A good place to live?' I say he asked the right customer, the man who built it. I extol its many features. He looks at the yarmulke on my head. He hesitates for a few minutes, as if he's gathering up courage to ask. 'Yes, you must be the right man,' he says. 'You would know if we are near a good synagogue.' " Stanley makes a wide gesture with both his arms, almost knocking his club soda off his little tray table. " 'Have I got a synagogue for you!' I tell him. With that, I insist on taking him upstairs for a cup of tea and to meet my beautiful Esther, who is already pregnant with our first child." Stanley's eyes tear up. "It was then I saw the tattooed numbers from under his shirt cuff. Those numbers from hell."

He shakes his head as if to push away the memory. I hold in my own tears.

With a quivering voice, Stanley continues. "He lost his whole family to the camps. Esther and I and the children became his family."

We stay silent and deep in our own thoughts, until the captain announces our plane is about to land in Tampa.

Stanley manages a small smile. "Oy, I talk too much."

I pat him on the shoulder. "Thank you for sharing this with me."

"Okay," says Ida, as the girls turn the corner to Phase Four. "This is where she lives. Though I'm telling you, this is a stupid idea."

Sophie sulks. "You said it fifty times already. You don't have to go with us."

"I do, because if I didn't, you'd do something dumb and Gladdy would be mad at me for not looking after you while she was away."

Bella is annoyed with Ida, too. "I wish Evvie had come with us."

Ida says, "She can't. She's with Joe.

Something about having to take him somewhere."

To spite Ida, Sophie knocks forcefully on
Margaret Ramona's ground-floor door.

The woman opens it and greets them with
that cigarette hoarse voice of hers. "Welcome, welcome. Madame Ramona and all
the spirits bid you come in."

Ida rolls her eyes. Once again the "Madame" is wearing large flamboyant clothes.
Ida wonders at it, because the woman's
hands and feet seem thin. She wears a lot of
makeup on her pointy-chinned face. And
has an unsightly big pimple — why doesn't
she do something about it? Her long gray
hair has pink ribbons entangled in it. Weird
broad, Ida thinks.

Madame Ramona leads them through her
living room, heading for the Florida room
in the back. Bella pokes Sophie, indicating
the paintings on the wall. Ida shakes her
head in disbelief. Each of them is painted
on a black velvet backdrop and has a gold
velvet frame. Elvis Presley with a guitar. Michael Jackson holding a teddy bear. Liberace seated at a piano with a lit candelabra.
Shirley MacLaine in a spaceship.

The Florida room looks like no other
they've ever seen. You would never know it
was meant to be a sunroom, since it is

painted all black, even the windows. The only light comes from white candles on a black chest. Four chairs surround a small table that is covered with a bloodred fringed cloth. On the tabletop is a crystal ball, which Madame Ramona turns over, making imitation snowflakes swarm about a Christmas tree. Next to the crystal ball is a deck of cards. Oh, yes, and an ashtray filled with cigarette butts. Bella and Sophie ooh and ahh. Ida smirks. A phony, no doubt about it.

"The spirits bid you welcome and wish you to sit down."

Sophie and Bella plop down immediately. Ida continues to stand, making sure she knows where the exit is if they have to make a quick run for it. She studies "Madame" for a moment. What's with the smug smile? Ida wonders.

Sophie attempts conversation. "So, is it true you come from Canada?"

"Shhh!" demands Madame Ramona. "You are disturbing the spirits." She quickly starts dealing from the tarot deck. "Queen of Wands," she intones melodiously, as she slaps that card down. "There is a woman in your life who holds power over you. The wand represents electricity."

Bella whispers to Sophie, "See, I told you

she'd know about Dora Dooley."

"Shhh!" Madame Ramona hisses again.

She deals another card. "Ahhh. The Fool. There is someone else in your life. You think he is a fool, but it is he who fools everyone." She turns over another card. "The Magician. Yes, he deals in magic. You will understand his kindness someday. Now you see him, then you don't." She whisks that card away.

Sophie and Bella stare, transfixed, even though they have no idea what she's talking about. Ida just keeps shaking her head.

Madame Ramona continues to deal. "The four of Cups. The Magician gives you a clue with this magical number. He says to think four."

Suddenly she reshuffles the cards and places the stack facedown in front of her. She shoves a cigarette into her mouth with one hand as the other hand snakes out. "Ten dollars. No checks."

"What?" squeals Sophie. "You said at the meeting the readings were free."

"That special offer ended yesterday." Her hand stays open.

"Go back to before," Bella says, upset. "What about that Queen of Wands? You know. Our queen of the remote. Our problem. We need you to tell us what to do with her watching all that TV."

Madame Ramona shakes the crystal ball dramatically, and when the "snow" settles down, she says, "The crystal ball has three words for you: *Pull. The. Plug.*"

She gets up, indicating it is time for them to leave.

"That does it!" Ida is incensed. She takes a one-dollar bill out of her purse and tosses it at Madame Ramona.

"You owe me nine more," Madame shouts, lighting her cigarette and coughing at the same time.

"Sue us," Ida says as she pulls both girls out with her.

Outside the door, Bella begs Ida, "Don't tell Gladdy. Please."

Lucy Blake Sweeney lives near the waterfront. This isn't the Tampa tourists see. These mean streets have seen hard times. Stanley and I knock at the door of the rundown cottage that is desperately in need of paint. The woman who answers is wiry and haggard. But her denim clothes are clean and her hair is combed. Her demeanor suggests she could be quite a scrapper when necessary.

Stanley introduces the two of us and Lucy invites us in. She looks sideways at Stanley's yarmulke and black outfit. She must be wondering what this man would want with her.

We sit at the edge of her rickety living room couch at her suggestion. "The springs sometimes just up and bite your . . . bottom, so be careful." Out of courtesy, she is watching her language.

She sits opposite us on the only chair in the room, a straight-back plain wooden one.

She leans forward. "I gotta admit you got my interest piqued. Ya want something to drink? I got some Cokes and beers."

Stanley answers for us. "No, thank you. We don't want to take up too much of your time."

She shrugs. "Been laid off again. Time's a'plenty right now."

"About your brother," Stanley begins. "We don't know whether or not we've come to the right place."

"I'll let you know."

He nods. "Your brother, Johnny, died many years ago. Very young."

"So far yer batting a thousand. The dummy went and left me alone. He was twenty and me nineteen. Never said where he was going, just told me he had to wander. I had no money. No support anywheres. He was all I had for a family." Her eyes tear in

262

memory. "But what does that have to do with you? Don't tell me you're from some bank and you just found a life insurance policy that's been lost for nearly fifty years."

I say gently, "Sorry. No."

Stanley continues. "There is no easy way to say this, so I shall just say it. We come from Fort Lauderdale and we have just suffered through a hurricane. A building fell down and we found a skeleton underneath." He pauses.

She shakes her head. "Now you lost me. What has that to do with me?"

Stanley seems tired, so I speak. "We think it was your brother."

Lucy gets up and slaps her thighs, amused. "Boy, are you in the wrong place. My Johnny is buried right here in the church cemetery, not five blocks away. And believe me, there's no doubt but that is his body in that there casket."

Stanley starts to get up. "Mrs. Sweeney, I'm sorry we bothered you for nothing."

"Wait," I say. "Would you fill me in on what happened to him?"

Stanley has no idea why I'm asking. Frankly, neither do I. I'm going on pure instinct.

"I don't mind," she says. "I haven't thought of the poor lad in years. I only found out later that he'd taken a job on a freighter that came all the way from Argentina. Guess he wanted to see the world." She takes a photo off a chest of drawers and shows it to us. "That was my brother. Tall, skinny, long drink of water, he was, with big dreams."

Stanley and I exchange glances. We are both remembering that the foreman, Ed, described his worker as "large, even heavy." Definitely the wrong man. Out of politeness, we wait for Lucy to finish her story.

"Anyways," she says, "the kid always had bad luck. He wrote to tell me he was on that ship and I was so excited finally hearing from him. The day his ship pulls into port, not eight blocks away from where we're sitting, I wait and I wait and there's no Johnny. Later on, I find out he fell overboard."

"Somebody see him fall?" I ask out of curiosity.

"No. The shipping company lied to me. They denied he fell from the ship. Insisted they signed him out that last day. But how could I believe a boy raised on the docks would just fall off of one? I knew something was screwy." She hangs her head, sadly. "He washed up on shore a month later."

We sit a few minutes longer, but there's

nothing left to say. Lucy shows us to the door. Stanley takes out his wallet and offers her some money for her time, what with her being laid off.

Lucy rears back, insulted. "I don't take charity." With that she slams the door on us.

Stanley and I walk to the nearest cab stand. "Sorry I dragged you along on such a wild-goose chase."

"That's all right. How often do I get to travel to these exotic places?"

"My pleasure." He smiles and follows me across the street. "So what now? Who is the dead man? Will we ever find out?"

31
DEAD END

As we sit at our usual picnic table late that afternoon, I report to the girls about the trip to Tampa. Behind them I can see yet another dump truck dragging away one more load of wrecked furniture. After I give them all the details, I say, "I guess he was the wrong Johnny Blake after all."

I pause. My brain is trying to come up with something.

"What?" Evvie asks.

"Something that woman in Tampa said to me that I'm trying to remember." I shrug; nothing's coming to mind. "And yet, the body was washed up a month later. After being in the water so long, how could they have been sure it was Blake? I'm driving myself crazy."

Evvie says, "Unless Morrie's lab can come up with something from the bones, we may never find out who was buried there."

"Speak of the devil," Ida says as she points

to Stanley walking toward them with Morrie in tow.

"Look who I found on my doorstep," Stanley says.

"I just dropped by to see how your repairs are going." Morrie gives the girls one of his delightful shy smiles. They eat it up. I can almost read their minds — they've got to find a girl for him.

"Going slow," says Sophie looking at Bella, both thinking of Dora. "Way too slow."

"I do have a report for you. From the forensics lab."

Ida says, "We were just talking about that."

The girls lean closer to Morrie to hear.

"My guys were so intrigued about having such an old skeleton on their table, they got right to work. Unfortunately I don't think it will help us find out who he is, but it tells us who he was not."

Evvie comments, "Sorry to hear that."

Morrie continues. "The bones tell us he was definitely male, approximately five foot seven inches tall. Probably between thirty and thirty-five years old."

"It doesn't match my foreman's description of a large, almost heavyset man." Stanley doesn't hide his disappointment.

"It doesn't match Johnny Blake's height

or age, either," I say. So much for my water-logged theory.

Morrie shrugs. "Sorry, they can't get much closer than that."

Stanley says, "Then we have indeed come to a dead end."

Our group is about to disband, when Joe shows up. He doesn't say a word. Evvie hurriedly gets up from the bench. "Gotta go. Need to pick up some groceries for dinner."

She moves quickly away. I look after her, wondering what is happening. Something is new with those two. It's unlike Evvie not to confide in me.

Stanley is about to head back to Phase Six, when Abe walks by carrying a shopping bag. Stanley looks surprised. "I thought you were coming to the family dinner tonight."

Abe smiles. "Would I miss a dinner at your home? Not to worry. I'm bringing along some noshes." Abe indicates Morrie, who is about to get into his car. "Any news on the skeleton?"

Stanley absently bends to pull a weed out of a crack in the driveway. "I think we're never going to know."

Abe tries to comfort his friend. "Maybe it's for the best. You have enough on your mind without this worry. Let the past keep its secrets."

"Gladdy." I hear my name being called and I turn around.

It's Jack, home from his work down at the police station. He waves to his departing son and Morrie waves back.

"Grand Central Station around here." Jack kisses my cheek. Bella and Sophie grin at that, vicariously enjoying our happiness.

I explain. "Pre-dinnertime gathering. Happens every evening around now. Just look up. Lots of noses peering out of windows to see the comings and goings."

"Sounds familiar. Like my Phase Six. Seemed like you were having a party."

"More like a wake." I take his arm and we head for my place.

I see Louise Bannister leaning over the railing of the third-floor walkway, watching us. I keep up a light banter so Jack won't look up.

At the mailboxes next to the elevator, I check my mail. What with leaving so early this morning, I'd forgotten. "Well, well," I say, looking at the familiar white envelope.

Jack looks at the envelope, too. "Not your Grandpa Bandit again?"

I open it up, and there's the green feather. "Guess so." I glance at it and wait as I see Sophie and Ida nearing us, heading for their apartments. When they are close I wave the letter, then read it out loud. " 'Hello, ladies. Things are seldom as they seem. Skim milk masquerades as cream. I'm back in business. It's going to be the Lauderdale S and L on Hallandale. Getting old means life is too short for us to save for a rainy day. The good news for me is that their alarm system works only half the time. And don't expect lunch. There's no deli around. Won't tell you the time. Tuesday's the date. Don't want to make it too easy-peasy. Or, then again, maybe I won't show up and this is a wild-goose chase.' "

Ida growls. "This is the last straw. We're gonna get him this time."

No moon shines in Enya's apartment. The curtains are tightly drawn. Blackness everywhere except for the small candle that burns on the table at the opposite wall, above which hang the family pictures. Of all the dead children. The shrine will be lit as long as Enya lives.

In her "bed of nails" Enya flings her tortured body from side to side. Over the decades she has managed to strangle most of her memories out of her conscious mind. If she hadn't, she would never sleep. She would go mad. She has prayed for death many times, but her prayers were not answered. None of her prayers were ever answered.

Now these memories from hell seep back into her dreams, forming beads of sweat on her face. She sees rivers of blood. A barking German shepherd, his gums slathered with spittle. A body, like something crucified, plastered across an electric fence, the zigzagging lights patterning a macabre dance as the man dies hideously. The coward. She spits with venom. How dare he take the easy way out, her husband?

More twisting, clutching at her pillow, holding on for dear life. Dear life it is. Here he comes, *Oberführer,* as she will learn to call him. And fear him with every fiber of her being. It's him! She screams aloud while staring into the deadness of his eyes.

There is a sharp ringing and a banging noise. She awakens, aware of her body pounding itself against the backboard of her bed, which hits the wall behind her over and over.

Her phone is ringing. It's Evvie. "I just walked by your door and heard some noise. Are you all right?"

I'll never be all right, Enya thinks. She sits up. "I'm sorry. Forgive me if I disturbed you."

"Do you want me to come over and stay

with you?"

What for, she thinks, leaning her exhausted head back against the now motionless headboard. Nothing will wash away this sorrow. "No, thank you, dear. Just a bad dream."

"You phone me if you need me. I'll come and sit with you anytime you want. Promise?"

"Yes, I will. Go back to sleep." Sleep easy, you people in this country who take for granted the peaceful lives you lead. You have no idea.

Enya stares at the shrine across the room. The light flickers back at her. No, my precious ones, I will never forget.

Evvie puts down the phone in her kitchen. The call upsets her. Enya sounded so very sad. She takes off her jacket, then heads quietly into the living room, where Joe is asleep on the couch. Evvie walks over to him and looks down, watching him breathe. He seems so helpless lying there. She bends to fix his blanket.

Her presence wakes him. "How was the lecture?" he asks sleepily. He squints at the clock on a side table. "It's late."

"We went for coffee after."

Joe looks at her, not knowing what to say

272

or do as she continues to stand there.

"Joe. Comfort me. Please."

He hesitates for a moment, not sure she means it. He sees the tears in her eyes. Then he jumps up and puts his arms around his ex-wife. Together, they head for her bedroom.

Where his kitchen wall backs the kitchen of his neighbor, Abe Waller sits at the small table, vaguely aware of the sounds coming from next door through the walls. He sips his scotch and stares grimly at his bible. Maybe he should move out. This crying of hers is not good. Too many memories, he thinks. I don't need this.

32
GRANDPA BANDIT
STRIKES AGAIN

We go over last-minute instructions as we wait for the bank to open. Standing in the parking lot behind the bank, we are a group ready for action. We are well organized this time. Since Grandpa knows who we are, we wear assorted disguises — hats, scarves, sunglasses, etc. Eight can play at his game — one of him and seven of us.

We have our own extra crew of volunteers, since Jack and Joe have joined us. But they defer to me as team captain.

"Everybody have their whistle at the ready?"

The girls nod eagerly as they feel for the whistles round their necks. They are hyped for this day of possible excitement.

"Cell phones?"

They all pat at where said phones are located on their bodies.

"Remember not to use them unless necessary. Joe, here, has volunteered to be rotating messenger. He'll go around to each of you to find out if there is something you need."

Joe smiles happily at finally feeling like he belongs. He gets to spend a day with Evvie, which obviously thrills him. Evvie is still not giving anything away. I guess she'll tell me what's going on when she's ready.

Out of the corner of my eye I see my Jack looking amused and pleased at watching his woman in take-charge mode. Another check on the pro side of his balance sheet. He isn't threatened when a woman is the boss. He winks at me. I bet he knows what I'm thinking.

"Everybody know her assigned exit?" Each of the girls has an exit to guard.

Bella raises her hand. "I don't know where the northeast corner is."

"I'll escort you," says Joe willingly.

I continue. "We know how Grandpa likes to trick us, so be on guard. And he might just wait for closing time, hoping to find us weary and careless."

Ida puffs her chest out. "He won't get by us this time."

"Just keep in mind, he knows what we look like. But then again, he might be someone we know, so be alert."

Evvie looks sternly at Bella and Sophie,

who are giggling. "He'll look for the weak-est link."

Bella sighs. "That could be me."

Sophie pats her on the arm. "I'll watch your back, *bubbala*. If you faint or some-thing, I won't let you fall." They grin at each other.

Evvie and Ida roll their eyes at the *two* weakest links.

"Don't forget to take turns for lunch breaks." Oh, yes, we have backpacks with food and drink — this army always marches on its stomach.

"And remember, Jack and I will be con-stantly on the move, visiting each of your checkpoints. We plan to walk in and out of the bank as pretend customers. Later we'll use the desks we were offered and playact as bank employees."

When we told Morrie, he believed it was another false alarm. But when I told him Grandpa *had* been there the last time, he took it a little more seriously. He promised he'd warn the bank officers so they'd be prepared. But his tone told me he thought we're wasting our time.

The bank managers have thoughtfully provided chairs at all the doors so we "elderly folk" have a place to rest.

It's ten A.M., the bank is open, and we

join the waiting group in front.

The girls march in, heads high and spirits good. The bank is in pretty good shape despite the hurricane of ten days ago. A few taped-up windows are all I notice as I look around.

"Look alive," I instruct them. "Get to your battle stations."

Everyone is eager. Even the bank employees, all of whom know what's going on, share in our anticipation. I don't expect any action right away and we don't get any. Eleven A.M. comes and goes. Joe walks over to where Jack and I are playing at being bank officer and customer.

"Message from Sophie. She says her feet hurt."

I sigh. "Tell her to take off the stiletto heels and put her sneakers on."

Joe salutes and heads for Sophie at the northwest door.

An hour later, Bella, taking a turn as a customer while Joe mans her post, walks in with a poodle. She stops to "chat" with me at my desk.

"Where did you get a dog?" I look at the froufrou white standard poodle covered with purple bows.

She giggles. "A lady outside loaned it to me when I said I wanted to impress someone." She turns and waves to the dog's real owner, standing at a desk where she is filling out a bank form.

By two o'clock everyone's beginning to sag. I shrug and say to Jack, "I can tell the girls are getting bored."

"Yes," he agrees, "too many bathroom breaks. And lunch breaks. And lolling about on chairs."

"Dangerous time, and I bet that sly old codger is depending on it."

At two forty-four, all hell breaks loose when we hear what sounds like gunfire coming from near the bank-vault area. The place is in a sudden uproar. People yelling in fear, running out, pushing and shoving others out of their way. Total panic.

Guards rush toward the noise, guns drawn, as all attention is on what's happening. In moments, the guards have the culprit on the floor and cuffed. From where I stand I hear him shout, "Leave me alone. Don't shoot!"

I stay at my post, but not my girls. They run to see what's going on. I suddenly have a funny feeling the real show is somewhere else. I scout all the tellers for unusual activity.

Joe and Evvie show up, out of breath. Evvie announces, "It's a teenager setting off firecrackers."

"No Grandpa, I bet," I say.

"Doesn't look like it." Evvie starts to catch on.

The thin, wiry boy, wearing gang-style low-riding pants, is being dragged away yelling, "Don't hurt me. Some old guy gave me ten bucks to do it as a gag!"

The noise level is high, almost high enough to muffle the alarm going off. But not quite.

Jack and I exchange glances, then he starts running toward the front door. He tells Joe to try a different door.

A shout comes from the teller farthest from where I am. "Help. Stop him! He's getting away!"

We are flummoxed. People are running every which way. Get who? We didn't see any of it. We have no idea where Grandpa went. Everywhere it's total chaos.

Sophie and Bella come running, all at sea.

"I was so scared," says Bella, shivering.

"I thought we were going to be shot dead," Sophie says, waving her arms agitatedly in front of her face.

I scowl at them. "It was Grandpa, diverting our attention. And it worked. You all left your posts."

Evvie, Sophie, and Bella hang their heads

in shame.

"Did anybody see anything?" I ask, knowing the answer. A lot of shaking heads. They were all watching the action with the kid. As I was. I should have known.

"What do we do now?" Evvie asks dejectedly.

I say, "We can all run outside and look around, but don't bother. He's far away by now. That shrewd old geezer has beaten us again."

Jack and Joe come back in, shaking their heads. Jack says, "Too many exits, too many streets to follow."

Joe agrees. "Just a lot of people milling around to catch the action. Easy for him to lose himself in that crowd."

At that moment Morrie walks over to Jack. "I just got here. Fill me in."

Jack walks off with his son. "See you back home," he says.

We stand there not knowing quite what to do. I count heads. Someone is missing. "Where's Ida?"

At the sound of the firecrackers, Ida looks in the direction of the noise, as does everyone else. But she stands her ground. Peripherally, she realizes that someone has just run out her exit door — a man wearing a windbreaker and a blue baseball cap. Everyone is running toward the sounds. This guy is running from. Quickly she races outside in pursuit. She has a vague memory of something else as the person runs by, but she doesn't know what.

Her exit door leads to a quiet side street. She looks both ways. The only person she sights is the back of a woman, carrying a Macy's tote bag, strolling away from her. The woman has long gray hair with ribbons. She is about to put on a big floppy yellow hat. A woman who looks vaguely familiar. On impulse Ida hurries after her.

Ida smiles as she catches up. "Well, fancy seeing you here. Madame Margaret Ramona, I presume?"

Madame Ramona turns an icy stare at her. "Do I know you?" She keeps walking.

"Of course you do. I was the one who paid you a dollar for your phony tarot reading."

"Which was very rude of you, cheapskate."

Ida keeps up with her. She glances toward the tote. "Been shopping?"

"Yes, and it's none of your business."

"Been banking as well?"

"No."

"Well, you just missed a bank robbery."

"Really. How thrilling. I'll read about it in the papers tomorrow." Madame Ramona turns a corner, takes her keys from her pocket, and moves quickly to where her Honda Civic is parked.

Ida makes a grab for the woman's tote bag. "Love to see what you bought."

Ida is fast, but Madame Ramona is faster. Ida manages to pull one thing out — a Florida Marlins navy blue baseball cap — just as Madame Ramona shoves her forcibly toward the wall. She climbs quickly into her Civic. Ida struggles to regain her balance.

As the car whooshes past her, Ida shouts, "Now I know what I saw when you ran past me — I'd know that pimple anywhere!"

With that she runs back toward the bank, blowing her whistle!

33
GOTCHA!

We meet up with Ida, still blowing that whistle, standing next to where our cars are parked in the rear of the bank. We surround her, the girls all talking at once.

"What?" asks Bella. "Where's the fire?"

"What are you doing out here? All the excitement was in there," says Sophie.

"Did you hear the firecrackers?" asks Joe.

"I caught Grandpa Bandit," she announces proudly, twirling a blue baseball cap with her finger.

We all look around. Nothing to see but parked cars and hurricane-damaged backs of buildings. Ida grins from ear to ear.

"What! You kidding us?" This from Sophie.

Ida raises her hand. "Scout's honor."

"So where is he?" Evvie demands.

"Grandpa drove off in 'his' car."

"You let him get away?" Bella asks.

"I had no choice. Grandpa knocked

me down."

I ask, "Are you hurt?" I can't figure out why Ida emphasized the *his.*

She's still grinning. "Nope."

What's going on? I wonder. But Ida is having a good time with this and she's going to do it her way.

"How did you know it was him?" Joe asks.

"By the pimple on 'his' face."

"Huh?" That comes from all of them. Ida can hardly contain herself. She does a little jig. Evvie chews her nails in frustration. Bella and Sophie are just flummoxed.

I ask the practical question. "Did you call the police?"

"No, not yet," she says. "Later will be soon enough."

Evvie, even more annoyed, asks, "What's so funny?"

"You'll see."

"You know who he is, don't you?" I ask.

"We all know 'Grandpa,' " she says, accentuating the name.

"Spit it out!" chorus Bella and Sophie.

She looks directly at the two of them. "Didn't Madame Ramona tell us we were chasing a magician? Didn't she say we thought he was a fool, but he really wasn't? And four was a number to remember?"

The two of them slowly nod their heads

in unison.

"She told us all about him. I wondered how she knew," Ida says.

Evvie, puzzled, asks, "Isn't she that weirdo with all the flamboyant clothes? What's she got to do with this? When did you learn all this . . . this magician stuff?"

Ida says, "You drove off with Joe the morning Gladdy was on her way to Tampa. We had a tarot reading at Madame Ramona's."

Bella's feelings are hurt. "You said you wouldn't tell."

"Well, now I have to."

Evvie glares at Bella. "What for? What silliness were you up to?"

I say, "Never mind that. Where is Grandpa Bandit?"

"Let's go ask the Madame." Ida turns to Joe, since she knows we have to leave Jack's car. "Onward to Phase Four. Magic number four."

"Wait a minute," I say. "You're taking us to the man who just robbed the bank? Don't you think we should get Morrie? And Jack?"

If Ida smiled any harder, her teeth would hurt. "Trust me," she says.

We follow Ida as she leads us to a ground-floor apartment. Evvie glances at me as if to say "What is going on?" I shrug. I don't have a clue.

Bella is quaking. "I don't want to go back in there."

Sophie whispers, "Me, neither. She's crazy." They cling to each other.

"Yeah," Ida says, "crazy like a fox."

We all crowd behind Ida as she pounds on the door. No response. She rings the bell, and then pounds on the door again. Still nothing.

Ida shouts, "I know you're in there, 'Gramps.' Open up. We're not going away, even if we have to stand here all day and all night."

The peephole finally opens and we see an eye. A voice whispers, "You have a reading with the Madame?"

Ida demands, "Just open the damn door."

"I won't," says the voice.

"You will," says Ida.

Evvie shakes her head in wonderment.

"Get out of here or I'll call the police," yells the hoarse voice.

Ida puts her hands on her hips. "Why don't you do that? And ask for Detective Morgan Langford. His stepmother is standing next to me."

I shoot her a look.

"To be," Ida adds.

A silence, then we hear many clicks of many locks and finally the door opens. To our surprise, a rather tall, skinny man — in his mid-sixties, I would guess — is standing there, in an undershirt and shorts. He's almost bald, with just a ring of gray surrounding his scalp. "You can only stay a few minutes," he tells her. "Madame has a client coming very soon."

"Can the act," Ida says, pushing her way in. We follow Ida into the living room. This is her show. Bella and Sophie linger behind. Evvie and I have not been here before, and we stare about this room, fascinated by the velvet paintings.

"Sit down," Ida demands.

We all hurry for seats. I find myself seated on the couch under Liberace and his candelabra. Evvie and Joe land on a love seat under Michael Jackson. Bella and Sophie huddle in the hallway, obviously hoping for a quick exit.

Ida shakes her head in disbelief. "I meant for *him* to sit, not you."

Joe smirks. Evvie hides a smile. I'm speechless. The bald-ish man sits down opposite us, on the edge of a straight chair, nervously picking at a large red pimple. He's seated under Shirley MacLaine, who looks down on him from her velvet spaceship.

"Tell them who you are," Ida demands.

"I'm . . . I'm Madame's boarder."

"And when you put on your outfit, which always has big ruffled blouses, and you pull out of your pants a colorful skirt, and then add your long gray wig with ribbons, you're also chubby Madame Ramona." She twirls the blue baseball cap in front of his face.

Eyes open wide at that. Even mine. Bella gasps.

She turns to Evvie. "Give a quick look around for a Macy's tote bag." I watch clever Ida as she watches the man, whose eyes immediately dart to a closet in the room. "Try that closet," Ida says, pointing. He starts to get up, but Ida pushes him back down.

Evvie retrieves the bag from the closet and upends its contents onto the floor. Out falls the windbreaker. The big sunhat, dark sunglasses. The long gray wig and the frilly blouse and skirt. And a wad of money. Ida tosses her the blue Marlins cap. "That goes with it."

The old man looks chagrined. Evvie turns to him and recites his own lines back to him, "Things are seldom as they seem. Skim milk masquerades as cream. Gilbert and Sullivan."

He tries for an impish smile at me.

288

I say, "Why did you do all this? Why the green feather?"

He remains quiet. Ida says, "You might as well tell us. They'll get it out of you at the police station."

"Yeah," says Bella, from the hallway, suddenly brave. "You might as well, 'cause you're no good as a psychic. Your advice didn't work. Dora's still in my apartment!"

Evvie and I look at him, and he shrivels up, realizing he just gave himself away. So that's how he did it.

There is a knock on the door. The man jumps up. Ida pushes her thumb into his chest. "Stay down." She walks into the hallway. Sophie and Bella move out of her way. She peers out the peephole.

A voice outside asks, "Izzy here?"

Ida, confused, replies, "Is who here?"

The voice repeats, "Izzy. Izzy here?"

Our thief says, "He wants me. I'm Izzy."

Ida shuts the peephole, and opens the door to let the visitor in. He is a small, nervous man in shabby clothes. He is bent over, carrying a cane made from a branch of a tree. And he's quite old. His watery eyes squint to seek out "Izzy." "Sorry," he says in a shaky voice, "but I don't mean to intrude when you're having a party."

"It's all right," the man we now know as

Izzy says.

"I'll just get what I came for and leave. You got the money?" the newcomer asks pleadingly.

Izzy gets up. Ida doesn't stop him. He goes to the tote bag on the floor and takes out the cash. He hands all of it to the man. "It's time?" Izzy asks him.

"Doc says I can't wait any longer." He hugs Izzy tearfully. "You're a saint. God bless you. Otherwise, I'm a dead man," he explains to us.

With that he turns and heads for the door. "Happy birthday," he announces, making an assumption, and leaves.

I jump up. "Wait a minute, that's stolen money . . ." I stop. Do I grab the money out of the hands of some pathetic sick man? Who might die?

The girls all look to me, aghast. Breathlessly awaiting my decision.

I sit back down. I'm glad Jack wasn't here. I sigh. Let the police unravel this later.

Izzy also sits down again.

Ida says, "Izzy. Are you going to give us a last name with that?"

No reply. Only silence.

Finally I say, "The green feather. You're playing Robin Hood? Steal from the rich, give to the poor?"

He corrects me. "Steal from the young, give to the old. Who takes care of the lost old people?" he asks. "The ones under the radar. Who cares if they live or die? They live in places you would run screaming from. They eat cat food when they can get it. They have no one. Then they get sick. And then they die. Alone. I pay for their needs the only way I can. The fourteen hundred I stole today is for his gallbladder operation. I steal only what I need for each individual case."

That explains the odd amounts.

"But why don't these people go to the proper authorities for help?" Evvie asks.

"Yeah, sure. *These* people don't know from how the system works. They don't know from papers to fill out. They're barely able to read. Or even see the fine print without any glasses. Folks who barely function at all. Old and infirm. Where's the health care for them? I do what little I can do."

I ask, "How long have you been doing your" — I grope for a word — "your charity work?"

"Many years. Since the day my sister died of a brain tumor because she didn't have any money to pay for doctors." He chokes up. "I had no way to save her."

Evvie walks close to him. "I don't get it. Why did you write to us? Did you want us to capture you?"

He glances up to her and shrugs. "Maybe I'm tired. Maybe . . ." Then he grins mischievously. "Maybe I was bored and I needed a little excitement. Pit myself against you to see which of us is smarter. I found out you were helping older people, so maybe I just wanted to reach out — one old professional to another."

I hear Bella and Sophie sniffling behind me.

I don't want to say it, but I know Jack would have. "But what you do is against the law. It's a federal crime to rob banks."

He cries out to me, "It should be a federal crime in such a rich country for only the wealthy to afford health care. It's enough to make a man turn into a Communist." Abruptly, he grins at me playfully. "Better he should be a bank robber."

He's getting to me, but I keep on. "We have to turn you in or we're aiding and abetting a criminal."

"No!" Sophie cries out.

What a terrible dilemma. My girls are in anguish. I feel awful, too. Evvie reaches out to touch my hand.

Ida comments, "And Madame Ramona

was your cover."

"An escape method. I knew the cops would never think Grandpa was a woman." The imp in him can't resist. "Now, aren't you sorry you only gave me a dollar?"

Sophie jumps up. "Wait just a minute. You weren't wearing a dress when you posed as the guy with no legs."

Bella sighs. "I wish someone would tell me how you did that."

He smiles. "I wasn't robbing the bank that day, either. I was there to watch how you operate, so I stayed a guy."

Bella says happily, "I still have your pencil."

I look to Evvie and Ida. "I don't know what to do."

"Don't sweat it," Izzy says. "I'll go quietly. But can I put some clothes on?"

"Of course," Ida says quickly.

He heads into his bedroom and Ida follows him to the door. He grabs some clothes from the bed and waves them at her as he enters his bathroom.

We wait for him in the living room. I see tearful faces and listen to the unhappy murmurings around me.

"Do we have to turn him in?" Bella wails.

Ida says stiffly, "We have no choice."

Evvie says, "I wish he had never written to us."

Bella asks, "Do you think we'll get a reward?"

"Don't hold your breath," says Ida.

Evvie helps Ida pick up Izzy's disguises from the floor as they repack the tote bag. Wait 'til Morrie hears this, I think ruefully. He's not going to be happy at how easily they were all fooled. This is not a win-win situation.

Ida gives me the tour of Madame Ramona's all-black office with the crystal ball, Ouija board, and tarot cards.

We wait. And we wait. Ida knocks on the bathroom door. "Let's go, Izzy."

No answer. It dawns on me; he's just pulled the oldest scam in the world. And we fell for it. Joe hurries into the bedroom. Of course the bathroom door is locked.

Joe rolls up his sleeves. "I'm gonna break the door down!"

As he starts to sprint, shoulders pointing, Evvie grabs him by the arm and pivots him around. "Are you crazy? What do you think this is — like the movies? It's not so easy to knock down a door."

"I can do it," he says, but his voice betrays him.

"You're an old man! The only thing you'll

break is your neck."

"He's gone," Ida announces as she walks back into the apartment. "I looked outside and the bathroom window is definitely open, and bye-bye, Bandit."

I sigh. I've watched this scene in a lot of movies, too.

But everyone is smiling. And Joe actually winks at me.

Needless to say, Izzy didn't leave anything in the apartment that will give us his real name or any other information. The Madame Ramona name is obviously phony. The apartment is a rental. Even if Morrie checks out Izzy's fingerprints, I'll bet he has no police record to match them against.

Bye-bye, Grandpa. I wonder where you'll turn up next. You wrote us that getting old was not for sissies, and you were right.

I can't wait 'til Jack gets home so I can tell him that the Grandpa Bandit case is solved. More or less.

And Morrie will have a fit that we let him get away. Oy!

34
AN UNEXPECTED VISIT

The doorbell rings. Enya, on her way to her kitchen, is startled. Hardly anyone ever comes to her door. Which is just the way she likes it. She peers through her peephole. To her surprise, Abe Waller is standing there, holding a small bouquet of flowers.

She doesn't answer, standing still, almost holding her breath. Maybe he'll go away. What does he wants from me? she wonders.

He rings again.

She hesitates, unconsciously smoothing her skirt down with her hands. He must know she's in here. She can't be rude. As she opens the door she sees Abe glancing at the mezuzah on the right side of her door frame.

He smiles ruefully. "It is a very strange feeling living in someone else's home. I have never lived anywhere without a mezuzah. May I, Mrs. Slovak?"

Of course she knows what he is asking —

permission to pay his respects to God. Her second husband, Jacov, whom she met after the war, himself a survivor, put the tiny box up when they moved into the apartment. She protested; she cared nothing about religion anymore. She looks at this pious stranger. Let him do what he wants. She nods.

He touches the sacred parchment scroll gently, then places those fingers to his lips. Then he hands her the flowers, which she accepts in puzzlement.

"What did I do for you to bring me flowers, Mr. Waller?"

"It's what *I* did. I felt I did not treat you kindly in the laundry room the other day. Perhaps I was too abrupt?"

At that moment, Evvie and Joe come out of the adjoining apartment. There is a moment of awkwardness, but quickly and at the same time they all nod. Then Evvie and Joe walk off.

Enya, not knowing what to do, and feeling obliged, says, "Perhaps you would like a cup of tea?"

"A glass of water, maybe." Abe says, following Enya inside.

"Well, that was interesting," Evvie says to Joe as they head for his car, out to a restaurant to celebrate their capture of Izzy. "Bringing flowers? How romantic."

"I brought you flowers a while ago. You gave them away."

Evvie flicks an imaginary bit of dust off his shoulder. "Don't go there, Joe. That was then and now is now."

With that she flounces into his car before he has a chance to open the door for her.

Across the way, Jack turns from the kitchen window. "Well, well," he singsongs, "love is in the air. Tra-la-tra-la. Just saw Abe bring flowers to Enya, and Evvie actually touched Joe's shoulder."

I come over, wiping my hands on my apron, and put my arms around him. "It's catching, isn't it?"

He pulls my arms even tighter, closer. "What is?"

"Being a yenta and spying on people. Like everyone else does around here."

He swivels around 'til he's facing me and gives me a playful swat on my rear. Then he goes over to the stove and sniffs what I've cooked for dinner.

"Decisions, decisions," he says. "Food or sex? Sex or food?"

"I thought you wanted to hear more about our Grandpa Bandit story?"

"It can wait." With that, he drags me out of the kitchen and I toss my apron behind me.

Enya stares at the few photographs on her small kitchen table. They are very old, tattered, practically shriveled up. Abe's empty wallet sits beside them.

Abe points to his photo of a young boy with a bicycle, and says, "We wanted Max to play the violin; he was interested only in sports." He manages a small smile. "I was a musician in the old country."

As he talks about his children, she thinks of the photos on her bedroom wall. For a moment, she is tempted to get them, but she can't bring herself to share them. She politely listens to him, sensing how much it must mean to him to be able to talk about his family. But something won't let her open up to him.

He reaches over to touch her hands, but the moment he does, she pulls away. "Sorry," she says. He gestures by raising both hands aloft, as if to say he understands. "You had children?"

She can barely speak. Her throat seems to be closing up on her. She doesn't want to talk about them. But she doesn't know how to be rude. This very kind man is sharing his pain with her. She whispers, "Rebecca was four and Micah was five. My babies . . ." The tears start to flow. He hands her a handkerchief.

He indicates the numbers on her arms. "When were you there . . . Auschwitz?"

She says, "Forty-two to forty-five. Sometimes in my dreams I imagine it never happened . . ." She moves a teacup around in its saucer, but doesn't drink. "In my nightmares there is no doubt it did."

"You know the strange thing?" Enya understands he is changing the conversation away from the personal to make her feel more comfortable. "I only found out afterward. It was only Auschwitz that tattooed the numbers. None of the other camps ever did."

"I never heard that," she says.

"Your husband. You. What work did you have in Prague . . . before . . . ?"

"Jacov and I both taught at the university."

"I was never there. I never traveled far from Munich."

They sit still for a while. Enya watches the second hand on the kitchen clock move round. She wishes he would go away. Her body is sweating; she wants to wash.

Abe finally gets up. "I will leave now. You must have your dinner to prepare. Thank you for the water." He gathers up his photos and places them gently into his wallet. He walks to the door, and as Enya moves around him to open it, their arms touch for a second. Enya's body goes rigid.

Abe opens the door, bows, and leaves.

Enya slowly returns to the kitchen table and sits down. She lifts the bouquet of flowers from the vase in which she placed them and buries her face in them. She remains there, sobbing until it gets dark.

35
GLADDY HAS A HUNCH

I wake up abruptly; something in a dream startles me into consciousness. Jack turns, opens one eye, and says, "What?"

I pat his shoulder gently. "Go back to sleep. It's nothing."

The phone rings. Jack groans and puts his pillow over his head. I look at the clock. Eight A.M. Has to be one of the girls. I'm up already, might as well start moving.

I answer the phone in the kitchen so as not to disturb Jack. It's Sophie.

"News," she says. "The pool is fixed and they're putting water in it. Everyone's going to watch."

"Everyone? How many calls have you made?"

"I didn't. Bella called me because Ida called her because Evvie called Ida." And she adds petulantly, "We always used to get up this early anyway to do our exercise."

She's speaking in past tense because since

Jack moved in, our early-morning routine has vanished. There's a tiny bit of complaining in Sophie's voice. I have to pay attention to this.

"Okay," I say, "I'll meet you down there soon as I get dressed."

"Don't bother wearing your suit. I don't think we can swim yet. Something about chlorine."

I hang up. Why are we all going to the pool if there's no water? I hum a few bars of "Tradition" from *Fiddler on the Roof*.

As I grind my coffee beans it hits me. Why I woke up so abruptly. I phone Stanley. I know he gets up early to supervise the repair work. Maybe I can catch him before he leaves.

Too late. His wife, Esther, tells me I just missed him.

I say, "When you hear from him, please tell him to find me. I need to talk to him about something important. If I'm not in my apartment, I'll be at the Phase Two pool."

I enjoy my coffee and toast, get dressed, and leave Jack a note. It says, "Not going swimming, but will be at pool. Don't ask. Love and xxxx." I leave the note and a camellia on my pillow. I'm really getting into this living together stuff.

■ ■ ■ ■

What a sight! Everyone sits in his or her usual place, facing the pool. Well, not everyone. Our Canadians won't be back for a while. But here they are, our regulars, staring at a pool slowly being filled with water. Comical, really. Seems as exciting as watching grass grow. Nothing too much is happening.

The difference is we have our new temporary neighbors, and even they have come down for this non-event. First face I see is Louise's. She immediately looks behind me to see where Jack is. Maybe she's hoping we had a fight and he's up for grabs. Not a chance, lady.

Dora Dooley has pulled a patio chair next to Bella and Sophie, even though they try to avoid her existence by chatting with their backs to her. Dora's deep into a *TV Guide* magazine, marking shows she wants to see. Ida knits, ignoring all of them.

Joe has a chaise next to Evvie. He's glued to her side. The way he watches her makes me imagine how a starving man might look at a steak. Evvie pays no attention to him and is engrossed in a book.

Tessie sits on the edge of the pool, her

feet dangling in air, as she stares down, watching for the water-level changes. Being the only real swimmer, she can hardly wait until the pool fills. Her hubby, Sol, is a different person since their marriage. The talkative Sol has turned very quiet. As Evvie said to me a while back, she'd love to be a fly on their wall. I'm curious, too.

In between slathering suntan lotion on each other's backs, Casey and Barbi sit directly in the sun, playing gin rummy.

I note that Enya is not here. However, her new neighbor, Abe, who brings flowers, sits in the shade behind the small wrought-iron gate, away from us, reading a newspaper. Abe is fully clothed, wearing his usual black suit. He doesn't seem to mind the heat. I'm surprised he's even there.

And last and never least, Hy and Lola.

It's as if he's been waiting for me to arrive. "In honor of the return of our pool, I got a new joke, folks."

Sol says, "Hah! Like we care."

Tessie gives her darling a little pinch. "You tell him, honeybunch."

No one shows any enthusiasm at all, but Hy is never bothered by opposition. In fact, he thrives on it. He gets up and emotes:

"A young woman brings her fiancé home to meet her parents. After dinner, the mother tells the father to find out about the young man. The father invites the fiancé to his study for a drink. 'So, what are your plans?' the father asks the young man.

" 'I am a Torah scholar,' he replies.

" 'A Torah scholar. Hmmm,' the father says. 'Admirable, but what will you do to provide a nice house for my daughter to live in, as she's accustomed to?'

" 'I will study,' the young man replies, 'and God will provide for us.'

" 'And how will you buy her a beautiful engagement ring, such as she deserves?' asks the father.

" 'I will concentrate on my studies,' he replies. 'God will provide for us.'

" 'And children?' asks the father. 'How will you support children?'

" 'Don't worry, sir, God will provide,' replies the fiancé.

"Later, the mother asks, 'How did it go, dear?'

"The father answers, 'He has no job, he has no plans, he has no ambition, but the good news is, he thinks I'm God.' "

There are a few small laughs. Abe gets up without a word and starts to leave.

"You insulted him," says Evvie, "using the name of the Lord in vain."

"What's the matter, a man can't take a

joke?" Hy says, offended.

As Abe moves out of the perimeter of the pool area, he meets Stanley, who is hurrying in. That stops him. "Is something wrong?" Abe asks worriedly.

"I don't think so, but" — he glances to me — "Gladdy said she needed to see me about something important."

I am now the center of attention. I try to underplay it. "Just some thoughts I wanted to share with him."

Sophie claps her hands. "I bet it's about the skeleton."

"Yeah," says Bella excitedly. "I bet you figured out who he is."

My girls are about to move in my direction as I head toward Stanley. I wave them down. "Relax, everyone. Let me chat with Stanley. If there's anything new to report, you'll hear about it."

They are disappointed. Everyone stares after us as I lead Stanley out of earshot.

We find a bench to sit at near the duck pond. The ducks are slowly returning after our disaster. I wonder how many were lost forever. We settle ourselves under a tree that is split in half, another result of the hurricane. Stanley shakes his head at all the damage to plants and trees. "So many years this tree was here. I remember we planted it soon after we finished the construction. Now it's dead."

I commiserate with him. He changes the subject. "Never mind, you have information? I thought our case was over."

"Just a hunch, Stanley. Something's been bothering me ever since we came back from Tampa. We finally decided that this Lucy Blake's brother, Johnny, was not our skeleton. But his sister, Lucy, said something that stuck in my head. She questioned the way he died. Falling off the dock immediately after a long voyage? Lucy was informed that her brother definitely left the ship. But what if he didn't? What if somebody wanted to steal his papers? Somebody trying to get into this country from a foreign country? He would wait until they were near port because he couldn't move around the ship before that. Suppose he threw Johnny Blake overboard the day they docked, and used his papers to get off the ship?"

"A stowaway, you're thinking?"

I nod. "Yes. Once onshore, he could have been moving around, using Johnny's identity, and somehow ended up here and got the job working for you."

Stanley is eager now. "And this stranger is

the one buried under the cement."

"Maybe," I say, "and maybe not."

He looks puzzled. "What do you mean?"

"I don't know. But it's something to think about."

Stanley paces back and forth in front of the shattered tree, his hands behind his back. "How can we make sure that it is the same Johnny Blake who is the connection? How can we find out?"

I shrug. "You got back the items you gave Morrie for the testing?"

"Yes. As a matter of fact, this morning. They are in my apartment. I was trying to figure out what to do with them. I almost threw them away."

"I'm glad you didn't. Would you please bring them to my apartment? I want to look closely at them. Perhaps there's something we've missed."

We reach my building. I'm about to go upstairs and Stanley is starting to head for Phase Six, when we run into Abe again. He's standing at his mailbox. He must be eager for something to arrive. The mail doesn't come for another hour.

Abe asks Stanley, "Is there a problem?"

Stanley pats him on the shoulder. "Everything is under control, old friend. This brilliant lady doesn't give up easily."

Abe gives me a bright smile. "That is good news indeed."

36
PUTTING IT
TOGETHER

We're seated around my dining room table eating lunch. Everyone's a little nervous. This is the first time the girls have gathered in my apartment since Jack moved in. They are on their best behavior. Sitting up tall, like elegant ladies, eating slowly, positively dripping with good manners. Jack is cramping their natural style.

"Would you please pass the salt?" Sophie asks ever so politely. Their usual behavior is boardinghouse style — reach over and grab.

Bella daintily lifts the salt shaker with pinky held high and passes it to Evvie, who gives it to Ida, who places it in Sophie's outstretched hand. What a performance.

Jack smiles and mimics them. "Glad," he says, "would you do me the honor of handing me the pepper?"

"Sure," I say. I lift the shaker and toss it to him. He grabs it and I smile back at him. For a moment, the girls are bewildered, but then they get it and start to relax.

By now I've filled everyone in and we're waiting for Stanley.

Stanley is excited. He can hardly contain himself. He comes in waving a tattered old envelope. "You are so smart, lovely lady. I never paid attention. The Christmas card to a Lucy Blake came with an envelope. And an address." His hands are shaking as he passes the envelope to me.

I scan it quickly and read, " 'Lucy Blake, P.O. Box . . .' " And I stop, chagrined. "Oh, Stanley, it's a fifty-year-old post office box number!"

The girls get it immediately. Then Stanley's smile fades. "I didn't think."

I pace for a few moments, exchanging glances with Jack. "Hold on, maybe all is not lost. Maybe she'd remember her old number."

Evvie isn't convinced. "You really expect that Lucy woman to remember a post office box number she used almost fifty years ago?"

Sophie chirps, "I remember the first phone number I ever had, when I was twenty. Tivoli two four eight five . . . three."

Ida says, "I lived at thirteen forty-five Manor Avenue, apartment four-J, in the

Bronx, until I was sixteen."

"Come to think of it," Evvie says, "I remember the first driver's license number I ever had." She gets up and pours coffee for all of us.

"Okay, okay," I stop them. "You made your point. Maybe she'll remember and maybe she won't. We'll soon find out."

Bella giggles. "But don't ask me what I just ate for breakfast." Then she says, "I still don't get it. This boy, Johnny, dies because a man kills him for his identity, so why isn't the bad guy the skeleton?"

Jack says, "Let me try to explain, Bella."

Bella practically bats her eyes at him. She's his number-one fan in my motley group of P.I.'s. I know Sophie also adores Jack, and Evvie finally is happy about my relationship with him, acknowledges it as the real thing. I watch for Ida to respond. Is she going to be my only holdout in accepting Jack, who seems to be infiltrating our investigating team? Not a hint does she reveal on her face. Her arms are crossed, however.

Stanley says, "You've obviously done some thinking. Fill me in."

Jack attempts to simplify it. "Lucy Blake told you, her brother Johnny was on a ship coming from South America. A bad guy, probably trying to get into our country il-legally, steals his papers and kills him. With me so far?"

Bella practically gurgles.

"The bad guy throws Johnny overboard near shore. Does it just before they dock. The authorities insist Johnny left the ship with all the others. The fake Johnny uses the confusion of docking and rushes off the ship as fast as he can, flashing the stolen papers. After the real Johnny's body washes up, the police figure he must have fallen off the dock. His sister doubts it."

Evvie has to jump in. "Okay, so he wanders around as Johnny Blake and ends up working on Lanai Gardens. It was a dark and stormy night." Evvie smiles; she's imitating a classic mystery novel beginning. "Someone comes to the construction site. And ends up murdered and thrown in the hole."

Bella raises her hand. "Stop. That's what I don't get. How do we know it wasn't the phony Johnny Blake that died?"

My turn. "I'm making that assumption. The bones found do not match the description that Stanley's foreman gave of the man he hired as Johnny Blake. Also, we now realize the impostor has already committed one murder. My supposition is, whoever came upon him that stormy night was the one killed. The bad guy already murdered one man; it wasn't a big jump to suppose he could murder another. Besides, the bones describe a much smaller man."

Good. Here comes Ida, joining in at last. Her curiosity overcomes her misgivings. "But why?"

I lean back and sip my coffee. "That's the big question."

Sophie offers, "A robber came to rob him or to steal building supplies?"

Ida says, "Doubtful. What with how bad the weather was that night."

Jack says, "Perhaps it was someone who was looking for him and finally found him."

I add, "And they had a fight?"

Evvie shakes her head. "So if that's true, now we have two unknown men. The bad guy and the mysterious stranger. How can we possibly figure out who they were?"

Ida says, "Sounds like another dead end."

I say, "I'm hoping Lucy will recognize the post office box number. If so, it will be definite proof the bad guy is connected to this Johnny Blake. We need to narrow that fact down."

Stanley looks at me doubtfully and shrugs.

"It's all we have to go on." I hand him my phone and I turn on the speaker so we can all hear. He takes a card from his pocket and dials Lucy's number.

We're in luck, Lucy's home.

After Stanley explains why we're calling, he repeats the number on the old, crumpled envelope.

For a moment, she's surprised. Then I can almost hear the smile in her voice. "Funny you should ask," she says, "I happen to be very good with numbers. I had that box number for years. Why do you want to know?" But she speaks before we can answer. "The man you found had Johnny's belongings, didn't he?"

Stanley says, "We think so. There was a Christmas card with your name and that post office box number."

"I knew it," Lucy says. "I was sure somebody killed my brother. Please," she begs frantically, "promise me you'll find him, so my brother can have justice."

Stanley looks at me and I nod. "We promise. We will do everything we can to find him."

He hangs up and I'm exhilarated. "Now we have proof!"

Stanley says wryly, "All you have to do is solve the crime. Identify the other dead man and a murderer who's gotten away with it for fifty years."

Everyone looks to me, as usual.

Jack raises his eyebrows. I know what he's thinking. "What has his Gladdy gotten herself into this time?"

37
WHEN NIGHT FALLS

First rainy day we've had since the hurricane. It's the three D's out there. Dreary, dark, and depressing. I have every light on in the apartment to chase away the gloom.

I wait for Jack to come home. He's late tonight. Though things have calmed down, I guess there are still many neighborhoods that are far from being repaired and that's where the extra police still guard for trouble.

It's my night to cook. Jack has made our cooking evenings a fun contest. Surprise Night: "I'm not telling you what I'm making, see if you can guess by the way the kitchen smells." No White Food Night; not a bad thing, leaves out lots of starches. Or Competition Night; "Who makes the best lasagna?" Not that we have lasagna two nights in a row. The competition is two weeknights apart.

Instead of *having* to cook, cooking has become fun. *Fun* is the operative word. And he is a fun companion. Why, oh, why did I wait so long? I could have had this life a year ago. Why didn't I follow my own rule of *If not now, when?* I was so afraid to give up what I had in favor of the unknown.

The key turns in the lock and I hear, "Honey, I'm home." He is determined to say that silly thing every time. And I meet him at the door with a kiss and say, "Hard day at the office, dear?" A new tradition.

And of course he heads directly for the kitchen. It's Soup from Scratch Night, and I have a hearty vegetable soup on the stove. To be served with a French bread and Brie. The secret of my vegetable soup is to sprinkle grated Parmesan cheese on it when serving. Jack lifts the lid, takes a spoonful, and smiles his approval.

"You're late. Any problems?"

"Nope. I had to make a stop."

He goes into the living room, where the table is elaborately set. BJ (before Jack), a tacky placemat, paper napkins, and any old silverware. AJ, need I say Martha Stewart would be proud?

He lights the candles in my fancy silver-plated candelabra, which had gathered dust for ten years in the hall closet until now.

And then he places a small box on my plate.

There should be a crash of cymbals. The first four notes of Beethoven's Fifth at least. Something. I examine the box from every angle. It looks like a small ring box. "Is this what I think it is?" I ask.

"It is," he replies. "Exactly what you said you wanted. A garnet instead of a diamond."

"This is it, then?" I ask, stalling.

He removes the ring from the box and places it on my finger. "Last chance to run. I would get down on my knees, but you'd have to pull me up." He beams. "Hope you like the design I picked. You can always get it reset, though."

It's beautiful, but what engagement ring isn't beautiful? I can't believe how corny I feel. There must be something of a universal subconscious that prompts this response in women when they get "the ring." Tears in my eyes, a blush on my cheeks.

He kisses me. "I'm only marrying you because you love to cook."

I burst out laughing. "You're trapped, too."

"I hope forever."

I bask in the joy of the moment. I wish everyone I love could be so happy.

They sit on the couch, side by side. Joe eats a TV dinner: roast beef, mashed potatoes, green peas. Evvie eats home-cooked lemon chicken with Brussels sprouts and a salad. They watch *Jeopardy!* Evvie calls out the answers when she knows them. Joe stares ahead and seems to be watching. But he is thinking.

"Evvie," he says. "Can't we divide up the chores? I can cook one night, and maybe you the next."

"Hah," she says. "When did you learn to cook?"

"I manage."

"You just want me to wait on you hand and foot, like I used to. And that's not going to happen."

He sighs. "I wish we could try to make things pleasant."

"Maybe your apartment will be fixed soon, so this'll be a moot point."

He picks up her plate and his aluminum foil wrapping and brings them into the kitchen. He washes up what little there is. He calls to her, "Want me to go out and get some ice cream?"

"It's raining," she calls back.

"So what?" he says, "I won't melt."

"All right," she says grudgingly. "Make it chocolate almond fudge."

"I know. I know what you like." He grabs his raincoat from the hall closet. And like an eager puppy dog, he races out.

Evvie tries to concentrate on the TV show. She calls out an answer. "Spain." She's wrong. It's Portugal. She shakes her head, disgusted with herself. Why am I so damned stubborn? Why can't I bend a little? He's trying so hard. Stupid. Stupid. Stupid.

Enya wakes up, disoriented, not knowing where she is. The room is dark. She reaches for the lamp and turns on the switch. She shakes her head to clear it. She had fallen asleep on the couch. Getting up slowly, she makes her way into the kitchen. From her window she sees Joe hurrying past. He is smiling. She puts up the kettle for tea.

Glancing at the clock she realizes it's past dinnertime. What does it matter, she's hardly ever hungry these days. She tells herself she must eat. But what for?

It's the nightmares. They won't stop. Eyes everywhere. The eyes of her husband and the children. Eyes pleading. Eyes filled with dirt and crying. Eyes dying; the light going out. Eyes of an assassin who terrorizes her.

She can't stand it, but what can she do? She needs to talk to someone. Throwing a shawl around her shoulders, she walks outside. She hesitates at Evvie's door. Then, not wanting to disturb her, on impulse she turns next door and rings Abe's bell. Immediately she regrets her action.

Abe, wearing a tallis, his praying shawl, answers and is startled to see her. "Mrs. Slovak, do you need something?"

She moves away, shaking her head. "A bad idea." She goes back into her apartment. How could she think of even going to that man? He's a stranger. And she realizes something about him makes her nervous. She drinks more tea and stares at her white kitchen wall, hoping for serenity.

Fifteen minutes later Abe knocks at her door. This time, he is wearing a jacket. He tells her, "You came to me in need and I should have helped you then and there. Forgive me."

"I'm all right. It was a moment of weakness."

He tries for a smile. "Perhaps I should have brought more flowers. I seem always to be apologizing to you."

She lets him in. She asks herself why. She feels she is not in control of her actions. Once again they sit at the small table, her hands clasped, his on his lap. He waits.

She blurts it out, "It's the nightmares. I see eyes and they are always accusing. I thought I buried those dreams, but they are back." She leans her head tiredly against the white wall.

"There is only one answer. You must forgive and forget, or you will live in agony all your days."

She throws her hands into the air in frustration. "How is that possible? How can I ever forget?" She jumps up, puts her cup in the sink, needing something to do.

He speaks quietly. "You place it in a compartment in the back of your mind. And you lock the door. You find solace in God. Otherwise, there is no peace in you."

"Peace? I don't want peace. And don't you dare say to me that my family would have wanted me to forget. That they would want me to be happy! I've heard it a thousand times, said by people who could never imagine hell on earth. You know better. You lived in the same hell."

Her face is close to his. "I wanted to die with them."

"But God chose you to live."

"And God chose them to die?"

"He had His reasons."

"Oh, yes, And what was His reason for me? To live in agony! There is no limit to the agony I must suffer, and it will never match what my family went through."

"Yet you knocked on my door because you could no longer stand the pain. Enough,

Mrs. Slovak. Enya. You've paid your penance long enough."

She shakes her head violently from side to side.

"God would not want you to suffer like this."

She screams at him, "God wanted my babies to suffer?" She drops to her chair, but falls instead to the floor. He reaches down to help her up. She pushes his hands away. She stays there on her knees.

Abe leans down to her and recites gently, " 'When I believed He saved me. I will say of the Lord, He is my refuge and my fortress, my God, in him will I trust.' "

"No! No! No!" Enya shouts. "Leave me alone!"

He drops down on the floor in front of her. "You must forgive. You must forget. You must!" He, recites, louder, with zeal, " 'O Lord my God, I cried unto thee, and thou hast healed me.' "

"Stop it!" she shouts, and covers her ears. "I can't. I won't!"

His voice lifts higher, becomes more passionate. He grabs her shoulders and makes her sway with him. " 'O Lord, thou hast brought up my soul from the grave: thou hast kept me alive, that I should not go down to the pit . . .' "

"Stop it! Stop it!" Enya, unable to bear another moment, pulls away with all her strength and flings her arm out. She slaps his face, accidentally knocking off his glasses. For a moment, they stare into each other's eyes. Both wild with rage and astonishment.

Then Enya faints.

When she comes to, Abe is gone and the front door is wide open.

38
TREMORS

"Go on out there, my pretty coward." Jack comes up behind me as I look out the window, and nuzzles me. "You can handle it."

The girls are already outside warming up for our morning exercise. I've reinstated our old routine and they are happy indeed.

"All right, already. I've got it on." I wiggle my ring finger. "But I guarantee it'll open a heap of aggravation."

Today, I intend to wear my engagement ring. It's taken me a few days to work up the courage, because I know what will happen. Instant need to make plans. Instant tumult. I shudder.

I dig my heels in, but Jack gently pushes me out the door.

Ida and Sophie perform their stretches on our landing and I join them in their warm-ups.

Across the courtyard, Evvie and Bella are

doing the same. Once that's done, we head downstairs and meet for the rest of the routine of walking the paths.

As we do, we discuss our day's plans. Bella and Sophie are going to a Hadassah luncheon. Ida will teach her baking class. Evvie and I will meet up with Jack at Morrie's office and see what he can do to help solve our skeleton mystery.

I keep waiting for someone to spot the glitter of my ring. But they are looking up and looking down and looking around; Bella, of course, always keeps her eyes on her feet to make sure she doesn't trip.

I need to get this over with. "Look what I have," I say, flashing my garnet ring. I had chosen my birthstone rather than a diamond. First there is a casual glance and then it sinks in. Bella and Sophie grab my hand for closer inspection. Ida's eyebrow goes up. Evvie looks at me, sees my eyes shining, and she is happy for me.

Sophie and Bella then join hands and dance around me, jumping up and down. Next words out of their mouths will be "When's the wedding?"

"When's the wedding?" Sophie asks.

"We need to have a party" will follow as day follows night.

"Yeah," Bella says joyfully. "We need to

make you a party."

"Party, party, party," sing my dancing girls.

"Congratulations," Ida says. The words must be closing down her throat. I know she loves me and wants my happiness, but this is clearly churning up old bad memories for her. Someday I hope she'll feel free to confide in me.

Evvie comes to the little dancing circle and gleefully pulls it apart. She hugs me, with tears in her eyes.

"Okay, okay," I say, "but first walking, walking, walking."

The rest of the walk is plans, plans, and plans.

Evvie glances at me slyly. She knows how much I hate being the center of attention.

We are on our way to Morrie's, Evvie and I, where we'll meet up with Jack. I've had some of the worst dings taken off the old Chevy, so it doesn't look as awful as it did.

Evvie says from her seat next to me, "What's different?"

"When? Now?"

"Yes."

"I don't know. What?"

"When's the last time we've had time to spend time together alone? Since before the hurricane."

"Come to think of it, we haven't."

"My point, exactly. Now that we have men in our apartments and our lives. In our kitchens, in our bathrooms, in our closets —"

I stop her hyperbole. "Now, now." She would go on forever if I let her, my drama queen sister. I glance at her face. Her lips are tightly pursed. "Well, you know what's been going on in my life. You just got the latest update this morning. I haven't a clue what you're about. With Joe."

Evvie looks out the window, not answering. Finally, she says, "University Drive is still a mess. The city looks like a war zone."

"Old news. And windows are still shuttered and stores are still closed. Yada, yada, as Seinfeld used to say on TV. You're stalling. Out with it."

She faces me. "Joe doesn't want anyone to know."

"I'm your sister. We don't keep secrets from each other."

She blurts, "He's got cancer and he's decided he wants to spend what time he has left with me!"

I almost lose control of the wheel. I turn to her in anguish. "Oh, Evvie."

Now the two of us are silent.

"I've hated him for years," Evvie says.

"Now I'm not allowed to hate him because he's dying."

"What kind of time are we talking about?" I ask softly.

"Maybe six months. Prostate. And now . . . *now*, he starts to be nice to me."

"Can't you forgive and forget?"

"All those years of treating me like dirt. He and his family making me feel small and useless. Dumping me on a New Year's Eve in front of everyone —"

"Ev," I stop the litany from continuing. "I know how much pain he caused, but get a little perspective here. Think of that old saying: I complained because I had no shoes, until I met a man who had no feet."

"Yeah, yeah. I know I should count my blessings."

"Think of Enya and what she went through."

She sighs. "You're right. My new mantra: Forgive and forget."

"Just keep saying that to yourself. Turn things around. Change the negative into positive. Find what's good in him."

"Why do you always have to be so damn smart?"

"Because I am." I smirk. She grins.

We arrive at the police station. Evvie and I hug each other. I wait a few moments until

331

she wipes the tears from her face, and we get out of the car.

We fill Morrie in, Jack, Evvie, and I, as we sit in his office. He has this habit of tapping his desk when he's impatient, and he's doing it now. I speed up my dissertation. All of it. My trip to Tampa with Stanley, meeting the sister. We track the Johnny Blake line from there to Lanai Gardens. Reminding Morrie that the forensics lab report on the skeleton proves it's not anyone already identified.

Now he pays close attention. "So you have two unsolved murders from fifty years ago. In two different counties." He looks at me.

"I know."

Morrie looks at Jack.

"She knows."

"We need you to take up the slack," I say.

"Nice of you. Thanks for giving me an ice cold case to handle."

I pinch his cheek. "No statute of limitations on murder. We already did the hard stuff, *bubbala*."

Evvie gets her dig in, too. "All you have to do is find out everything about that ship, and how and where the guy got on, and who knew about it. A piece of cake."

With that, we take our leave, with me saying "I know you'll want to get on this right away, so off we go. Ta-ta."

With those long legs of his, he gets to the door before we can. "Not so fast, Gladdy Gold. Don't think I haven't noticed. You aren't getting out of here that easily." He lifts my left hand. "Nice ring. When's the party and when's the wedding?"

Jack, Evvie, and I exchange glances. "I told you so," I say with my grin.

Denny waits at his truck in front of building Q. Sophie and Bella, all dressed up, hurry to him.

Bella says, "I hope we didn't keep you waiting."

"No problem," he says, opening the door for them. "I got all my chores done already, so I got time."

"Denny, a moment, please."

The girls turn at the sound of the voice. It's Abe Waller, hurrying toward them. He seems agitated. "I have a problem. My faucet just broke off in the kitchen and water is gushing. I'm glad I caught you before you left."

Denny is chagrined. "I'm taking Mrs. Fox and Mrs. Meyerbeer somewhere."

Abe seems upset. "But what can I do with all that water running?" He looks at Bella and Sophie. "So sorry. Didn't mean to interrupt. Where are you lovely ladies going?"

Sophie preens. "Were going to a luncheon. In Margate."

"Margate? Really?" Abe says, "I'm on my way there now myself. May I give you a lift?"

The girls and Denny are at a loss.

"Well, I don't know . . ." Sophie says.

Abe bows to her. "Please, it would be my pleasure. Then Denny will fix my faucet."

That old-country-style charm works. The girls melt.

Abe asks Denny. "Do you need my key or do you have a master?"

Denny says, unsure, "I can let myself in."

"Then it's settled. Ladies, my car is right here. Allow me to escort you."

Bella and Sophie smile at each other. They wave at Denny. "Thanks anyway, Denny," Sophie says. "We'll call when we need a ride home, if that's okay."

Denny nods. "Lots better than a ride in the truck," Bella says, seating herself in the backseat of Abe's comfortable Pontiac.

Sophie sits next to Bella. They giggle. "This is like having a chauffeur," she says happily.

As they drive off, Sophie gives Abe the street address. Abe turns on a music station for them. "Classical all right?" Abe asks.

The girls nudge each other. They are enjoying this. Bella says, "We like anything."

Abe makes conversation. "These have been very exciting weeks, have they not? I, myself, never experienced a hurricane before. Were you frightened? I know I was."

Sophie gushes, "You bet. We were scared out of our wits."

Bella adds, "I thought we were going to die."

Sophie says, "We were lucky. We got to stay with Gladdy and she kept us calm."

Abe turns slightly to them. "Your friend is a very smart woman, is she not?"

Bella says, "She sure is. She knows about everything."

Abe comments, "She even seems very well informed about the skeleton they found."

"Didn't it creep you out?" Sophie asks. "Finding out you lived with a dead guy right under you all those years?"

"Certainly gives one pause," he answers. "My dear friend Stanley told me he and Gladdy went to Tampa and found out the skeleton wasn't really that Johnny Blake person. So, I might assume the trail ends there."

Sophie beams. "Not with our bloodhound-dog leader. Even as we speak, she's at the police station with Detective Morrie Langford, Jack's son. Now they know for sure that the real Johnny Blake is buried in Tampa and she figures someone stole his papers when he was on a boat and then someone must have known the guy and he came to find him . . ."

She's out of breath, so Bella eagerly continues. "And that guy got killed, too. So the way she figures, there are two murdered men. Johnny Blake and the poor guy who became our skeleton." She grins, proud of being able to remember it all.

For a moment, there's silence. Then Abe says, "Yes, your friend is very smart."

Bella smiles with satisfaction. "That killer better watch out — our Gladdy's on his trail."

A few minutes later they arrive at the Chinese restaurant where their luncheon meeting is being held. Abe gets out and opens the doors for them. They thank him profusely.

Sophie and Bella are pleased to see he is watching them walk to the door. Probably to make sure they get safely into the restaurant. "Such a gentleman," Sophie comments.

39
BREAKDOWN

Darkness outside. Darkness in. From where she lies on her bed, Enya dreams she is tied down. A movie appears on all four of her bedroom walls. Black-and-white. No color. Except for the blood. Shouts she knows well. *"Achtung! Rause!"*

The lights from the towers zigzag, splashing grays and sharp whites from one side of the room to the other. She ducks her head to keep them from finding her.

Schweinhund!

The dogs bark and bare their slobbery fangs.

"Vyhlizet!" someone cries out to the others in their filthy shack. Look out!

Inmates who can still move run quickly. Others barely crawl. Confusion everywhere.

The boots march relentlessly. *"Achtung!"* Halt!

The machine guns chatter. Rat-a-tat. Rat-a-tat.

Splazit se! Hide!

Schvat se. Run!

Nein! Das zaun! The fence! *Electrfiziertes!*
Electric!

Banging

Tearing.

She needs to run. To hit!

To smash back at them.

She can't . . . She must.

She closes her eyes. She cannot bear to
look into his eyes again.

She moans.

She screams.

Evvie wakens abruptly, hearing the hard
knocking on her door. She struggles into
her robe and hurries to answer. It's Denny,
looking wild-eyed and frightened. "Something's wrong with Mrs. Slovak," he cries.

Denny's apartment is directly below Enya's. He continues breathlessly, "There's
banging and screaming. I can hear it from
my ceiling. It's scaring me. I don't know
what to do."

"Okay," she says, "wait here." She dashes
into her living room, where Joe sleeps on
the couch. She shakes him awake. He is
groggy. "What —"

"Come. I need you," she says. He grabs
his robe and they rush outside. At Enya's
door she and Joe can hears sounds of things

breaking. And Enya shouting.

Evvie pokes Joe. "Go back to my place and call Gladdy. We may need her help." As he runs, Evvie moves to Enya's door and rings the bell.

Hy and Lola, also in robes, call from their doorway at the other end of the same floor. "What's going on over there? Why is everybody up?"

Evvie says, "We don't know. Go back to sleep. We'll tell you tomorrow."

Hy is about to protest, but Lola pulls him inside. Denny, glad not to get involved, goes downstairs to his apartment again.

Evvie rings Enya's doorbell again and again.

Joe comes out of her apartment. "Gladdy's on her way."

"Joe, grab the master keys on the hall table."

Joe once again is happy to do her bidding.

It looks as if the place had been robbed and tossed by vandals. Chairs are knocked down. The pillows on the couch have been thrown every which way. Books are ripped and hurled from overturned shelves. The curtains are torn from the living room windows. From the kitchen door Jack and I see dishes smashed, cupboards open, pots and pans flung across the room.

I call, "Evvie, where are you?"

"In the bedroom. Hurry."

We rush to the bedroom, where Evvie and Joe are gently trying to stop Enya as she tears her bed apart. I am surprised — such unnatural strength from so fragile a woman.

"Enya, dear," I say firmly, "let us help you."

Between the four of us we get her to sit on the edge of her bed.

The dresser drawers have already been upended. The bedside lamp lies on the floor, spotlighting the ceiling.

She stares at us, befuddled. "He's come," she says. "I won't let him take anything from my home. I leave him nothing."

I find a blanket to wrap around her. But Enya pulls her arms out in order to grab my hands and clutch them. "I am going crazy. Help me. Madness. All I see is madness! Put me in an asylum in a straitjacket."

From the wildness in her eyes, I'm afraid she's telling the truth. She drops her arms; her eyes seem blank and far away.

Jack says, "I think we should take her to the emergency room."

"Even the smell of him," Enya cries out. "How can I remember? Such a thing as a smell? Can a smell last so long?"

"Who are you talking about?" I ask quietly.

Enya cries out to me imploringly, "He was fatter then. Fat with his importance. How he loved to see the skin cling to our bones. It gave him such an appetite."

We look from one to another, not knowing how to help her. She is shaking now. I'm at a loss to know what to do, other than let her talk.

"His face. The beard. I did not see it because of the beard."

Joe says, "Should I get some whiskey?"

Evvie nods. "We have to try something."

Joe runs out again to go to Evvie's.

Enya asks pleadingly, "Where are his boots? I was always so frightened of his boots."

I say, "Maybe we *should* get her to the hospital."

Enya's eyes seem to whip about. "How is it possible? Such a nice man. Such a religious, good man. What can I be thinking?" She stares at the wall leading to the kitchen. "It can't be. No. It's me. I am crazy."

She is sobbing by now. "It's the scar. Under his eye. It's the scar!"

Jack tries. "Enya, please," he says softly. "Tell us who you're talking about."

She walks out of the bedroom, into the living room. We follow her. She continues walking until she reaches her kitchen.

Joe returns, whiskey bottle in hand. All of us watch as Enya points to the kitchen wall. The one that connects to Abe's apartment.

She wipes the tears from her face, then whispers in an almost childish voice filled with awe, "Shhh, it's him. Don't let him hear you. *Er ist Der Oberführer. Er ist Der Bösewicht,* the evil one with the evil eye. He will be very angry."

40
WHAT CAN IT MEAN?

There's a knock at the door. Jack goes to answer it. It's Mary, our nurse friend who lives right above Hy and Lola. She carries what looks like a doctor's bag. She says, "Lola called me and said there was a problem. Perhaps I can be of assistance."

I'm very glad to see her.

Evvie says, "They shouldn't have wakened you."

Mary shrugs. "Comes with the territory." She glances around, taking in the mess and the near-hysterical woman on the couch, who sits there with a coat around her shoulders.

Joe says, "We were just about to take Enya to Emergency."

Enya rears back, terrified. "No, I don't want to go."

Mary examines her. Takes her pulse, her blood pressure. Listens to her heart.

"Mary."

Enya begs, "Don't let them take me away."

"It's all right, dear," she says. "Maybe you just need to sleep."

Enya nods, childlike. "I haven't been able to sleep."

"Do you have any prescription pills?"

"The doctor gave me some, but I was afraid to take them."

Mary looks to us. "See if you can find them."

Jack and I go into the bathroom and look through Enya's medicine cabinet. We bring back the few bottles we find there and hand them to Mary.

She picks one out. "This will do fine." She tells us, "Mild tranquilizers."

Evvie goes into the kitchen and brings a glass of water. Mary hands Enya a couple of the pills. "These won't hurt you. I promise. And you'll be able to sleep."

Enya takes them and pats Mary on the cheek. "You're a good girl. Thank you." She leans over as if to impart a secret. "He had this terrible scar, you know. It circled his left eye. From a knife fight, perhaps. He was very lucky not to lose the eye."

With that, she lies back and turns her face into the pillows.

"I'll stay with her," Mary says. "You all look exhausted."

Mary walks us to the door. We stand there whispering. Mary asks, "She tore the place apart herself?"

"Yes," I say.

"Hopefully it's not a psychotic episode," Mary says. "Seems like she's having some kind of breakdown. I'll get in touch with her doctor as soon as I can."

We thank her profusely as we go outside. She closes the door behind us.

The four of us stand there, utterly done in. Joe scratches at the bald spot on the back of his head. "Wow, that was bizarre. What got into that poor lady?"

Evvie sighs. "God only knows."

Jack puts his arm around me. "I don't know about the rest of you, but I can't think clearly right now."

"Let's meet in the morning with the girls and discuss this," I say needlessly. With last-minute hugs, we head for our own apartments.

As we head downstairs, I can hear Joe saying, "I don't get it. What's with the pointing at Abe's apartment?"

"Want me to make some coffee?" Evvie asks as they get inside.

"No, I wanna crash," Joe says, yawning, heading for the living room couch. "I desperately need to sleep."

"Joe," Evvie says quietly. "Sleep with me."

He looks at her for a long moment. "And then the next night back on the couch? No thanks. I feel like a yo-yo."

She goes over and pulls him along to the bedroom. "No more yo-yo. Just yo."

"Yo, toots," he says. Now he's pulling her.

Back in bed, I find it difficult to relax. I can't even begin to process what just happened. "Maybe we should have taken some of those 'tranks,' too," I say.

"Nonsense," he says. "I'm better than a pill." With that, he puts his arm around me and I cuddle into him, grateful for the comfort he offers.

By ten A.M. we're gathered in my apartment for a late breakfast. My puzzled girls can't figure out why Jack and I slept so late, until I fill them in on the night we had with Enya. They need only to look at the circles under our eyes to believe it.

We are seated around the dining room table. With seven in that small space, we are crowded together. But no one's complaining as Jack serves us all a wonderful vegetable omelet.

"Take lessons," Evvie tells Joe.

"I already memorized the recipe," he says, smiling at her.

Now it's my turn for eyebrows to go up. These are two self-satisfied après-sex type grins. Hmmm. I sure hope so.

As we dig in, Jack still standing, he says, "Let me try to sum up what we know so far about the two of them. Abe Waller moves in next door to Enya. Enya has nightmares about the camps."

Ida interrupts. "She started having nightmares before he moved in next door, even before the hurricane."

Joe says, "Premonition?"

I say, "Let's table that for a moment."

Jack continues. "They have conversations a few times."

Sophie jumps in. "It looked like a romance brewing like a teapot. Didn't it?" Sophie and Bella exchange nervous glances. I wonder what that's about. Sophie takes seconds of the eggs. Looks like nervous eating to me.

Ida says, "All it means to me is that having talked to someone who also survived the camps brought back her own horrible memories. She's never spoken about her experiences to anyone. She keeps to herself. Obviously she never got therapy. All that guilt-of-the-survivor pain building up for so many years. Now it's come to a head and she's having a nervous breakdown."

I say, "I'd agree with you, but she keeps repeating she recognized him by his eyes. Something about a scar around one eye. She called him by a name. I don't think it was a person's real name. Perhaps some kind of German title? *Der Bösewicht?*"

Jack pours refills of coffee for everyone.

Ida shakes her head. "Crazy talk. It's too much to believe. Just by coincidence a German soldier from a concentration camp now lives next door to her? And for this sick fantasy, she picks on Abe Waller, a deeply religious Jewish man, for heaven's sakes."

There is silence for a few moments as the girls, while thinking, busily fix their coffee refills with their choice of low-fat milk and/or sugar.

Jack and I both say it in unison, "But what if —"

We stop, surprised at having similar thoughts, and he indicates I should go on. "What if it's true?" I can't believe I'm saying this. "What if he's not Jewish. What if —"

Bella drops her coffee spoon. It clatters to the floor. She looks horrified. She pokes Sophie, who pokes her back and says, "Shh."

"What!" Evvie says, annoyed. "What's

with you two? You're like cats on a hot tin roof."

Always the literary one, my sister. Not that they know the reference.

Bella blurts, "That we rode in a car with . . ." She can't even say his name.

All eyes turn to the two now cowering women.

"Spit it out." Ida says, "Or you'll choke."

Bella is tongue-tied. Sophie is forced to talk. "You remember yesterday, we were off to Hadassah. Denny was going to drive us, but Abe did instead. No big deal."

"You got into a car with Abe Waller?" Ida says, surprised.

"And?" Evvie says, annoyed. "What's with the two-second explanation? Why didn't Denny drive and why did Abe?"

Sophie, putting her hands on her hips, continues reluctantly. "Abe said a pipe burst in his sink and he needed Denny to fix it right away. And Abe asked where we were off to and then he said he was going to Margate, too, and gave us a lift. End of story."

I pick up the phone and dial Denny's number. Since he is our fixer-upper, I have his number memorized. Denny answers.

"Hi, Denny, it's Mrs. Gold." I listen. "Yes, I think Enya's much better. Thank you for asking. Just have a question. Did Abe Waller have a big problem with his kitchen sink yesterday? I heard it was flooding." I listen again. "Thanks a lot. Bye."

When I hang up, I say, "Denny said the washer came off. It took him a minute to put it back on, and there was never any flooding."

"Wow!" says Joe.

Bella shakes Evvie's arm. "What does that mean? What?"

Jack says, "It means that Abe might have taken the washer off himself and left the faucet running."

Sophie, arms still crossed, says, "So?"

Ida pokes her in the shoulder. "So it means he might have lied, and why do you think he might have done that?"

Sophie says, "I have no idea. You punch me again, I'm gonna punch you back."

Evvie says, "It could mean that he wanted to get Denny away from you so he could drive you to Hadassah."

Bella is practically in tears. "How were we supposed to know that?"

Ida is next. "How come it didn't make you wonder? Abe is not friendly. He never talks to anyone, except for Stanley. Have you ever seen him have anything to do with any of us?"

Sophie says nastily, "Big deal. We needed

a ride. He offered."

Jack says gently, "Bella, Sophie, try to remember what you talked about in his car. You did have a conversation, didn't you?"

Bella nods eagerly. She can handle that. "He wanted to know what was happening with the skeleton and we told him Gladdy was still on the case, and he said Gladdy is real smart and we said she sure is and she's at the police station right now telling Morrie what she knows. And then when we got there, he opened the door for us like a gentleman." She stops, out of breath.

"Oh, my God," says Evvie.

"The skeleton?" Joe says, surprised. "He wanted to know about the skeleton? And if he wanted to know about the skeleton, why didn't he ask Stanley?"

"Precisely why he got the girls in his car," I say. "He's already asked Stanley about it too many times. He didn't dare arouse Stanley's suspicion."

Ida mutters under her breath, "He went to the two weakest links."

Sophie glares at her. Bella hangs her head.

We all look at one another. The skeleton. No more coincidences. In my mind I can already connect the dots.

41
THE SKELETON CONNECTION

We've gone back and forth on this subject ad nauseam and discussion is still going strong. The noise level is high. Everyone talks at once. Lots of churning emotion in the air. To move around and stretch their cramped legs, the girls remove the breakfast dishes, but that doesn't stop conversation — they use the see-through cut in the wall between kitchen and dining room. Joe moves into the living room area and stretches out on the couch, still close enough to keep up his share of opinions.

"You shouldn't have gone into his car," says Evvie. "Big mouths, both of you."

Ida adds, "And then you don't tell us about it?"

"Enough already," says Sophie, thoroughly disgusted. "You never would've cracked the case if we hadn't. So as far as we're con- cerned" — she puts her arm around Bella — "without us, you never would've made the skeleton connection!"

"Yeah!" echoes Bella, "we're the heroines here."

"Some heroines. You've put Enya and Glad in danger," Evvie says angrily.

Joe says, "We're close. We'll watch over Enya, won't we, sugar pie?" Evvie nods in agreement.

Ida adds, "And I'm sure Jack will take care of Gladdy."

I glance over at her, listening for her usual sarcasm, but I don't detect any. Maybe she means what she says.

Jack salutes Ida.

We're spinning out of control. I rap on the dining room table. "Enough with the bickering. Let's put our thoughts in order." Jack leans back in his chair, watching me trying, yet again, to keep the girls on track.

Evvie reaches in her purse for the notebook that's always there. "Okay, shoot. I'll get it all down."

"First," I say, "and most important — as far as everyone outside this room is concerned, Enya did not have an . . . episode. She has the flu. All that banging was a call for help. We need a cleanup crew to put her apartment back in some order. Anyone asks questions, repairs are still from the hurricane."

Ida comments, "Lucky you were the only ones to walk in and see the mess. Hey, what about Mary?"

Evvie says, "We can trust her to keep quiet." She glares at Sophie and Bella. "Unlike some others."

Joe says to her, "Don't start again."

"Okay, okay." Evvie backs off.

Ida paces. Everyone watches her do laps around the table. She says, "What did she say, his face was different?"

Evvie says, "That could have been because of the beard." She starts to do stretching exercises. And of course her shadow, Joe, leaps off the couch to follow suit.

Now Sophie moves into the living room area and jumps up and down in place. And here goes Bella, who has to copy her actions.

Evvie adds as she does neck rolls, "And she said that he was big and heavy."

Sophie says, puffing, "So he lost weight by the time he got here."

By now they are all moving in different directions. "Could we all stay in one place?" I ask. "You're making me dizzy. Do you want to take a break?"

Everyone hurries back to their seats. "No, let's keep on," Evvie says.

However, we do take a few minutes to

refill coffee cups and water glasses.

"But Abe is Orthodox," Bella says.

Evvie says what I guess some of us are thinking: "What more evil way for a Nazi to hide?"

We are quiet for a few moments, imagining the horror of that.

Jack asks, "What are your thoughts on discussing this with Stanley?"

Again everyone talks at once.

"He'll have a heart attack," says Bella.

"He won't believe us," says Joe. "Not in a million years."

"He'll go right to Abe and tell him!" Ida says. "Stanley will never forgive us."

I hold my hands up. "Okay, table that. We don't say anything yet."

Jack says, "Let's review our logic. The skeleton is unearthed because of the hurricane. Stanley assumes, by where the body was found, that it had to have been buried at the time the condos were built, in 1958. A worker, a guy named Johnny Blake, went missing, so it was deduced that it must be his body. First we suspect some kind of accident. The police tell us, no accident — his head was crushed — it was murder.

"Gladdy and Stanley go to Tampa and find out Johnny Blake died six months earlier than that fateful night, right off the dock near where he lived and his body was found, and buried at a nearby church. His sister, Lucy, says she believes foul play.

"The forensics lab reports what they discover from the bones. Their findings show that it couldn't have been Johnny Blake of Tampa, nor could it be the man posing as Johnny Blake here. However, because of Lucy's P.O. box number, we know for sure there is a definite connection. So now let's call this unknown man X."

I add, "Lucy also tells us the ship her brother was on came from Argentina."

Sophie jumps in. "I read that that's where the Nazis went to hide from being caught as war criminals."

Jack continues. "Maybe X realizes somebody's stalking him in Argentina. So he stows away on the ship and picks Johnny as the one to kill to get a new identity. He throws him overboard and easily makes it off the ship with Johnny's ID. He wanders around and arrives at Fort Lauderdale, gets a job working on building these condos." Jack stops to take a drink from his glass of water.

I continue for him. "But maybe this stalker catches up to him. It could be someone from the camps who wanted revenge for killing his family. A Jewish man named Abe Waller."

Bella gasps. Hearing his name in this manner is chilling.

Evvie can't wait. "X probably murdered the entire Waller family so nobody ever comes looking for the real Abe Waller."

Jack continues. "We can imagine that in the middle of a terrible storm the two men fight to the finish. X is the stronger and he kills Abe Waller. So X has killed two men to keep himself safe."

Ida says fervently, "All right. But why didn't X keep using Johnny Blake's ID?"

Jack says, "My guess is, he kept track of Tampa news and found out about Johnny's body turning up. Here was a golden opportunity. He can't remain Johnny Blake, so now he becomes Abe Waller. When he leaves Johnny's stuff behind, it probably must be because he couldn't get back into his locker and he figures those old clothes would get thrown out."

Joe says, "Which Stanley, the pack rat, never disposed of. Safe for fifty years until you, Gladdy." He tips an imaginary hat to me.

Ida says, "But why would he do something so crazy and then move in and live where he buried the body? It doesn't make any sense."

I say, "We can only speculate. He comes back a year later, thinner and with a beard and mustache. No one would recognize him as the guy who worked on the construction site. Maybe he decided to hang about awhile to make sure the body wasn't found. Then he just stayed on. It's amazing how utterly realistic he's been playing the part. I mean, why take on such a difficult role? Fifty years of going to temple consistently with Stanley. Not just being Jewish, but Orthodox, the most rigorous and devout form of Judaism. Why didn't he leave when he was sure he was safe?"

Jack says, "Maybe he thought this was the ultimate disguise. No one would ever again recognize him. And he was right."

It gets very quiet and I say, "Time for a reality check. What if we're totally wrong and our imagination made up this entire scenario? What if Enya's behavior *was* irrational and we're reading Abe's actions incorrectly? Maybe Enya, cracking up, is delusional and for some sick, sad reason, she's picked on Abe. And what if Abe's innocent? This man has lived an impeccable, faith-filled, decent life. What if our carefully built-up assumptions are just that, assumptions — and we are about to destroy a man's life?"

"One thing's for sure," Jack says, "without knowing his real name, we have nothing to go on. We have no proof. It's all conjecture. But I have an idea . . ."

"Well?" says Evvie, never known for her patience. "Tell us. What?"

Jack looks at me and smiles. "We need to buy time. Glad, you're not going to like this, but we have to get people's minds off hurricanes and Enya and skeletons. Something to make Abe — if guilty — think he's safe. Only way to do that is give everyone something else to get excited about. An event that will make them happy. Now we spread the word about our engagement and upcoming wedding. And have a party to celebrate. That will give us time to come up with a plan."

That startles me. I had no intention of having any kind of party, that's not my style. I'm not thrilled with the idea, but Jack makes sense. I dread having to give the pool gang that ammunition. There goes romance. Good-bye, privacy.

Ida bursts into the laundry room on our floor, in a robe and with her bun unpinned, letting her salt-and-pepper hair fly. "What's with the call to come over here right away? I was just about to take a bath."

359

Now that our final partner is here, we turn to Evvie, who called this meeting for eight-thirty this evening. As if we hadn't had enough discussion today. She's busily filling a second washer with a load of clothes. "Thought I'd kill two birds with one stone," she tells us.

Ida says, "It couldn't keep 'til morning?"

With four of us girls already crowded in this small space, there's hardly room to move an arm or leg. We all push backward to make room for Ida.

"I had something on my mind," Evvie says, "and I wanted it settled tonight."

I come to my sister's aid: "Ev suggested that we cast our votes for whether we believe Enya is right about her fears. Or whether we don't believe Abe is really a wolf in sheep's clothing, so to speak."

Ida shakes her head. "But why here, now?"

Evvie shrugs. "I didn't want to hurt Joe's feelings by telling him he didn't have the right to vote." She pushes her garments around in the tub so they fit in evenly.

Ida tries to put her hands on her hips. There's no room, so she drops her arms.

Bella and Sophie watch the two of them bicker. Sophie gets bored and she examines her face in the small utility mirror, looking for new wrinkles. Bella plays with the coin lever, pulling it in and out.

"All right already, vote. My bathwater's getting cold. And what's with you and Joe anyway? Since when do you worry about his feelings?"

"Don't ask," Evvie says, looking toward me, who understands.

Sophie says, "My hand is ready to lift up, so let's go."

"Ditto," says Bella, "not that I'm in a hurry to go back to Dora. She's watching the reruns of the shows she watched this morning. I have such a headache from all the TV fighting and kissing and slamming doors."

They all turn to me as usual, their reluctant leader, so I proceed. I guess it's a good idea to see where we stand. "We heard a lot of stuff today and there was plenty to digest. If you're not sure yet, say so. Okay, who believes Enya is right about Abe being the Nazi she knew in the camps?"

Sophie's hand shoots up first. "I believe."

Bella is next. "I believe."

I say, "I believe."

Ida hesitates, and then her hand goes up, too.

Evvie laughs as she raises her hand as well. "I believe, and now all we need is for Tinker Bell to show up."

We all smile at that. A buzzer sounds to tell her the first load is dry.

"We done now?" Ida asks.

Evvie lugs out her dry clothes. "Done."

The secret society meeting is over and it's time to head for our homes. Except for me. Evvie beckons me to stay. She says, "We should go over and tell Enya. She must be on pins and needles. First I gotta finish my laundry."

It's past ten o'clock by the time Evvie's laundry is done. Lights are out everywhere. Evvie and I tiptoe along the second-floor landing where Evvie and Enya live. I take a quick look at Abe's kitchen window. No light there. Evvie leaves her filled laundry basket in front of her apartment.

Enya's been told we're coming, so she is waiting right at the door.

We slip into her apartment quickly. Enya looks a little better now that Mary is taking care of her.

"I'm so ashamed," she says. "About the way I behaved."

"Nonsense," says Evvie. "You had good reason."

Enya leads us to the living room. Evvie and I sit down on her old horsehair sofa. "Do you want anything?"

"No, thank you," we say.

Enya sits down at the edge of her chair and looks at us like she's a prisoner at the dock, waiting to hear the verdict.

I say, "Enya, we believe you. But we have a very big problem. Without knowing his real name, our hands are tied. We have to have proof."

Enya shakes her head. "If only I could remember. There were so many of them. We never knew their names. But this one, *Der Bösewicht* — we gave him that nickname because he frightened us more than any of the others — he was truly evil."

Evvie adds, "We aren't giving up. We'll find a way to prove you're right."

Enya's tears start to flow. The tension this woman has to be under must be unbearable. She comes over to us and grabs one of my hands and one of Evvie's. "Thank you. Thank you."

Still clutching our hands, Enya is lost in her troubled thoughts for a few moments. "The things they did, he did. I cannot bear to speak of them. I will not put you through having to listen to these abominations." She pauses, wipes the tears from her eyes. "That he has lived freely among us for nearly fifty years horrifies me. That he lived as a Jewish man is unbearable."

She stares into space. How she survived what she went through is almost unimaginable to me. I say, "I know you're exhausted. Try to rest. We'll keep bringing food to you. Stay put. Do not go out, and be very careful before you answer the door."

"I am so frightened. Does he know I recognized him?"

She walks with us to the door. "Bless you for caring."

We hug and kiss her and tiptoe out.

42
Party, Party, Party

Good news travels faster than the speed of light. At least that's the way it seems in Lanai Gardens, Phase Two. This beautiful morning at the pool is the perfect place to hand out invitations to the Gladdy-Jack engagement party, which we had made up a few days ago. Bella and Sophie are assigned one end of the pool to dole them out, as far from Abe as possible. Evvie and Ida take the section that includes Abe, seated as usual behind the little black metal gate in the shade. Watching us, I now realize, always watching us.

My job is to wander about, showing off my ring, wearing a silly grin.

Sophie and Bella have on large, floppy sun hats, and huge wraparound very dark sunglasses, terrified of letting their faces show their fear. Any more mistakes in what they do or say could be dangerous. They're in trouble, as it is, for spilling the beans to Abe.

They especially won't look in our alleged Nazi's direction, afraid he can read them like a book.

From what I can see of his eyes, behind the thick glasses, they seem hooded. You don't fool me, *Oberführer*. I know you're watching us like a hawk. But you've met your match in Evvie Markowitz, who is heading over right now to hand you your invitation. I leisurely stroll by to catch the action.

He will try to stare Evvie down, but she, who believes she might have been an Oscar-winning actress had life not tossed her into marrying Joe, won't blink. "This is for you, Abe," says Evvie, playing an older Little Miss Sunshine. "And don't you try to wiggle out of coming." That's said with a waggling hand demonstrating the wiggle. "Stanley and Esther already RSVP'd because they know we're doing it right. Steinberg's kosher restaurant is catering."

Stanley was happy about my news and told me how he and Abe sometimes after temple go out for lunch at Steinberg's, their favorite eating place. Perfect.

Abe manages what I read as a slick smile. "I wouldn't think of missing it."

Tessie arrives at the gate, carrying a now empty soup tureen. I knew she would be passing by, since it was I who planted this idea in her head, to bring the poor "flu" victim some chicken soup.

"How's Enya doing?" I say, not looking at Abe. I have to keep calling him Abe and thinking of him as Abe or I'll lose my cool.

"A little better," Tessie reports. "Poor thing. I can't believe how high her fever went the other night. Lucky she didn't die."

Well done, Tessie. I couldn't have scripted it better myself. But, of course, we've been spreading that "dangerous case of flu" story with "Enya becoming delirious" for days. Since Tessie knows nothing, she reveals nothing.

Hy, after immediately responding yes to the party, announces, "For this great occasion, a toast." He lifts his Dr. Brown's Cel-Ray tonic bottle and points toward Jack and me, the engaged couple. Jack, from where he lounges, reading a Michael Connolly detective novel, nods. I perform a silly curtsy.

I look around to see the response. Mary and Irving smile happily. Barbi and Casey grin slyly. Tessie sits down next to her hubby and shouts, "Hooray!" Sol shakes his head sadly. I guess marriage isn't agreeing with him. Aha, Louise is sitting there with her mouth wide open in shock. Close your mouth, lady. As my mom used to say, You don't want to let the flies in. Tiny Dora is jumping up and down. I can't believe it, is that a TV clicker in her hand?

Directly across the way, in Denny's garden, he and Yolie stop their planting and pay attention to what's going on. They are thrilled at what they hear.

Tessie takes another look at her invitation. "Wait a minute. This Friday. So fast?"

Hy, annoyed at being interrupted, says, "At our age, who makes long-term plans?"

Tessie, suitably chastened, shuts up.

Hy instructs, "Those who have bottles to raise, get 'em up." Water bottles and juices wave on high. Those without beverages just wave.

"To the engaged couple . . ." He indicates we should come to him. In order to make this plan of ours look like all is back to normal, we agreed earlier to put up with whatever nonsense comes up. Naturally, it would be Hy who finds a way to torment us. Jack rises from his chaise, and he and I walk over to where Hy is now standing. Jack kisses me and whispers, "Any excuse, babe."

Hy hands Lola his drink and puts one arm across my shoulders and one across Jack's. I grit my teeth.

Hy stares into my eyes and speaks loud

enough for all to hear — and believe me, everyone is zoomed onto us and listening. "Here's to the love that lies in a woman's eyes — and lies and lies and lies."

I try to pull away, but he doesn't let me. Everybody laughs. He leers at Jack, whose turn it is. Watch out, Hy, Jack's no pushover.

Hy's eyes practically twinkle. Lola stands behind him, ready to save him from Jack if necessary. He says, "Here's to the happiest days of your life, spent in the arms of another man's wife!"

Hy pulls his hands away, fast. Jack shakes his fist mildly in a pretense of anger.

Hy pulls Lola in front of him for protection. Jack wouldn't hit a woman, would he? "It's your *mother*. In your *mother's* arms," Hy croaks. Then weakly, "She's another man's wife, right?"

Jack, who towers above little Hy, reaches past Lola and runs his hands playfully over Hy's balding head. "Good one," Jack says, laughing.

I'm glad that's finished.

On our way back from the pool, Evvie, as instructed, knocks on Enya's door. Enya peers through the peephole, then barely opens it.

"Are you all right?" Evvie asks.

Enya nods. "Yes."

"Need anything?" I ask.

"No, I'm fine. Tessie's soup will hold me."

"Just checking. Things are moving along."

"Thank you," she says.

They gaze at each other, lips smiling, but their eyes reveal their fear.

"He was there, wasn't he?" Enya asks.

"He always is," Evvie says. "Listening to every word we say, watching every move we make."

"Be careful. He is the Devil."

"We will."

43
THE PLAN

"Are you crazy?" Sophie asks. "Tomorrow?"

"He'll kill you if he catches you," Bella speaks up, shaking with fear.

"Yes tomorrow," says Joe, who seems to have slid into place as the newest addition to our investigating group, and nobody seems to mind. Neither is Evvie complaining about the fact that Joe sticks to her like flypaper. Hmm, whatever happened to that gooey, disgusting product? I wonder for no good reason whatsoever.

Evvie also agrees. "Yes, let's move it up."

Ida says, "I can't wait. I wish we could do it now. The tension is killing me."

We sit in a secluded area near Denny's beautiful garden. No one is around usually at mid-afternoon. It's rest time or preparing-dinner time or off to early-bird-dinner time. Quiet enough for what we're scheming. We even have knitting and crocheting stuff in our laps in case anyone does come by and is curious.

Evvie says, "Tomorrow, being just before the Sabbath, we know for sure Abe will be at the synagogue most of the day."

"But why would you want to do it on the day of your party? It'll be a zoo." Bella doesn't like any of this. Short notice always makes her nervous.

"That's what I'm counting on," I answer. "People will be too busy to see what we're up to. Besides, I'll be a wreck waiting for the party — I already have my outfit picked out, so at least this will keep me busy."

Joe has a worry. "What if he doesn't go to temple?"

"He always goes on Friday," says Evvie.

Joe can't let it go. "But what if . . ."

Evvie puts her fingers on his lips. "Shhh, worry-wart."

"We can always get him out on a pretense," says Ida.

"Like what?" Sophie asks.

"We can tell him there's a meeting of the Bund," Ida says wickedly.

Evvie, Joe, and I grimace. We're all old enough to remember there was once an actual club of members of the Nazi party right here in our country.

"Kidding," says Ida. "We'll think of something. But there's no reason for him to change his routine."

Bella raises her hand. "But . . . but I have to go to the beauty parlor."

Evvie says, "Bella, honey, you and Sophie always have early-morning Friday appointments. You'll have plenty of time to help us."

I cut in. "Let me say a few words here. I doubt that Abe has been fooled by our charade and I have a very strong feeling that he is up to something. I can't even imagine what he might be planning. Frankly, I'm afraid to guess. I feel we need to move fast and catch him off guard."

"Besides," Ida says, "we can't keep Enya locked up forever. We have to find a way to end this."

"Okay," says Evvie, "let's go over it again. Naturally, as president of the Condo Association, I have, like Denny, a master key of all apartments. We make sure no one's looking, and we sneak in."

I wait for Bella and Sophie to stop squirming, and I say, "Bella and Sophie are on watch, sitting in the back of my car with a cell phone."

Bella raises her hand. "I still don't get that."

Sophie pokes her. "I do. It's right across from Abe's parking spot, so we'll know exactly when he drives in. And he won't see us."

Bella nods slowly, digesting the information again.

I say, "Ida, Evvie, and I do the search. Joe waits with Enya in her Florida room, next door, in case we have to make an emergency exit. If so, we climb from Abe's apartment into Enya's, with Joe's help."

Luckily for us, the hurricane blew out all our sunroom screens and none of us have fixed them yet.

"What do we tell Enya?" Bella asks.

I say, "We tell her exactly what we're doing."

Sophie asks, "What if you don't find anything?"

"Honestly, I don't know," I say. "We just have to hope we do."

Joe says, "I have a question for you, Glad. What will you tell Jack?"

Before I can answer, a familiar voice is heard behind me. "Tell Jack what?" my beloved asks as he walks up to us. "I've been searching all over for you. What's this, some kind of class?"

Everyone freezes on the spot. I thought I'd be alone when I dealt with Jack on this subject, but no such luck. I take a deep breath. "We've been discussing a plan on how to prove Abe's guilt."

Silence as Jack looks from one anxious face to another.

"Speaking of guilt," he says. "May I make a guess?"

Sophie and Bella nod frantically. They squirm around in their chairs, wishing, I assume, that they were anywhere but here.

"What I read in your faces is that you've already decided on a plan."

More nods from those two. Everyone else remains rigid.

"And since I wasn't included in this get-together . . ." He pauses to address Joe. "Knitter or crocheter?"

Joe shrugs, flashing a silly grin along with it. "Family kibitzer," he explains.

Jack continues, "Perhaps this plan has something not quite kosher about it?"

Sophie and Bella nod again, their heads bobbing up and down like apples in a barrel.

Ida can't stand it anymore. She shrieks at the two of them, "Stop nodding!"

Both heads bow down.

I try to salvage the situation. "Jack, honey, shall we continue this upstairs? Alone?"

"Not really," he says. "Just go on with your meeting." He kisses me on my cheek. "Shall I start dinner, my love?"

"Whatever," I say meekly. Ooh, oh, I'm in hot water now.

I smell something wonderful cooking as I open the door and stand in the doorway of the kitchen. Jack is busy chopping vegetables.

"Lemon curried chicken?" I ask, in a most docile manner.

"Might be the last meal I cook for you if certain things don't change around here," he says without turning around.

This startles me. He says the words softly, but there's steel behind them. I feel my heart begin to pound. "May the condemned woman say a few words on her own behalf?"

Jack moves over and stirs something in a pot. "Might I suggest some words — like 'We changed our minds and are not going through with this dangerous plan'?"

"Jack, honey —"

"Or 'I hereby promise to discuss my plans with my future husband before, not after, deciding to break the law.' You do intend to enter Abe's apartment without his permission?"

I pause. I cannot tell a lie. "Yes. But Evvie, as condo president, has the right to enter an apartment if she thinks it's necessary."

"If I recall, for it to be legal, the tenant

must be given twenty-four hours' notice, and a reason."

I shrug. I know he's right. No way we can do that.

He turns and holds me by the shoulders. "It's one thing to go after an elderly guy robbing banks, which, by the way, was handled recklessly. You should have called for backup."

"But it wasn't clear what Ida was doing. It seemed odd that she was taking us to what seemed like a psychic. And besides, Grandpa wasn't dangerous."

"You couldn't have known that for sure, going to where he lived. He used a gun in those robberies."

I interrupt with desperation, "We didn't know if it was a real one."

"My point exactly. You didn't have enough information. You behaved hastily. And now, in this situation, you're rushing in again, without considering the terrible danger of going into this man's home. If you're right about Abe Waller, and clearly you believe you are, the man you're taking on is a mass murderer. A man trained to kill. And after leaving the camps, he murdered two other men, ostensibly simply to cover his tracks. Don't you think you're a little out of your league?"

"But you said it yourself: We have no name. There's no evidence."

"Let Morrie handle it. That's his job."

"There's no way to arrest Abe. Asking Morrie for help is useless. We don't have enough for him to get a search warrant. This Nazi has outsmarted everyone for fifty years."

Jack drops his hands and looks deep into my eyes and I see such worry in his. "And you believe *you* can outsmart him?"

I don't know what to say. I don't know how to plead my case. He is absolutely right, of course. Am I guilty of arrogance? I feel like I'm walking on quicksand. "Is what we're having called a serious quarrel?"

"You could say that."

I blurt, "Big enough for you to break off our engagement if I don't do what you want?"

He is almost surprised at my outburst. "Careful, dear, you're dealing in absolutes now. Do you want me to lay down an ultimatum?"

I sit down on the kitchen chair and hold my breath. Will what he says next determine the course of the rest of my life? I'm amazed at how scared I am. The silence is so long, I can hear my teeth clench.

He sits down next to me. "I have one last

question." He reaches over and takes my hands in his. "Answer carefully."

I gulp. "Shoot," I say with false courage.

"If I were not in your life, if we'd never met and it was just you and your girls living the way you used to, would you be going through with those plans tomorrow?"

I hesitate and think long and hard. I look him right in those gorgeous eyes. I know I'm getting too emotional, and I could possibly lose this man I love, but I have to make him understand how strongly I feel. "Damned straight I would. As the Jewish people of the world said after the war, 'Never again!' "

Jack doles out our dinner and brings our plates into the dining room, where he has already set the table. I think about what I might lose. I shudder. I ask, and I'm terrified of his answer, "What are you going to do?"

He sits down and says, "You do what you do and I'll do what I do."

With that, he digs in.

Dinner is very quiet; bedtime, even more so.

44
A Date to
Remember

I didn't sleep much last night, but when I finally did and woke up after eight, Jack was gone. I'm sure he didn't sleep too well, either. Nor, I imagine, did the girls. What have I gotten us all into? How can I put my sister and my dear friends at such risk? Should I call it off? I can't be angry at Jack. Everything he said was right. But what's my alternative? Tell Morrie to take it over and hope that someday, someway, he'll find out the truth? Doubtful. Besides, will anything we discover be admissible in court? But there is a higher court out there. And the groups, started by Simon Wiesenthal, to this day track down Nazis as war criminals. They won't give up until the last one is dead or caught. But I'll come across as an idiot when I turn in a religious Jewish man in his eighties who has done good deeds all his life, and has papers that prove he is Abe Waller. I'm sure the numbers he tattooed on his arm nearly half a century ago belong to the real Abe Waller. I'm betting he hasn't made a single mistake.

Will Enya dare to come out of her apartment until Abe finally goes back to Phase Six when it's rebuilt? But that could be six months or more. And even then? The voice in my head says this man will not sit still. We haven't fooled him. He is planning something. We must find a clue. I've opened a Pandora's box and I've got to close it somehow. The truth is, I'm terrified. And I'm so tired, I can barely move my aching body.

We meet, as planned, in Enya's apartment, right next door to his. Everyone looks tired and drawn. Joe, imitating Jack, made us breakfast. It was only cereal and toast, and very kind of him, but no one eats a bite. We drink coffee, too much. Enya has gone to her bedroom to lie down. Needless to say, she is very stressed out.

Ida says, "Jack was sore, wasn't he?"

I nod. "He thinks what we are doing is foolhardy and very dangerous. I have to ask this before we go any further — do you want out? I'm sure it must be on everyone's mind."

The girls, one by one, shake their heads slowly.

Bella shivers. "But what if we fail you?"

"You won't," I say. "You can't miss watching his parking spot."

"What if the cell phone doesn't work?" Sophie asks.

"I've thought of that," I say. "I've brought another one for you. They're both charged and ready. Just make sure you aren't noticed."

"What if someone sees us anyway?" Sophie asks.

Ida answers, "Then make up something, like you're waiting for us and we're late."

Sophie comments, "Yeah, right. Only an idiot sits in the backseat of a hot car doing nothing for an hour."

Ida says, "I rest my case."

For a moment Sophie is angry, then Ida shrugs and grins. "I'm pulling your leg."

We all smile and it relaxes us for maybe a second.

Joe speaks to Sophie and Bella. "I'm volunteering to be your backup. I'm going to be watching from up here, from the living room window. Then, if anything goes wrong, I'll know, too."

Bella sighs, relieved.

"Besides," Evvie says, "hopefully we'll be through in less than an hour."

"Last instructions," I say to Evvie and Ida.

"I'm repeating myself, but I can't say it enough: No matter what happens, every single thing you touch must be left exactly as you found it. One tiny mistake and he'll know we've been in there."

They both nod vigorously.

"We better get started. He's already gone two hours; it looks good to go." In my head I'm wondering where Jack is. But don't go there, I tell myself, I've got to keep my head very clear.

Everyone hugs and kisses. Even Joe. Enya comes out of her room to watch us leave. She seems as frail as an eggshell.

As planned, Evvie goes first, glances around, then quickly uses her master key and slides into Abe's apartment. Ida's next, she looks, too, then I follow.

"My heart's hammering like crazy," Evvie whispers as we look around Abe Waller's meticulous apartment. The Canadian family, the Dumas, who owns the condo, only uses it as a vacation home, so thankfully there is very little furniture, other than the basics, to deal with.

I blab, also whispering, "Don't miss ice trays, hollow legs of chairs, in bottoms of socks, coffee cans, inside lamps — underneath drawers, for taped stuff. Probably never under mattresses. Too obvious."

I feel a calm coming over me. Now that we're here and committed, I breathe easier. We can handle this. We'll be all right.

We walk slowly from room to room as a first survey. Evvie manages a nervous smile. "You get that stuff from all those mysteries you read."

"You bet," I say.

Ida heads for the kitchen. Evvie, the bathroom, to be followed by the bedroom. I take the living room and then the Florida room. We work slowly and methodically.

I hear Evvie say, "This is so spooky."

For a long while that's the last thing said, as we intensely examine everything. Every drawer, every cupboard. All the places I thought might be hiding places. But nothing speaks of Abe. There were only the possessions left by the Dumas. Surely he must have personal things somewhere. Not even a toothbrush, reports Evvie from the bathroom. How is this possible?

We take a very short break after half an hour to stand in the kitchen for a drink of water. Then, carefully, we wash and dry our glasses and put them exactly where they were.

"Weird," says Ida, "it's as if no one lives here. There doesn't seem to be anything of his own. Not even a piece of mail to be found."

I say, "Well, don't forget, he lost his things in the hurricane."

"Yes, but they were all allowed to go back to Phase Six and get whatever stuff wasn't ruined," Evvie reminds me. "I'm sure he found some things."

"Even if he didn't, it still seems strange. Not a book or magazine? Not a careless shirt, or whatever, tossed over the back of a chair?" Ida says.

"And nothing in the bathroom medicine cabinet? Not even a bottle of aspirin? No dirty clothes in the hamper?" Evvie is incredulous.

"Okay, back to work," I say.

Evvie tries for a joke. "I can't wait to see what his underwear looks like."

We disperse to our areas of search.

A few minutes later Evvie utters a small scream and comes running out. Her eyes glitter. "Get in here, now!"

She runs back to the bedroom with the two of us racing after her. She indicates the open closet door. In the corner is a large suitcase.

"At first I thought it was just parked there, but when I started to move it, it was heavy."

Pull it out," Ida says excitedly. "Maybe

that's where he hides his stuff."

"Carefully," I say, "watch exactly how it was placed in the closet."

Evvie tries to lift it. She can't. I help her pull it out. "Fingers crossed," I say as I reach for the snaps to open it.

I try a few times, but it's locked. "Bad luck. I bet he has the key with him."

We are let down.

I feel for an outside pocket. "Wait, there's something . . ." I pull out a long, narrow, black leather folder and open it.

"Oh, my God," Evvie says, over my shoulder. "Airline tickets. To where? When?"

"Buenos Aires," I read. "Tonight. Late."

"We knew it! We knew he was up to something. He's gonna make a run for it." Evvie jumps up and down in excitement. "No wonder we couldn't find anything personal. Everything he owns must be in here!"

Ida leans over me, squinting without her glasses. "What's his name?" she demands of me.

Disappointed, I tell her, "It says Abe Waller on tickets and passport."

"Damn," says Evvie. "And we dare not break the lock open."

I dig deeper into the fold. Something is lodged down there. I pull it out. It's a small patch of cloth wrapped around a signet ring. Evvie grabs the patch; Ida, the ring.

"There's a large cross on here," Evvie says.

"And one on the ring."

"I've seen this before," Evvie says, "in movies."

"It's called the Iron Cross," I say in wonder. "I read about it a long time ago. I think it's the highest award German soldiers ever get."

We look at one another, happily astonished, big smiles on our faces.

I look on the back of the Iron Cross patch. "We've got him!" I say. "There's a number. I bet somewhere there's a match with his real name. We've got to copy down the number."

Evvie grins happily, grabbing the patch from me so she can examine it more thoroughly.

My cell phone rings. Evvie actually jumps. The three of us stare at the instrument with foreboding. He can't be back! He mustn't! I answer. Sophie and Bella are screaming into our ears. "He just drove in! He's back! Get out! Get out!"

At the same time we can hear Joe shouting Evvie's name from Enya's rear sunporch.

■ ■ ■ ■

I feel like I'm moving in slow motion as I shove the black folder back into the side pocket.

Ida is quietly hysterical. "I don't remember which way the suitcase went in!"

Evvie, breathless, pushes it in the corner.

"The zipper part was in back!" I say, terrified now. "Wasn't it?" Evvie's not sure, but we're out of time and we leave it.

We close the closet and run from the bedroom to the Florida room. Please, God, don't fail us now.

What a crazy idea, I think, looking at our escape route. What could I possibly have been thinking! We have to climb through the windows where screens used to be and jump two feet over air to get next door.

Trying to hide his fear, Joe thrusts his arms out Enya's window as far as he can reach, and grabs Evvie by her forearms as she balances herself on the window ledge. She looks down at the empty area between both screened porches.

"Don't look down," Joe says, too late. "When I say three, jump toward me!"

Evvie looks at us, eyes wild, then to Joe.

Ida and I hold our breath as Evvie jumps.

Joe pulls her through Enya's side window, but for a moment, it looks like Evvie is flying.

All I can think is, I'm looking at a seventy-five-year-old man's flabby arms, unused to exercise, along with his arthritic hands. Will he have the strength to pull all three of us?

Ida gives me a panicky look, and then focuses on Joe. She bends her knees, waits until Joe has her arms in his grasp. She leaps out and up toward him. She's so fast, the two of them fall backwards into the room.

Now it's my turn, and Joe's arms are shaking from the strain. I call to him, "Joe, get Ev and Ida behind you, and have them both hold on to your waist. Hurry."

He doesn't stop to question me; he understands how weak he is now. He turns inside to tell the girls.

My eyes dart toward the front of Abe's apartment, expecting any second for him to come in and find me there with no place to hide.

Joe turns back to me. "They're ready."

I step out on the ledge. I look down in spite of myself. If I fall I'll probably break my neck dropping two stories, or at least my legs.

I reach my arms out. Joe grabs on to them, gripping me as tightly as he can. He looks at me and I can see the fear there. He counts to three.

I jump.

And miss Enya's window ledge. Suddenly I'm hanging straight down, with nothing but air under me. I feel Joe's arms sliding down my arms, to my hands. I clutch his hands tightly.

"Pull!" Joe screams to Evvie and Ida behind him. "Pull me inside!"

Within seconds I am jerked up the side of the building and into the room, just as Joe loses his grip.

All four of us fall to the floor, one on top of the other, panting breathlessly.

My stomach and legs are scratched and bloody from bouncing off the building. But at least I'm in one piece.

Evvie throws her arms around Joe, laughing and crying at the same time. "My hero," she says, hugging him tightly.

I see Enya standing in the doorway, holding her breath.

"I'm all right," I tell her to allay her fears.

"The bastard came back early," Ida mutters. "Why?"

Joe tries to calm us as well as himself. "But it's okay, you got out safely. And you left everything the way it was. Right?"

"I think so," Ida says unsteadily.

Evvie stares down at her hands. "Oh, no," she cries out. We look at her, still clutching the small patch of cloth in her left hand. The small patch with its distinctive Iron Cross.

45
ENGAGED

Hearing a commotion coming from down-stairs, we hurry to the living room window and stare out and down. A group of people are gathered and chattering directly under us.

Ida says, "They're circling around Abe's car."

"Something's blocking our view. I can't see what it is," says Evvie.

Ida points. "Look over there. It's Abe. And he's talking to Jack!"

Abe is still downstairs? With Jack? What's going on?

Evvie rushes to the front door. "I can't stand it. I've got to see what's happening." She opens the door and rushes out onto the landing.

Ida and I are right behind her. Not only can we see, over the balcony, but we can easily hear. I feel Joe and Enya peeking over my shoulder. I can see Sophie and Bella standing near my car, watching anxiously.

Jack, my ex-cop, seems to be in charge. I hear him say to Abe, "I can't imagine how it happened." He looks around. "Anybody see how this big thing got here?"

What a sight before our eyes. A huge garbage Dumpster that, according to the letter on its side, belongs to R building has somehow managed to roll forward and smash the front of Abe's Pontiac, denting the hood severely.

Abe is angry, but he's trying to hide it. "How is it possible? That Dumpster is always at the side of the building. How could it get from there to here?"

Lots of surprised shrugs. Apparently, none of the gawkers had seen anything, since no one ventures forth with information.

Evvie whispers to me, "Jack must have done it. He stopped Abe from coming upstairs."

"Yes," I say, choked up. He might not have approved of what I was doing, but he wasn't about to let anything happen to me, either. But I shudder to think what would have happened if Jack hadn't been watching our backs. We've just had a very close call.

"I'm a witness," says a familiar voice behind me. I hadn't even heard Hy approach us from his apartment down the walkway.

We turn. "What?" I say, nervously.

Hy speaks very softly. "Your boyfriend is the culprit. I saw him roll the Dumpster over earlier, and as soon as Abe drove in Jack leaned down behind the Dumpster and pushed it hard. Anybody want to tell me what's going on?"

Oh, no, I think to myself. Not Hy, the town crier!

A chorus of six (which includes Joe) says in unison, "No!"

Hy performs a zipping motion across his lips. "No problem. Your secret is safe with me. If Jack is into car demolition, he must have a very good reason. Let me in on it when you're ready."

He pauses, and grins. "Here's a joke for you. Husband comes home. His wife's wearing a sexy negligee and is all tied up with ropes. She says seductively, 'You can do anything you want to do.' So he walks back out and goes to play golf." He laughs at his own joke. "I got dozens more. Saving 'em for tonight's engagement party!" With that he struts back toward his open door, where Lola stands watching.

Ida says, "I can hardly wait."

We hear Jack saying in a loud voice, "Just call your insurance company, Abe. Bye, see you later." He's warning us. Abe is climbing up the stairs. We scurry back inside, fast!

Once inside, Joe asks, "What do we do now?"

"Talk to your Jack," Enya says. "He'll know."

I lie on my couch with a cold compress on my eyes and forehead. I have a bad headache that makes me see stars; it hurts that much. My left eye keeps twitching and it won't stop. Jack brings me another wet towel to exchange for the one I have.

"Feel any better?" he asks.

"No," I groan.

"Maybe if we talk about it, your pain will go away."

"Ouch," I mutter. "I doubt it."

"You can't go to your party like this, so let's try. I'll start first. I want to tell you how *I* feel. Waiting helplessly downstairs while I knew you were in Abe's apartment reminded me of Faye. I finally truly understand — I mean, I thought I understood, but I didn't, viscerally — what Faye felt all those years being married to a cop. She told me she would worry every day, with panic rising — would I come home, still in one piece, or would it be one of my pals from the precinct at the door, to tell her how I died."

I lift the compress and turn my throbbing head to see him better.

"Today, I was Faye. Waiting to see if you came out alive. I couldn't stand it. In all my years as a cop, I was never as afraid as I was this morning."

I weakly reach over to take his hand in mine. "I'm sorry I put you through that. But I felt I had to do it. And we succeeded. We have proof. Finally." I look at him, pleadingly. "Doesn't the end justify the means?"

"Glad, that's not the point. It could have ended very badly, and —"

I interrupt. "But didn't you push the Dumpster into his car? And bought us time to escape? Wouldn't you say you broke the law a bit, too? Didn't the end justify the means then, too?"

He sits me down and pulls me close. "I wouldn't be able to stand it if I lost you."

"Please say you forgive me. Please?"

He crushes me closer. "I do, but promise never to scare me like that again."

"I do. I do." We rock back and forth in each other's arms. This is no time to tell him about how I got scratches on my body.

A few moments later, he asks, "How's the

headache? How do you feel now?"

I think about it. My headache is nearly gone. "Better. Much better."

I kiss him long and hard. "I absolutely give you permission to save my life any chance you get."

I make two phone calls.

"Morrie. Big news. We have the proof we need on Abe." I fill him in on the iron cross without mentioning where and how I got it — later for that. And also about Abe's plane reservations.

Morrie says, "I'll alert the airline not to let him on the plane tonight."

"You've got to catch him before he can get out of the country."

"I'm on it," Morrie says.

The second call is to Stanley. "Can you meet us at the clubhouse an hour before our party? Without Esther?"

"What? Is something wrong?"

"Yes," I say. "Something is very wrong."

We need to inform Stanley before the police do.

46
SHOWDOWN

So here we are in the clubhouse, dressed in our finest. We, who live in sundresses and shorts, had to dig through our closets for cocktail dresses and heels. I'm wearing a peach organza dress, last worn for my daughter Emily's wedding, in New York. It still fits, thank goodness. Evvie is wearing a multi-colored caftan-type dress, all swirly, with lots of folds. Sophie and Bella have matching lemon and lime outfits they bought for a bar mitzvah years ago. Sophie tugs at her dress, realizing she's gained a few pounds since the last time she wore it.

And Ida — well, Ida owns one basic black dress, and that's that. We were going to go shopping, but what with Enya's problem, we decided to make do with what we had. Frankly, I'm just as pleased. I confess, I don't like shopping. And besides, Jack, having never seen me dressed up, whistled when I modeled the peach number to get his opinion.

Jack looks wonderful in a dark suit and tie. Joe, who insists he threw out every tie he owned when he moved here, wears a sports jacket.

We're surrounded by cheerful decorations put up by an energetic, romantic group of Phase Two friends. Lots of balloons and greeting cards with congratulations. There is a large shoji-type screen off to one side with smiling photos they've gathered of me, then Jack, then both of us together. The catered food sits on tables, waiting for the party to begin.

We may be dressed for a party but anxiety is the group emotion. The seven of us are standing, facing the front door, waiting for Stanley. Enya, dressed simply in a beige dress, sits on a chair, all by herself, away from us. There is a strange kind of calm about her. What must she be thinking?

Stanley will arrive any minute. I'm not looking forward to breaking this man's heart.

There's the expected knock on the door and Stanley enters, a puzzled look on his face. "Esther doesn't know why she should stay home and I come an hour earlier."

"You'll explain later," I tell him.

Stanley looks from one face to another.

He sees worry, concern, fear, nervousness. "I better sit down." He uses one of the folding chairs facing us. "You all look like somebody died."

Jack moves behind me and rubs my shoulders. I take a deep breath. "Someone did die, but it was fifty years ago. And we found his skeleton recently."

Stanley is ready to smile. "You've solved it, haven't you?" He half stands, about to come forward. "Congratulations."

"Don't!" Evvie blurts. "Please sit back down."

Startled, Stanley lowers his body once more, worry furrowing his brows.

I go on. "Stanley, dear, I have to warn you, it's taken us a while to be able to believe what we now know, and I expect it will be very difficult for you to accept. But we found proof."

Bella nervously needs to get water from the drinks table. I wait until she comes back. This time, she takes a seat. I can see her trembling.

"You know the name of the dead body?" Stanley asks eagerly.

"Yes." I close my eyes for a moment, not wanting to see the expression that will be on his face in a moment. "Abe Waller."

A deadly silence sinks in. Sophie gasps as

Stanley clutches the sides of the flimsy wooden chair for support. His face has gone pale.

Bella rushes forward to give him her water, but he shakes his arms in refusal.

"What do you mean?" He is alarmed now. "What can you possibly mean?"

I twist around to Jack and indicate that he should take over.

"It means," Jack says, "that the man who murdered Johnny Blake in Tampa, and took his identity, murdered another man, that night at your construction site. His next victim was a survivor of the camps who tracked down the Nazi who killed his family —"

A new voice interrupts, "Very bad manners to talk about a person behind his back."

We all spin around quickly, to see an unfamiliar man standing in the doorway. He enters and shuts the door behind him. It takes a few moments to realize the large, slightly bent over, clean shaven, no longer bearded man, sporting a barber-styled haircut and wearing a tan suit and tie, is the man we've known as Abe Waller. Now that I can see the face, it's an ordinary face, but it reveals hardness. He's no longer wearing glasses, and the scar that circles his left eye is faded, but still identifiable. I glance at his

401

hands and, to my horror, he's wearing the signet ring.

Stanley looks mystified, unable to comprehend what he sees.

"There I was, ready to take my leave, when I see my dear friend Stanley hurrying to the clubhouse, looking very perturbed. I couldn't resist following him."

Stanley, now realizing who this apparition is, almost falls off his chair as he jumps up. "No!" he shouts, righting himself. "This cannot be."

I look at Enya, who remains calm amid the chaos in the room. Bella and Sophie are clutching each other. Ida and Evvie are rigid, eyes darting. Joe takes a few steps, bringing him next to Evvie. Jack removes his hands from my shoulders and I can practically feel his body move into alert mode. He takes a stance in front of us. "Jack, dearest," I whisper desperately to his back, "don't do anything foolish."

The man we knew as Abe moves to the side of the room. I see what Jack sees. The Nazi is nearing Enya.

He smiles. "You might as well hear it, from what you call the horse's mouth. As you probably guessed, I came back to Lanai Gardens all those years ago, to make sure Abe Waller's body hadn't been unearthed."

I look at Stanley, hoping he won't have a heart attack. Stanley appears numb.

I wonder what Jack is thinking. We didn't expect this. But we should have.

"Abe" smiles at Stanley, and it isn't a pretty sight. "And lo and behold, the first person I meet standing in front of the pristine building Z is Stanley. I am wearing a fake beard and dark clothes to make sure no one recognizes me as the former Johnny Blake, and Stanley immediately assumes I am Jewish. What an amusing joke. I have a Jewish man's identity in my pocket and now I'm being welcomed with open arms because Stanley thinks I am like him. How can I resist such friendship? I get my brilliant idea. I'll live here among them for a while to make sure no one is looking for Abe Waller and then I'll leave."

My girls, behind me, must be holding their breaths, listening to this, realizing we're in terrible trouble. I hear one of them gasp.

What goes through my mind, based on reading hundreds of mysteries, is that killers never confess unless they are sure they will leave no witnesses. What will Jack do? What *can* he do? I'm sure the Nazi has a weapon, and Jack will die first! God help us.

As if reading my mind, Abe says, "By the

way, allow me to introduce myself. My name is Horst Kolb. Formerly of Munich, Germany."

Enya sighs deeply, and then calmly says, "Formerly *Oberführer* Kolb, known as *Der Bösewicht,* of Auschwitz," as if a great secret has finally been revealed and a huge weight lifted.

Stanley's face turns ashen.

I groan. We are going to die. All of us.

Horst Kolb, as I might as well call him, seems very relaxed, but his clenched fists betray him. "At first I am highly entertained, wearing Jew clothes and going to temple with my new best friend." He glances at Stanley, whose body begins to sway and his lips move in fervent prayer.

Now Kolb looks toward Enya, who hasn't taken her eyes off his face. "But something unexpected happened to me. I don't know when or how," he says with great earnestness. "The religious teachings took, and over the years, as I found God, I felt guilt over the crimes I committed. I became Jewish in my heart and soul. I spent these many years doing penance for my sins. I, too, share your nightmares of the dead bodies, Enya Slovak." He entreats her. "Can you find it in your heart to forgive me?"

Our heads whip back and forth as we look

to Enya, then Kolb. I notice Jack moving forward slightly. Kolb moves, too. Toward Enya. My heart is pounding. This is when he'll pull out the weapon.

Kolb says it again, his tone cooler. "I need your forgiveness."

She says nothing.

"Your fault," he shouts at her, losing control. "If you'd only let it alone!"

Enya finally speaks. Her voice is flat. "There is no room for forgiveness in my heart. Forgive you? Never!"

Kolb is swift. In seconds, he grabs Enya off her chair, and there it is — the gun comes out of his pocket and he presses it to her head.

Sophie screams. Bella whimpers. The girls tumble into one another, clutching at their friends for comfort. I am still watching Jack move a little more. What was it he said this morning? *He was never so frightened in his life?* As I am now.

Jack quickly whispers to me, "When I tell you, grab Stanley and the girls and run for the side door. Warn them if you can. If not, push them."

"Jack, you can't."

"Shh," he says.

Kolb is furious. "Give me back what

belongs to me," he shouts at us. "I want the patch!"

Evvie gasps behind me, clutching her purse close to her side.

"We don't have it with us. We hid it," I say, but my trembling voice betrays me.

"Liar," he says.

"I'll kill her if you don't give it to me right now." He pushes the gun farther into Enya's hair.

"Do it," Enya says calmly. "I died the day my babies died. Destroy this shell that feels nothing."

She turns to us. "Leave. Let him kill me. I don't care. I am no longer a victim and he no longer has control over me."

Kolb nudges her with the gun. "If you don't value your life, then I'll kill one of your friends. They care about living."

Enya and Kolb look in each other's eyes. His voice is shrill. "Tell me you forgive me!"

She laughs, but it is a sob. "A good Jew, ready to commit murder?"

To our utter astonishment, Enya raises her hand and smacks him. "May you rot in hell!"

Jack yells, "Run!"

I react instantly. I pull Stanley along and shove the girls and Joe toward the nearest side door, shouting, "Move. Move!" Yet I'm still watching what's occurring behind us.

Amazingly, these things happen all at once. Enya calmly walks away from Kolb, not looking back. Jack picks up a heavy glass ashtray from a side table and lobs it along the floor toward Kolb as if it were a bowling ball. At the same time as Kolb is distracted by the runaway ashtray, Jack races toward him, zigzagging every which way, head lowered, as if he were on a football field, trying to confuse the opposition so they would be unable to pin him down.

As Kolb whips the gun around, trying to aim at the ever-moving Jack, the front door swings open.

"Drop it! Drop the gun!" Morrie Langford says, as he and Oz Washington rush in.

Jack reaches Kolb, tackles him, knocking him down. Jack instantly rolls away. Morrie reaches Kolb and kicks the gun out of his hands. Oz grabs Kolb to his feet and cuffs him. Morrie says, "You are under arrest for the deaths of Johnny Blake and Abe Waller."

Jack catches up to Enya and leads her far out of danger. As he does, he says to Kolb, "Not only doesn't Enya forgive you, but the state of Florida won't, either. Neither will the war crimes commission. They will be very happy to close the books on Horst Kolb, once and for all."

The girls are screaming and crying at the same time.

If I had to guess who among us would faint, I wouldn't have picked Stanley Heyer, whose inert face now lies flat across my shoes.

Jack runs to me and hugs me. "How?" I begin to ask.

He grins. "Something else about me I haven't gotten around to telling you. I was a football jock in college."

And to all of us who complained to the clubhouse hospitality committee that we wanted the ashtrays removed because nobody smokes anymore, give thanks they didn't get around to it yet.

Jack has saved my life again. That's two I owe him.

At that moment, appearing at the open front doors, are the beautifully dressed engagement party guests. They begin to file in.

Hy, looking very dapper in a pearl gray Armani knockoff, looks around eagerly and says, "What did we miss?"

47

THE PARTY

It takes a while to quiet down the incoming guests as Horst Kolb is taken away by Morrie and Oz and other police. Questions fly, and I am sure the girls and Joe answer as best they can.

Outside the clubhouse Stanley and Esther take their leave of us. Jack holds tightly on to my arm, as I'm still shaken from the last few minutes. The Heyers cannot bear to stay, but shakily, they extend their congratulations. Stanley has tears in his eyes. I am thinking as I look at that dear man that it will take a long time for him to recover from this shocking news. A man he knew and trusted as his dearest friend. How difficult it will be to face his congregation. But he surprises me. He tells me that I will always be a heroine to him for what I did. And that brings on my tears.

We go back inside and there is much hugging and kissing from the amazed guests. A night to truly celebrate. It's wonderful seeing all my friends and neighbors dressed beautifully and wanting to share our happiness. For their sakes, I must put away my feelings about this momentous day to be able to process later. Enya comes to me and embraces me. It's as if she never wants to let me go. I can feel the wetness of her cheeks. Jack gently moves in and kisses her as well.

The engagement party is a huge success. So much color and laughter and happy music. Everyone eats too much and drinks too much. There is something about having looked into the jaws of death that whets the appetite. One is determined to live life to the absolute fullest.

Highlights of the evening:

Enya leads us in dancing the hora. She looks ten years younger as she weaves in and out of the dance, everyone bending and swaying to her direction.

As I walk by him I'm amused to hear Hy, now retelling latecomers the capture-of-Kolb story, building up his part.

"I could have turned Jack in for smashing Kolb's car. I watched him do it but not a peep out of me, no siree. I could see how he was planning to stop the Nazi from going back into his apartment. I was with him one hundred and ten percent!"

Jack and I do a mean East Coast Lindy Hop and finally sit down, out of breath, to much applause.

He's gasping for breath. I grin. "Football star, indeed."

Evvie starts the clapping and everyone follows with the clinking of spoons on glasses. Voices ring out. "Name the date! Name the date!"

We look at one another and then I call out January first, and that gets even more applause.

Morrie and Oz return, their arms filled with presents for us. Naturally, we hug. I try very hard not to whisper I told you so to my future stepson.

He beats me to it. "Well, you were right, Gladdy." His tone a little forced.

"As usual," I say sweetly back.

While we are strolling around outside with our drinks and food, I spy Evvie and Joe having drinks around the pool. Evvie reminds Joe that this is the very spot where he dumped her years ago on that miserable New Year's Eve.

Joe apologizes. "I'm sorry. I'm sorry. A hundred times over I'm sorry."

"I forgive you," Evvie says, and promptly

pushes him into the deep end.

I hear Sol whisper to Barbi and Casey, "I saw what you do through your windows. You should pull your shades down." Egad, is the Peeper back in action?

I forgot to mention, in all the tumult today, that there was a picture postcard in the mail. It was postmarked Atlanta, Georgia, and has a lush photo of ripe peaches accompanied by greetings from Grandpa Bandit. He wrote, "Seventy is the new fifty. Gray hair is the new black. Hang around long enough and you'll be a teenager again." Signed with a drawing of a green feather.

A great evening was had by all.

In a quiet corner, Jack and I toast one another with champagne. I say happily, "Nothing will ever part us again."

ACKNOWLEDGMENTS

Evan Baker, Ph.D.: thank you for the German words. Much appreciated. And for all the great photos you take.

My New York team:
Caitlin Alexander
Nancy Yost
Sharon Propson

The 580 team:
Camille Minichino
Jonnie Jacobs
Peggy Lucke

As always, to my family and friends for their continuous support.

And
In loving memory of Bronia

ABOUT THE AUTHOR

Fate took **Rita Lakin** from New York to Los Angeles, where she was seduced by palm trees and movie studios. Over the next twenty years she wrote for television and had every possible job from freelance writer to story editor to staff writer and, finally, producer. She worked on shows such as *Dr. Kildare, Peyton Place, The Mod Squad,* and *Dynasty,* and created her own shows, including *The Rookies, Flamingo Road,* and *Nightingales.* Rita has won awards from the Writers Guild of America, the Mystery Writers of America's Edgar Allan Poe Award, and the coveted Avery Hopwood Award from the University of Michigan. She lives in Marin County, California, where she is currently at work on her next mystery starring the indomitable Gladdy Gold. Visit her on the Web at www.ritalakin.com.

The employees of Thorndike Press hope you have enjoyed this Large Print book. All our Thorndike, Wheeler, and Kennebec Large Print titles are designed for easy reading, and all our books are made to last. Other Thorndike Press Large Print books are available at your library, through selected bookstores, or directly from us.

For information about titles, please call:
(800) 223-1244

or visit our Web site at:
http://gale.cengage.com/thorndike

To share your comments, please write:
Publisher
Thorndike Press
295 Kennedy Memorial Drive
Waterville, ME 04901